A camera flash ... *and Emma. Oh* ... *really not good.*

Ducking their chins to their chests, they walked out, keeping their backs to the camera. Recognising the woman behind the camera had Chloe's stomach knotting. Rubi, the "In the Know with Rubi Cho" gossip columnist for the *New York Reporter*.

"This way," a man said.

Chloe looked up and saw her eye candy. He shielded them from Rubi all the way to the street, preventing any more photos. The limo stood by the kerb with the door open.

Chloe hesitated and turned to the guy. "Thanks."

He smiled and touched her cheek. "You're welcome."

Breathless, she couldn't move. He had the most gorgeous eyes she'd ever seen on a man. A striking grey that mesmerised and somehow haunted.

Impulsively, Chloe brushed a quick kiss to his lips.

His knees folded under him.

"Oh, God!" Emma shrieked. "He's out cold. Damn it, Chloe, you kissed him?"

"I forgot about the tranquilliser film in my lipstick, okay? I didn't think about it, I just did it."

"Well, you'd better think now. What the hell do we do with him?"

Available in January 2007 from Silhouette Sensation

The Heart of a Ruler
by Marie Ferrarella
(*Capturing the Crown*)

Hard Case Cowboy
by Nina Bruhns

In Dark Waters
by Mary Burton

Pawn
by Carla Cassidy
(*Bombshell*)

Third Sight
by Suzanne McMinn
(*PAX*)

Bulletproof Princess
by Vicki Hinze
(*Bombshell*)

Bulletproof Princess
VICKI HINZE

First published in Great Britain 2007
Silhouette Books, Eton House, 18-24 Paradise Road,
Richmond, Surrey TW9 1SR

© Harlequin Books S.A. 2006

Special thanks and acknowledgement are given to Vicki Hinze for
her contribution to THE IT GIRLS series.

ISBN-13: 978 0 373 51392 5
ISBN-10: 0 373 51392 5

18-0107

Printed and bound in Spain
by Litografia Rosés S.A., Barcelona

VICKI HINZE

is the author of fourteen novels, one non-fiction book and hundreds of articles published in over forty countries. Her books have received many prestigious awards and nominations, including her selection for *Who's Who in America* (as a writer and educator) and a multiple nominee for Career Achievement Awards as the Best Series Storyteller of the Year, Best Romantic Suspense Storyteller of the Year and Best Romantic Intrigue Novel of the Year. She's credited with having co-created the first open-ended continuity series of single-title romance novels and with being among the first writers to create and establish subgenres in military women's fiction (suspense and intrigue) and military romantic-thriller novels.

Acknowledgements

My thanks and gratitude to:
Evan Fogelman, my agent. You're the stuff of heroes.

The entire Silhouette team, with special thanks to Cindy Watson and the eHarlequin.com staff for their work on the free online IT GIRLS series prequel, *Invitation to a Murder*.

Lorna and Marge, and my friends William Olsen and Troy Burkett at Writers-in-Motion, who have given me the privilege of sharing their innovative, grand adventures.

My beloved family, who knows my every flaw and eccentricity and manages somehow to love me anyway.

Sandie Scarpa, my amazing assistant, a godsend.

Karen, Pam, Deb and Laura, Noveltalk.com gurus, who work tirelessly on both the bombshellauthors.com website and my own.

My fellow IT GIRLS authors: Erica Orloff, Michele Hauf, Nancy Bartholomew, Sylvie Kurtz and Natalie Dunbar.

Mary Elizabeth and Edna Sampson, extraordinary women forever in my heart.

To Madeleine Grace

Welcome to the world, Little One!

May blessings shower your life,
Wisdom keep you at peace,
And love always fill your heart.

I'll love you forever!
Gran

Prologue

In the Know with Rubi Cho

Two nights ago, New York's elite gathered in the main dining room at the exclusive Manhattan restaurant Perrini's to witness the familial blessings of the engagement of Gotham Rose Club charter member Chloe St. John, Princess of Astoria, principality of Denmark, to one of the A-List top five most eligible bachelors, Marcus Abbot Sterling, III, the notorious attorney who has lost but one case in his illustrious career: that of Preston Sinclair, husband of Gotham Rose Club owner Renee Dalton-Sinclair. Through her Rose heiresses and debutantes, Ms. Dalton-Sinclair has raised millions for charities to better the lives of women and children across the United States.

Today, the late Marcus Sterling will be buried in a private graveside service. His elegance and wit will be missed in high society's social scene.

Authorities are not yet releasing specifics on the case, and reports from those close to the couple conflict. Multiple sources state that Sterling was the victim of an apparent kidnapping by men posing as NYPD officers. An eyewitness says that the pseudo-officers abandoned the patrol car, and Sterling, handcuffed to the rear door, was attempting to free himself when the vehicle exploded.

Other reports indicate that Princess Chloe had broken her engagement to Sterling the same night as the familial blessing. They say that she was the kidnap victim and that she had escaped her abductors and discovered Sterling was responsible for her abduction.

For now, the truth remains elusive…and the princess remains unavailable for comment.

Chapter 1

Chloe awakened with an elbow in her ribs.

She turned over and found herself nose to nose with Jack Quaid, the man she'd been crazy about since the summer she'd turned sixteen but had only connected with days ago when the mob had pegged her for assassination.

Within hours of a drive-by shooting attempt, the press had dubbed her the Bulletproof Princess. Laughable, because all she had done was duck. Yet if she hadn't, it'd be her funeral as well as Marcus's that half of New York City attended today.

Jack's soft snoring stopped, but his eyes remained closed. She stroked his face, his black hair curling on his neck, the seemingly perpetual five o'clock shadow stubbling his strong jaw, and pressed gentle kisses to his wide brow. He didn't rouse, and she looked beyond him to the clock on the bedside table. Marcus's funeral wasn't until two, but she and Emma Bosworth had a meeting with Renee at the Gotham Rose Club at ten.

Chloe crawled out from beneath the luxurious covers and walked to the bath, freshened up, then stepped into a closet that was half the size of her enormous bedroom and wondered. "What does one wear to one's fiancé's funeral?"

Normally, answering that wouldn't be difficult. But considering her *fiancé* had sacrificed her to the mob to save himself, had drugged and kidnapped her to force her into marriage to save her life because the mob had a rule against harming wives, and *then* had attempted to murder Jack by burying him in the concrete foundation being repaired in her building, Eleanor Towers, Chloe wasn't sure what to think or feel much less what to wear. All of which explained why she had a meeting with Renee Dalton-Sinclair, her boss and mentor. Renee would help her decide the best course of action for minimal damage and exposure.

Minimal exposure was essential to the Gotham Rose Club.

Of over 200 members who had joined the G.R.C. in its four-year history, Renee had hand-selected nearly twenty to become agents in a top-secret spy organization. While the other Roses didn't know the agency existed, the agent Rose speculated that it had originated high in the halls of Congress or perhaps even in the White House. Renee selected each recruit for a specific reason—Chloe for her title, of course, because it gained her access to places and people mere money couldn't touch. A fact proven on her last two assignments by aristocratic arrests.

The Rose agents were tasked with information and evidence gathering to affect the arrests of high-society criminals who thought they were too rich, too powerful or too smart to be held accountable for their crimes. Once the Roses had done their part, overt authorities such as the police and FBI stepped in and made arrests.

Chloe showered and lathered with the scented signature

soap she'd created on her last shopping trip in Paris. She inhaled its spicy scent. She'd chosen the distinctive chompas and patchouli scent to remind her that she wasn't the spoiled heiress her mother believed, but a strong and successful businesswoman inspired by Eleanor Roosevelt. Eleanor had had a fondness for patchouli.

Turning, she let the hot water beat the stress from between her shoulders. Okay, so she had trust issues with men who, until Jack, had never failed to disappoint her. They all wanted her money or her title. Even men like Marcus, who had fortunes of their own. But she stayed grounded and focused on what really mattered. That's the reason she'd bought Eleanor Towers and had been devoted to restoring it. It was physical evidence of her commitment to herself to live a life of substance.

Chloe closed her eyes and remembered the morning Madison Taylor-Pruitt, her sister Rose and a real-estate magnate had called.

"I found it, Chloe. The perfect building for you. It overlooks Central Park and has a wonderful history."

"Tell me about it."

A lilt settled in Madison's voice. "When Eleanor Roosevelt was working on the Human Rights agreement at the United Nations, she stopped in front of this building and told reporters that women weren't weak or ignorant, they didn't lack courage, and every woman should aspire to leave the world better than she found it."

"I remember reading that report!" Excitement flooded Chloe. This had to be the right building for her. "Everyone doubted Eleanor would get sixty-four nations to sign the agreement, but she did, and it changed the world."

"I still think it's a bit idealistic," Madison said, ever blunt.

"But way too many in our circle turn cynical young and stay jaded for life, so I guess we need it."

"It's realistic, Madison. It happened."

Madison paused, then skepticism tinted her tone. "Do you really believe every woman changes the world?"

Normally Chloe would keep her opinions to herself, but Madison had asked with a flicker of hope, and Chloe wanted to nurture it. They'd developed a bond of trust, and while a lot had improved in Madison's life, she still grieved her best friend, Claire's, death. That and the subsequent investigation into Madison's family company had led to Renee recruiting Madison into the spy world of the Gotham Rose Club. "I believe every woman changes *someone's* world for better or worse. If they realize it, maybe they'll try harder to make sure the change is for the better."

"Mmm… So do you want to see the building?"

"I want to buy it."

"It needs to be gutted, Chloe. There've been a lot of haphazard modifications."

"So I'll gut it and then restore it."

"That'll be expensive." Madison reeled off a sum that most would find staggering.

Chloe smiled. "Lock it down. I want it."

She'd signed the papers within weeks, buying the building from Marcus, which was how they'd gotten close. She'd then renamed it Eleanor Towers. In the months since, the work had been brisk. The building had a long way to go to regain its glory, but it would get there. Chloe loved Eleanor Towers, and it showed.

Then Marcus had gotten the mob involved. Dead bodies, trying to seal Jack into its foundation… She leaned her forehead against the limestone wall, held the scented soap against her chin and inhaled again, then rinsed, wrapped herself in a towel and returned to her closet. If Marcus weren't already dead, Chloe would kill him for making Jack a target to get to her.

Jack appeared at the closet door. "You okay, Chloe?"

Torn between tears and a hysterical laugh, she nodded. "I don't know whether to hate him, feel sorry for him, wish him alive so I could kill him myself, or what, Jack."

He walked over and put his arms around her. "I'd say any and all of it is valid, honey." He pressed a kiss to her neck. "Anything but you loving him."

"I don't love him." She looked up at Jack. "At one time, I thought I did, but I didn't and I don't."

"Are you going to the funeral?" Jack stood aside while she stretched for a black Vera Wang suit.

"I think I have to," she said, searching the rows of shoes for the right pair. "Going raises fewer questions than not going." Sighing, she looked over at Jack. "I'm dressing for it. Emma and I are meeting with Renee to discuss it."

He nodded. "I wish I could be there for you."

She sent him a look laced with gratitude. "I appreciate it, but that would just create another scandal. Erik will be with me," she said, referencing her brother. At least, last night on the phone he'd promised to be there. Heaven knew if he'd actually show up.

Jack grunted. "If he remembers to put in an appearance, you'll end up having to look out for him."

Erik wasn't responsible but, to their parents, he was the Chosen One while Chloe was a dismal failure at being "the perfect princess." Only two years separated them. Two years, and a world of maturity. "He's gotten a little nicer lately. I'm not sure why." Maybe because she'd been dodging bullets?

"He has to be trying to impress a woman. Nothing else motivates him."

Because that was true, Chloe sighed. "Probably."

Jack walked out and around the corner. She heard him turn on the spigot. Water splashed. "I'd feel better if Renee were going with you," he called.

"She is," Chloe said, sitting at her vanity to do her makeup. "Emma, too. I'm picking her up on the way to meet Renee."

Minutes later Jack's cell rang and she heard him take the call. "Quaid," he said, then paused. "This is a really bad time for me to leave, Henry. Isn't there someone else who can cover—" He waited again, then added. "All right. No, if his wife is due to deliver any day, he can't very well go. I'll be there by ten."

Chloe's heart sank. Jack was leaving. He was a reporter for *Architectural Restorations*, which is how they'd reconnected. He'd given her some free press on the restoration of Eleanor Towers. But he also owned a chain of newspapers and did a lot of field reporting, including a fabulous series on Africa.

She finished dressing then slipped into a pair of basic black Jimmy Choos and debated wearing a hat with a gossamer veil to obscure her expressions from the press.

"Damn," Jack said, obviously having ended his call. He stepped out from around the corner wearing only a towel, his broad chest glistening.

Chloe's breath hitched. "You have to leave." Sadness stretched and yawned inside her.

He sent her an apologetic look. "I'm sorry, honey. I'm sure you heard—"

"The daddy needs to be home to greet the new baby."

"Exactly." Jack looked down at her, worry in his gray eyes. "I have to go to London for two weeks. When I get back, we'll find out who killed Marcus. These men aren't playing games, Chloe. Promise me you won't investigate on your own."

They'd hired a pro to kill her once already, to force Marcus to bury evidence on a case. Expecting them to tie up loose ends with a second attempt wasn't a stretch. "I know. They could decide they still want me dead."

Jack rubbed her arms, shoulder to elbows. "So you'll leave it for when I return?"

"If I'm given a choice." At his six-six to her five-seven, she had to crank her neck to look up at him. "But if they come after me again, I'm going into full attack-mode, Jack. I'll have to if I want to stay alive."

"If that happens, you call me immediately and I'll come."

So would the other Rose agents—not that she could mention them to Jack. Instead, she nodded, touched at his willingness to put himself in harm's way for her. In the past, she'd cared for three men and all three had betrayed her. But even at sixteen, when she'd first felt a sizzling special attraction to Jack, she'd known that what was between them was a significant, once-in-a-lifetime experience. Now that they were together, she intended to move forward without fear of her past mistakes and errors in judgment. She trusted him completely. And of all the things she found attractive, respected and admired in Jack, trusting him ranked most important. With her history, she didn't think even love could compete with it.

On tiptoe, she kissed him. "You look pretty good in a towel." She tugged its edges and it slid down his thighs to the floor. "But even better without it."

Chloe sat in the back of her limousine, staring at the royal flag furling in the wind on the front of the car. She'd prefer to travel incognito, but her mother would consider it scandalous for her to drive herself to Marcus's funeral, and today Chloe just didn't have the extra stamina to fight all her own demons and her mother, too.

The meeting with Renee would be challenging enough.

"You okay back there, Princess?"

Chloe stared at the back of Frank's head. His gray hair was reminiscent of Albert Einstein's wired look. And though frail, Frank had an indulgent mischievous sparkle in his eye when he looked at Chloe. So long as he drew breath, Frank would put Chloe first. He had been her protector and her driver her entire life. "I'm fine."

"Uh-huh."

She grimaced. *Fine? Had she honestly said she was fine? To Frank?* She needed a serious internal-radar check. In her position, only a fool would be fine. "I'm sorry. I'm coping."

"That's better," he said, clearly glad to get the truth. "But don't you worry. Mrs. Dalton-Sinclair will help you set matters to right."

She would. Renee always had been wonderful to Chloe.

Frank drove to Sutton Place, a section on New York City's East Side, where Emma Bosworth stood waiting.

Wrapped in a velvety black cashmere coat and standing next to her bruiser of a doorman, she looked like a tiny, fresh-faced angel, gentle and approachable. Unlike Chloe's brown, chin-length bob, Emma's hair was long, naturally streaked auburn and pulled up in a loose knot. She always looked elegant. Today, she wore pearls—and a black raw-silk Chanel suit. With her sea-green eyes, the effect was flattering and dramatic…and deceptive.

Most of the Gotham Roses supported the G.R.C. with fundraising for their chosen charity. They had separate and varied careers, like Madison's in real estate and Chloe's in investing. Those things told Renee most of what she needed to know about which Roses had the character, connections, skills and the will to become successful in their top-secret endeavors. But Emma didn't have a career. With Emma, none of that was needed. She was born to spy, and both she and Renee knew it.

The limo stopped at the curb. Stern-faced and authoritative in his black uniform with looped gold braid at the shoulder, Emma's doorman left no doubt he was protecting the lady. That was endearing and amusing, considering the five-foot-three little lady could take the bruiser down in two moves.

He opened the door and Emma gracefully slid onto the seat. "Thank you, Daniel."

"Of course, Miss Bosworth. Have a good day." He shut the door and stepped back from the car.

Chloe grunted. "How do you do it?"

"What?" Emma asked.

"Pull off looking helpless. It amazes me."

"Fake it 'til you make it."

"I hate it when you say that."

"Okay, okay." Emma lifted a perfectly manicured hand. "The secret is what my mother called a demure demeanor." She dipped a pale pink nail toward Chloe's shoes. "Oooh, I *love* the Jimmy Choos. Are they new?"

"Yes, and they don't pinch," Chloe answered, anticipating Emma's next question, and then asked, "Demure demeanor?"

"It's like Jimmy Valentine taught us in training. You want your adversaries to underestimate you. The less skilled they think you are, the less effort you have to expend to kick their asses."

That Chloe understood. After boarding school in Sweden and the unfortunate experience at Harvard, she'd gone through years of personal training. Everything from basic self-defense and FBI incidental shooting to Secret Service and Special Operations training for handling toxic substances, including bio-contaminates, in case the need ever arose. But on a personal level, the growing-from-girl-to-woman kind of training had been absent in her life. The only personal training her mother had deemed essential for Chloe had been of the "how to be a perfect princess" variety. If not for Emma and

Renee, Chloe would have forever remained pathetically clueless in basic life skills.

"Better step on it, Frank." Emma checked her Cartier watch, which her parents had given her for Christmas. The diamonds set around its face caught the sunlight and filled the interior of the limo with rainbows. "Otherwise, I'll have to tell Renee it's your fault we're late." She sent Chloe an innocent look.

Frank grunted. "I'm damned if I'm taking the blame for you being tardy to tea with Mrs. Dalton-Sinclair, Miss Emma. It's cold out today and I don't see a thermos of hot coffee in your hands to keep me warm while you two go in and have your chat."

"Well, the truth is out now, isn't it?" Emma frowned. "Chloe, can you believe we've got to bribe Frank to cover for us? Where's the dedication? The loyalty?"

Chloe knew they were trying to cheer her up and calm her down. She loved watching Emma and Frank spar, but she couldn't bring herself to laugh.

Frank had known both women since they were babies, which was why he absolutely refused to retire. Precious man. "She's got convenient amnesia again, Frank."

"Damn right."

"I do not," Emma insisted.

"Then tell me this," Chloe said, putting challenge in her tone. "When we were at the country house, who sneaked us out to the stable at the stroke of midnight so you could ride that black monster horse while your Jupiter was perfectly aligned with your Mars?"

"Aspected," Emma corrected her. "And it was Saturn. Jupiter and Saturn."

"That Hellion earned his name, all right," Frank said, clearly remembering the horse and the occasion—and, no doubt, the stomped flower garden they hadn't been able to see in the moonlight but had heard plenty about it in the light of the next day. "Didn't tell on you two for burning down the playhouse, either."

"Damn right," Chloe said, echoing Frank's favorite expression.

"Oh, I remember that," Emma said. "We were smoking out there during a storm and, Frank, you pitched an unholy fit."

He had. And he'd threatened them within an inch of their lives if he ever saw either of them with a cigarette again. Emma only indulged now and then, but she still hid her smoking from him. "He lied for us, Emma, remember?"

"Ungrateful child don't remember nothing—including my damn coffee."

"I remember you lying, Frank." Emma got in her dig. "You told Chloe's parents a lightning strike started the fire."

"They believed him, too," Chloe said.

"Okay, okay, okay. *Uncle,*" Emma conceded. "You're loyal to the bone, Frank, and I'll love you forever for it."

"Damn right." He sniffed, affronted but sufficiently appeased, and eased down the tree-lined streets, past old brownstones and through Central Park to the East Side of Manhattan. "While you ingrates are all warm and cozy, sipping your tea and hobnobbing with your friends in the Gotham Rose Club, you spare me a kind thought for being out here freezing my bones and going thirsty 'cuz someone— *though I ain't naming no names*—forgot my damn coffee."

Emma pulled a gleaming brushed stainless thermos up from the floor. Laughter bubbled up from her throat. "Gotcha!"

Frank looked stunned. "How'd you get that past me, girl?"

"Daniel slipped it in when closing the door so you wouldn't see me carrying it." Almost giddy at getting one up on Frank, Emma passed the thermos through the lowered glass.

Disgusted, he snorted. "Won't be happening again."

"Nothing ever does," Chloe said and meant it.

"You should know I'd never forget your coffee, Frank." Emma's eyes shone with total affection. "Forget my head maybe, but never your coffee."

"It's happened." He hiked his chin.

"Not in years."

"True." He looked at her through the rearview mirror, and gave her a little wink. "I'll forgive you that one."

"Well, it's about time."

On the Upper East Side, at 68th between Park and Madison, Frank stopped the car and Chloe and Emma got out.

Chloe bent to speak to Frank through the window. "You go somewhere warm. I'll call you when we're ready to leave."

He looked at her as if she'd lost her mind. "I'll be parked right here, Princess, to take you to the funeral."

"I don't know if I'm going yet. There's no sense—"

"Mrs. Dalton-Sinclair will guide you right," he said. "You go on now. I'll be here when you're ready."

So fiercely protective, even now that she was grown. "Okay. But run the heater so your arthritis doesn't flare up."

"I will." He sounded cross, but his appreciation for her concern burned in his eyes.

"Enjoy your coffee—and no adding anything from the flask under the front seat."

"You know about the flask?" He sounded stunned.

"Of course, Frank." Chloe grunted. "Didn't you teach me how to spy?"

"Damn right." He unscrewed the cap on the thermos. "But drink and drive?" He grumbled under his breath. "Girl ought to know better."

Chloe stepped away from the car and turned toward the building. Her breath fogged the cold, crisp air and hitched in her chest. Most people looked at the Gotham Rose Club and saw

3734655

a beautiful brownstone with a white facade, a wrought-iron gate, and the understated quality that comes only with old money and generations of restrained taste. Chloe looked at it and saw the one sanctuary in her life outside of Frank's car where she was valued and accepted on her own terms and merit.

Emma reached the gate and tapped the buzzer. "So, are you wishing Marcus was alive so you could kill him again, mourning him, or what?"

"Yes."

"Damn." Emma frowned up at the security camera, then walked through the gate. "I figured. But you're not questioning your feelings for Jack, right?"

"No." Thank God. Chloe followed Emma and the gate closed behind her. "I don't trust many men—too many have put the screws to me. But I do trust him." A little chill crept up her spine and settled in her neck. "If this relationship doesn't work, none will."

"Don't be stupid. It'll work. Jack loves you, Chloe."

She felt it, but she didn't *know* it. "Does he?"

"Yes, he does," Emma said with resolute conviction.

"Time will tell."

"I guess it's inevitable that you'd be skeptical after Marcus." Emma walked up the steps that led to the front entrance. "Did Olivia tell you what this meeting is about?"

Olivia Hayworth was one of Renee Dalton-Sinclair's oldest friends and her personal assistant. Their ties went back to their post-college service in the Peace Corps down in Colombia. Unfortunately, Olivia was as closemouthed as Renee. "Just to come for tea at ten o'clock, but come on, Emma. This is about what I'm supposed to do now—about the engagement and Marcus and the kidnapping. What to keep quiet and what to tell."

"I know that." Emma stopped on the landing. "I just wanted

to make sure you were thinking straight enough to know it. All this likely has the honchos giving live birth to cows on their desks."

"Probably."

"Renee's going to tell you to go to the funeral as Marcus's fiancée, then to come back here for an updated briefing."

"Did she tell you that?"

"Of course not," Emma said. "But I feel it in my bones."

Chloe respected Emma's bones far more than her own judgment. They'd proven right more often.

"Play the grief-stricken fiancée. The press will be easier on you."

"The press is never easy on any of us." Especially that bitch, Rubi Cho. Maybe the Roses should get together and buy the *New York Reporter* and then fire her ass.

"Smile." Emma elbowed Chloe.

She looked up at the surveillance camera but didn't smile.

The front door opened and Olivia stretched out her arms to take their coats. "Renee is waiting for you in the sunroom."

"Has she noticed we're late?" Chloe asked.

"Of course." She lowered her voice and offered her usual friendly advice. "Apologize going in."

"We'll blame Frank," Emma whispered.

Chloe frowned. "You do and I'll tell him."

Moving to the left, Chloe paused to soak in the heat from the fire crackling in the huge walk-in fireplace.

The club's entrance was an expansive room meant to impress. It did so, quietly and completely. Sunlight streamed through its long windows and streaked across the intricately patterned parquet floor, and Renee's favorite Debussy played softly in the background, pleasing to the ear. Chloe never had pinpointed the location of the speakers, though Emma swore that Alan Burke, their resident wizard of all things electronic, had somehow fused them into the crown molding.

Her heels clicking on the floor, Chloe passed the streams of soft, flowing drapes and slowed her step at the grand staircase, unable to resist letting her gaze sweep up its exquisitely carved rosewood banister to the second floor.

The G.R.C. proper was on the first and second floors. Renee's private quarters were upstairs on the third and fourth floors. And, though few beyond the nearly twenty Rose agents knew it, several more floors built below the club formed a maze of secret offices and task-specific quarters, including a spa, a firing range and a research library. Those floors were protected by many of the same security systems used in the White House.

"Hurry, hurry," Olivia said, with a wave of her hand. "You've got twenty seconds before you're officially late."

Being "officially late" required the offending Rose to create two hundred twelve handwritten notes of apology: one to every Rose and member of Renee's staff. The heiresses might be overindulged elsewhere, but not in Renee's club. In four years, no Rose had been exempt, regardless of tragedy, trauma or upset. And not one Rose had committed the "thoughtless, ill-mannered, inexcusably rude" infraction twice—though Porsche Rothschild had made arriving at the last possible second a new art form. But she loved to push boundaries. Chloe was just fine with hanging between the established lines.

Picking up her pace, she rushed down the hallway to the back of the brownstone and breezed past the open French doors into the sunroom. "Sorry we're late." Chloe took Olivia's tip.

Emma came up from behind and stopped beside her. "We are *not* late."

"Almost late, then," Chloe amended.

"Very close, darlings, but you've made it on time." Renee stood and dropped a kiss to Chloe's cheek, then to Emma's. "Please, sit down."

"Thank God." Emma collapsed on the sleek sofa.

Chloe watched for Renee's reaction, but noticed instead her presence and royal bearing, both so natural they had to be instinctive and not learned. She was forty-one, classic and timeless in an effortless way, with flawless skin. Her rich auburn hair was styled in an elegant French twist that suited her bone structure as well as her amethyst Rucci suited her coloring. Renee looked exactly as she always had to Chloe: as if she, and not Chloe, should be wearing a crown.

"Are you all right, darling?" Renee clasped Chloe's arm.

"I'm fine." *Inferior, but fine.* She crossed her ankles and bumped her handbag. Fortunately, nothing spilled out.

Olivia came in pushing a teacart laden with Renee's favorite gold-rimmed bone china, Chloe's favorite blueberry muffins and Emma's raspberry tarts. She discreetly glanced down at a preprinted card telling her how Chloe and Emma preferred their tea, poured, served, and then addressed Renee. "Do you need anything else?"

"No, thank you." Renee clasped her cup and sent Olivia a nod so slight that even watching for it, Chloe nearly missed it.

Olivia caught the cue and closed the French doors on her way out. Chloe's heart beat a little faster. Emma's bones were right; this wasn't a personal advice session.

"There's no sense in delaying this," Renee said. "Chloe, I've discussed your situation at length with the Governess and her consultants, and they advise you to go to Marcus's funeral today as his fiancée. The press must not know what really happened to you."

"Okay," she said uneasily. The person they all knew only

as the Governess was Renee's boss, a high-ranking individual positioned somewhere in the labyrinth of government, whose true identity remained unknown even to Renee. That was for everyone's benefit and safety. "But why not?"

"There's been a development, darling. I'll explain everything after we return from the funeral. It's complicated."

"Complicated?" Emma's bones were batting a thousand. "Does it involve a mission plan?"

"Actually, it does. But I'd prefer to wait until after—"

"Just tell me, Renee." Chloe's nerves snapped. "Otherwise, I'll be thinking about nothing else but what's coming and imagining all kinds of horrible things."

"Not as horrible as this," Emma predicted.

Renee shot her a look to hush, and Emma shrugged. "You might as well tell her now."

"Sometimes you're too perceptive for your own good, Emma, dear. Work on that."

"I'll try." She reached for her teacup.

Renee shifted her gaze to Chloe, and her eyes filled with regret. "It appears that the Marcus situation is more complicated than we originally thought."

"What do you mean?"

"He may have been involved with the Duke, Chloe."

Stunned, Chloe tried to grasp that. The Rose agents were in constant pursuit of the criminal mastermind they called the Duke. The nickname had begun as an inside joke about the elusive lawbreaker's seeming arrogance, but over many years he had become the Governess's obsession, involved in all manner of dark activities. Many of the Rose agents' missions concerned disrupting his illegal practices and trying to bring him to justice. Thus far, they'd come close but he had eluded them.

Marcus didn't have the stomach for those kinds of activities. He couldn't have been involved with the Duke.

Okay, so as an attorney Marcus had represented half the mob, that was true, but none of the Rose agents had successfully tied him to even one illegal act. His refusal to withhold evidence was what had frustrated the mob into putting out a contract on Chloe. "I don't doubt you, Renee, but I just can't believe it."

"I know it's difficult, darling, especially considering that our initial investigation didn't reveal anything on this. But, as you know, the Governess has more extensive resources at her disposal, and she has multiple Intel reports suggesting it's highly likely that Marcus had direct ties to the Duke."

"Direct ties in what way?"

"Her sources believe the Duke is using an escort service that operates citywide as a front for a multitude of felonious activities."

"Escorts?" Shock flooded Chloe. "You think Marcus was involved in a prostitution ring?"

"We aren't sure," Renee said, tilting her perfectly coifed head. "While the escort service is a legitimate front and its clientele proves it, we suspect it has a dual function. Something Marcus may have known about."

She was afraid to ask. But Renee was clearly waiting, giving her time to assimilate the shock before giving her more information. "And the other function is…what?"

"The white-slave trade."

Chloe dropped her cup.

Chapter 2

Chloe endured the funeral wearing Marcus's engagement ring and avoided the prying eyes of the press afterward, thanks to Frank's pre-positioning the limo.

Erik had not shown up.

She, Renee and Emma were silent on the ride back from the Long Island cemetery to the G.R.C. It was late afternoon when they entered and walked past the huge fireplace and grand staircase, then disappeared into the closet—the entrance to the secret rooms. Rather than going to the conference room, they went to Renee's private office.

Chloe and Emma sat on a cream brocade sofa with dainty legs and scrolled arms. Renee poured each of them a glass of seltzer, passed the crystal glasses, then took her seat at a Renaissance desk. An original Dali hung behind her. "Are you still shaking, Chloe?"

She removed her veiled hat and set it aside. "No. I'm all

right. It was just…difficult seeing Marcus's parents there."
They'd been so devastated.

"I'm sure it was. Grief is as merciless as guilt."

Renee had known her fair share. Her husband Preston was
out of jail now, but only because Renee had cut a deal to work
for the Governess to secure his early release.

Emma nodded knowingly, sipped from her glass, then
asked, "Why isn't Tatiana here?"

Tatiana Guttmann, a natural beauty, second-generation
coffee heiress from Colombia, often worked as Emma's
partner on missions. Constantly underestimated, Tatiana used
her skills as a former model to mask the fact that she was very
smart and an amazingly gifted financial analyst. In her social
circle, no one would believe that she'd spent the past year
working for Renee as an agent, and that was an enormous
asset as well as a necessity. Only secrecy allowed the Roses
to function. Without it, they'd be stymied, completely unable
to perform and in definite danger.

Renee hesitated only a second. "I'm afraid, my dears,
Tatiana *is* the development—at least, in part."

"What do you mean?" Emma asked Renee.

"She was dating one of the men from the escort service."

Emma's jaw dropped. "You've got to be kidding."

Chloe couldn't believe it, either. Tatiana was aggressively
ambitious about two things: elevating her social standing,
and remaining a darling of the press. Dating an outsider—an
escort—wouldn't further either goal, and she was all about
furthering her goals.

"I wish I were kidding, but I'm not." Renee hid a frown
behind her glass. "She found the initial documentation that im-
plicated Marcus. It enabled the Governess's sources to decode
other transmissions, and the rest, as they say, is history."

"So if progress resulted, then why are you unhappy with the

situation?" Chloe asked. Tatiana *would* dig for dirt on Marcus. She believed Chloe loved him, and dirt on him would hurt her.

"Unfortunately, her personal association has created a situation that the Governess finds discomfiting. So we're making some adjustments."

"Renee," Chloe interrupted, firming her voice. "I want to know who killed Marcus. They tried to kill me and could try again." Another assassination attempt she did *not* need.

"I realize that, darling." Renee turned her royal blue gaze on Chloe. "I've pulled Tatiana off the assignment and inserted you to work with Emma."

Chloe looked over at Emma. "You've been working on this already?"

She nodded. "But only as Tatiana's backup. I've never been inside the escort service, and I didn't know about Marcus. I swear it."

Tatiana was just going to love this. She hated Chloe now. Replacing her would only make the rivalry worse. "What are the Governess and her consultants suggesting we do?"

"Identify the Duke, of course." Renee delicately cleared her throat then continued. "And confirm or dismiss charges that some of the women hired by the service as escorts *or* models are being sold into white slavery and shipped out of the country."

A chill shot up Chloe's spine. "There is no low with that bastard. The Duke will do anything. And you really think Marcus was involved with him?"

"We suspect the Duke is involved," Renee clarified. "And from the documentation Tatiana confiscated, Marcus was definitely in the middle of this."

"It wouldn't surprise me if the Duke is involved. He's neck-deep in every nasty high-society nook-and-cranny," Chloe said. The Roses had already tied him to money laundering, bribery, drugs and a host of other unsavory operations. If they could just catch the jerk, he'd rot in jail forever. "But Marcus?"

"She has a valid point. We can't ignore Tatiana's envy of Chloe, Renee."

"I'm not ignoring anything. Neither is the Governess and her consultants."

Emma reached for her glass. "Do we know how the service is choosing its victims?"

"Not with any degree of certainty, but an apparent pattern is forming." Renee set down her glass. "The known three missing women are all well-educated, well-spoken brunettes in their mid-twenties who can handle themselves in sophisticated settings. They're all beautiful, and they're all Russian."

"So they're targeting vulnerable women," Emma said. "Ones new to the States, or ones without families who'll report them as missing."

"The Governess and her consultants fear that's true, and I agree with them," Renee said. "Intel has the Department of Defense's top profiler consulting on this. She says the lone-victim target carries a high probability."

"Has Tatiana been exposed? Is that why you've pulled her off the mission?"

"We don't think so, but we can't be certain. That's why I've removed her." Renee was decidedly uncomfortable. "We would have preferred she not take on the added risks, but she made the connection and assumed she would be done with the mission and authorities would intercede to mop up."

"What didn't she know, Renee?" Emma asked.

Renee didn't respond.

Chloe's stomach suffered an uneasy pitch. "You and the Governess can't expect us to make ourselves victims they snatch up and export to only God knows where."

"Actually, we do," Renee said.

"What?" Chloe couldn't believe her ears.

"Renee, no," Emma protested. "Absolutely not."

Renee lifted a staying hand. "We won't let events progress to the point that we risk you being exported." Renee cocked her head. "But you do speak Russian, Chloe, which we need for obvious reasons, and you do have the ability to conduct yourself with royal decorum. Both of those assets fit the pattern as we've currently defined it—and they significantly increase your value on the black market. That makes you the perfect agent to partner with Emma on this assignment."

"You can't possibly be serious." Chloe looked from Emma to Renee. "What you're proposing is a lot more dangerous than investigating the high-society criminals we signed on to take down. We excel with the rich and famous, but this assignment reeks of mafia and hard-time criminals. It exceeds our scope."

"That's true," Renee said. "And it is much more likely you'll experience elevated levels of violent conduct. How elevated, we can't accurately predict. But Intel feels certain that the head of this ring is well placed in society—his methodologies are extremely sophisticated and expensive—and that puts this assignment firmly in our domain. I do believe this is the only way to prove or disprove the Duke or Marcus's involvement."

"Tatiana's evidence says Marcus is connected. Intel says Marcus is connected." Emma frowned. "But money-laundering, drugs, racketeering, bribery—those things are more the Duke's style than trading in human flesh. And I can't see Marcus involved in that either."

Chloe weighed that response, but the deductive reasoning didn't sit comfortably with her at instinctive levels. She remembered Marcus ordering her not to wear red, her favorite color for evening wear. How he'd threatened to ruin Jack and had tried to force Chloe to bend to his will. And when she'd broken their engagement, she remembered his warning her that he did not suffer humiliation well. "I can see him doing it, Emma."

"Who?" Renee asked. "The Duke or Marcus?"

Chloe hated admitting it, but she couldn't lie. "Both."

Emma paused. "Since the beginning of this assignment, I've had a feeling in my bones about the Duke."

That did it for Chloe, who'd learned the hard way to respect Emma's bones. "Did this assignment originate with the Governess?" It could have come down through another Washington powerhouse like Ellie Richardson, the senior senator from New York, or through the Joint Chiefs of Staff.

"As far as I know," Renee said.

Chloe sent her a level look. "Aside from what Tatiana has produced, is there any hard evidence implicating Marcus?"

"Hard evidence, no. But Intel does have circumstantial evidence it didn't disclose," Renee confessed. "Yet that isn't of notable consequence at this point. We need insight and evidence to stop this slave trade, if it's occurring. And if during the course of stopping it, we discover Marcus was active or inactive, then we've proven it. If the Duke is at the helm, then obviously we hope to discover his true identity. That's all."

"That's *all?*" Chloe couldn't believe her ears.

"Yes," Renee answered, ignoring the incredulity in Chloe's voice. "As soon as he's identified, the Governess will have the appropriate authorities move in, and our covert portion of this assignment will be done."

Chloe sat there, too stunned to speak. The entire four years the Roses had been in operation, they had been trying to determine the Duke's identity, but he'd always stayed a step ahead of them. And now, on this extremely dangerous assignment, Renee talked as if discovering his identity would be a cakewalk?

"I know it sounds simple, after all our years of profiling

and tracking this elusive man. But this is our first solid lead on a non-high-society crime, and the Duke won't be expecting us to look at him from this angle. He's finally exposed a weakness." Renee's expression sobered. "The report notifying us of the three Russian women's sudden disappearance came in late last night, Chloe. We think it's a new criminal venture. If this trade is occurring and we don't intercede quickly, then those women could very well end up being slaves—likely in the Far East."

Tense, Chloe lifted a questioning brow. "The Far East?"

Renee explained. "They're the world's most active buyer of sophisticated Western women."

The pressure against Chloe's chest doubled. Her emotions ripped between fear of getting caught up in the white-slave trade and fear that if she didn't at least try to do something then the three missing women would disappear and never be seen or heard from again. Her hand shook.

Inside, she shook all over.

Resigned, she set her glass down on a gleaming table that matched the desk in design, and swallowed hard. "I can hear the newsflash now. 'Chloe, Princess of Astoria, principality of Denmark, dead at twenty-six. The princess was murdered last night in New York City's Lower East Side while working as a professional escort…'"

"Chloe, don't even—" Renee started to object.

"No, Renee." Emma swept a hand across her brow. "She's right. It could happen."

Chloe frowned. "True or false, everyone, including my mother, will substitute 'prostitute' for 'escort,' and the royals will pitch yet another bloody fit. My parents will be humiliated, and I'll carry their censure for all of eternity." Chloe frowned and didn't bother to try to hide it. "It's humiliating, Renee."

"She's right about all that, too." Emma added her opinion.

"The Governess isn't playing fair on this one. This isn't the type of criminal activity we're trained to derail."

"I know it isn't." Renee laced her hands in her lap and let them see her worry. "The Governess knows it, too. But it is critical that we move quickly to protect these women and, frankly, the Roses have better odds of success than any other agency at her disposal."

Chloe didn't say a word. Emma let out a sigh that showed she, too, had conflicting emotions on this.

Renee leaned back in her seat. "When I opened Gotham Rose Club and approached you two about becoming agents, we discussed the possibility of this type of action. Then, you claimed you understood and agreed to do the work," she reminded them. "What's changed?"

It *had* been discussed—Chloe recalled it vividly—but then it had been a discussion of a far-fetched, hypothetical situation. Now there were women being restrained against their will and sold as slaves, and she damn well didn't want to be one of them. Chloe shook off an icy chill and shifted uneasily on her seat.

Renee lifted her chin, looked Chloe straight in the eye and then turned her unyielding gaze on Emma. "Are either of you refusing this assignment?"

Neither answered.

"You can refuse, you know," Renee said, her voice soft and without censure. "That's acceptable to do and, considering circumstances, certainly understandable."

Chloe wasn't fooled. Refuse, and horrendous consequences would follow—professional ones, certainly; and likely personal ones, as well.

The silence stretched, then stretched again, with Emma sitting statue-still, staring back at Renee.

To hell with it. Chloe caved. "We can refuse, but if we do, then these women will be dragged through the horrors of hell and it'll be on our shoulders."

"I would never say that, darling."

Renee wouldn't. But she wouldn't have to say it. Every time she looked at Chloe, Chloe would think it. *Damn it. Damn it. Damn it.* She hated guilt. "I'm in," she said. "But if I end up dead, Renee, you'd better swear on Preston's head that no one will ever know about this escort business." Bringing Renee's beloved husband into the mix should get Chloe some assurances. "I will *not* go down in the annals of Astorian history as its first prostitute princess."

"You have my word." Renee smiled. "I'll make you a saint they revere for the next twenty generations."

Emma sighed. "God, Renee. You're ruthless."

Renee ignored that, but wasn't offended by it, which meant she took it as a compliment. "God is already on the job, my dear." She turned a gently disapproving eye on Chloe. "When I told Alan to expect you two downstairs soon to pick up some special equipment, Jimmy overheard me."

"Why is that a problem?" Chloe asked, unable to see it. Jimmy "the Heartbreaker" Valentine overheard everything—and what he didn't overhear, he was briefed on. He had the security clearance, and needed it to appropriately train the Roses.

"Because he was so worried about you being put on this assignment, he took his lunch hour early."

Chloe was lost. "And this is significant because…"

"Because he did it to run over to St. Patrick's to light a candle for you and say a novena."

She had him on his knees. Guilt swam through her stomach. So did resentment. "Well, doesn't that just bolster my confidence?" Chloe said dryly. "Is there a special reason for all this drama, or is he just generally afraid of my incompetence?"

"You've missed your last three training sessions and

you're a wee bit heavier than he considers best for your optimum performance."

"It's only ten pounds."

Emma frowned. "Twenty."

"Okay, twenty." After that, Chloe didn't dare think about what was going on for dinner. "I'm not obese, and I haven't forgotten my skills."

"Which is exactly what I told Jimmy," Renee said with a lift of her hand. "But he worries, Chloe. Just as you consider the fate of the Russian women to be in your hands, Jimmy feels the fates of the Rose agents are in his. He's responsible for your physical training, defensive and offensive, and he takes that responsibility very seriously. That's what makes him the best. If you lose, then he's failed you."

She'd never thought about Jimmy's training from that perspective before, but doing so now certainly shifted her thinking. "I'll try harder."

Emma spoke bluntly. "It'll help if you show up."

Renee sent Emma a reprimanding look, then softened her gaze on Chloe and gave her a warm, glowing smile. "He'll be so pleased to hear that."

"So will the priest who hears his confessions at St. Patrick's."

"You do have a unique way of looking at things, Emma." Renee refilled her glass. The seltzer fizzed. "Will you be a dear and excuse Chloe and me for a moment?"

"Of course." She slid Chloe a sympathetic look, snagged her purse and then left Renee's office.

Renee had the grace to wait until the door closed to turn on Chloe. "Now, tell me, darling. Why have you gained this weight? Is your mother driving you to distraction again?"

"Only when she's breathing," Chloe confessed, having finally accepted that her mother would always drive her to distraction. She was thin as a reed and Chloe was naturally curvaceous—not fat, just not model-like, which rated as a mortal sin in her fashion-designer mother's eyes. She considered Chloe unforgivably flawed and extremely overweight and, diligently fulfilling her motherly duty, she rode Chloe constantly about it. It didn't matter that Chloe felt good and looked damn good in her clothes. She had meat on her bones, and that, to her mother, was disgusting.

Which was exactly why Chloe had studied eating disorders—her mother, not she, had one—and why she'd chosen to support the Women's Center as her pet charity. They sponsored an eating disorder program and so much more, offering shelter, career advice and job placement to women struggling to start over and build better lives. Last year alone, Chloe had sponsored events that had raised $14 million for her cause. The struggle continued, however, because the Center needed far more.

Renee let out a little sigh. "Darling, you simply must stop giving her this kind of power over you. I know it's difficult because, after all, she is your mother, but you can choose how deeply you let her affect you."

Chloe wasn't so sure about that. "She has a way of wearing you down, Renee." Especially when she'd spent a lifetime bouncing on your esteem.

"No, dear." Renee scooted to the edge of her seat, leaned toward Chloe and grasped her shoulders. "Look at me."

Renee's eyes were fired with determination. "There is strength in you, Chloe. I knew it the first time I saw you, and I've known it every day of your life since. You have all the assets you used to build your companies available to you to deal with your mother, too. Remember, you doubled your assets before you were twenty-one—tripled them before you turned twenty-five. These are not the accomplishments of a weak woman, darling."

"But that's different. That's just business."

"It's not different," Renee insisted. "Your strength isn't compartmentalized unless *you* compartmentalize it. Draw on it—you fought so fiercely for your silent partnerships in Perrini's and Adelphio, remember?" Chloe nodded that she did, and Renee went on. "Fight your mother fiercely, too. You can because you're not really fighting *against* her. You're really fighting *for* you. Princess or pauper, my dear, you control your life, and you alone are responsible for it."

Chloe heard Renee, knew she believed everything she was saying, but she was wrong. Chloe wasn't strong. Or brave. Or smart. And what did that leave her to fight with?

For four years, she'd been following Emma's "fake it 'til you make it" advice. And until today it had served her well. Even on dangerous assignments she could play the roles. Hell, she was good at playing roles. But they weren't real.

Her mother was real. This assignment was real.

And neither pretending to be strong and brave and smart nor confessing her fraud would save her or those Russian women.

Renee cupped her face and smiled. "You can do this, Chloe. I have every faith in you."

Renee did. It burned in her eyes, clear and certain. She always had believed in Chloe, even when she'd been falsely accused of possession at Harvard and had been asked to leave. Her own mother hadn't believed her, but Renee had. She'd been appalled, indignant at Chloe's mother's reaction to a daughter in trouble, and had appointed herself as a surrogate mother to Chloe. Renee had been one—a great one—ever since. Now, the fear of disappointing her, too, had Chloe sick inside.

"Believe, Chloe." Renee stroked her cheek. "See the strength I see in you."

Chloe's eyes stung. Renee made it seem so easy to see the best, to believe the best. "You're a wonderful mother, Renee."

"You make it easy, my dear." Renee smiled, patted her knee. "So Jack is with you?"

"He's gone to London on assignment for two weeks."

"Now?" Renee frowned.

"He had no choice," Chloe defended him. "He had to go or send an expectant father."

"Well, that's different, then," Renee said, drawing the same conclusion Chloe had. "Chloe, be careful on this mission, my dear. And don't let your preconceived notions about Marcus blind you to the truth, okay?"

Chloe nodded. She honestly had to worry more about going the other way and blaming the man for everything she saw.

Renee stood up. "Now, you'd better run. Kristi and Alan are waiting for you."

Chloe nodded and picked up her purse. Kristi Burke was the Roses' dresser, the queen of magical transformations, and her brother Alan was a master of electronics, all types of weaponry, high-tech tools and equipment needed to carry out undercover assignments. "I will do my best to be objective, Renee." Chloe promised but didn't smile.

Neither did Renee. "You always do, darling."

Chloe would try. But even with Emma's help, her odds on this assignment were dismal. To succeed, she had to actually become all the things she had pretended to be—smart, strong, cunning—and she had to do so fast, or she would die—or end up enslaved with the other women.

Given a choice, Chloe would rather be dead.

Chapter 3

On the way to the dressing area, Chloe received a cell call.

"Chloe?"

Jack. She smiled. "Where are you?"

"Getting ready to board a flight. I just needed to hear your voice." Husky. Sexy. "I miss you already."

Her heart fluttered, and she stopped and leaned against the hallway wall. "Me, too."

"This morning was…" He grunted in pure male appreciation. "Incredible."

She felt the sizzle, flushed from the heat. "Yeah." Kristi Burke stepped into the hallway and waved Chloe over. Chloe nodded, then said to Jack, "Definitely incredible."

"It's going to be a long two weeks."

A shot of pure pleasure rippled through her and settled in her chest. "Rush."

"I will," he promised. "Bye."

"Bye." She closed her phone and dropped it into her favorite Prada bag, sighing contentedly.

"Will you hurry up?" Kristi waved at her again. "We're running late."

"I'm coming." Chloe picked up her steps and entered the dressing room.

Ten minutes later, she was flushed again. This time there was nothing sensual about it. "Oh, no, Kristi Burke. No way." Dabbing on her signature fragrance, Remember Me, Chloe resisted an urge to shout. "I'm carrying a record twenty extra pounds and you want me to wear a skirt I can't bend over in, a red wig and fricking crystal-studded sunglasses?" Chloe glared at her dresser in the long mirror. "What are you trying to do, force me to put my mother in the grave?"

Emma folded her arms and groaned at Chloe's back. "Red wigs are Renee's orders. We're vulnerable, not well-heeled, remember? And those fricking sunglasses are Gucci, and very hot. Ash wore a pair at lunch yesterday."

Ashley Thompson, a fellow Rose agent, was also a fashion editor for *Chic* magazine and the undisputed queen of fashionistas. "Terrific." Chloe shot Emma a glare. "Then she can wear them."

Kristi sighed from the heart out, pleading for help, and Emma rescued her. "For pity's sake, Chloe, just put the damn things on. Alan's waiting and we're going to be late." She dropped her voice to a whisper. "Did you not hear me? We're vulnerable and broke. Escorts might not write apologetic notes, but they do suffer consequences for being late."

"What's wrong with crystals?" Fellow Rose Samantha Adams—whose hair was hunter-orange today and had been grape two days ago—peered over Emma's shoulder. "I love crystals."

Emma smiled. "You look adorable in them, too, Sami."

"Well, sure." She hiked her chin and exaggerated a look down her nose, then crossed her eyes. "I'm an adorable woman."

"And modest, too." Chloe rolled her eyes. Samantha loved anything funky. It suited her. But none of this suited Chloe. Not the escort cover, not the long red wig—though she had to give Kristi points for quality—and, while when it came to style she worshipped Gucci as a third religion, not the fricking crystal-studded sunglasses. "Nothing's wrong with them, Samantha, I just hate crystals and diamonds. They remind me of tiaras." And tiaras reminded her of being a princess, and that reminded her of all she wasn't and would never be.

Fingering a flowing, sheer white curtain, Tatiana Guttmann glided across the floor in her South American slink. Her killer eyes glittered gold. "So the It girl princess has a record?"

Oh, great. Just great. Chloe did not need Tatiana's claws in her back right now. She was nervous enough. *A fricking escort? Fricking Duke and Marcus? Fricking white-slave trade?* "That's old news, Tatiana." As old as her $500 million inheritance from her grandmother carrying a provision that Chloe never set foot in Denmark: a penalty due to her heir-to-the-throne father abdicating to marry a lowly fashion designer. The press had covered it all, in degrading detail.

Yet, even if the royals ignored her branch of the family tree other than to privately berate it, Chloe's special social standing awarded only to those in high society bearing a title grated at the mere coffee heiress in Tatiana.

Chloe often wondered why. Tatiana had a history rich in Colombian culture. The only thing Chloe had found being a princess good for was its use as a measuring stick, and considering she always fell short on the damn thing, she didn't need it. She had plenty of shortfall indicators without the title.

Emma leaned to whisper near Chloe's ear. "You shouldn't

have taken the hit for Boy Wonder then, and you shouldn't take it now. Set her straight."

"Shut up, Emma." Chloe dragged her lips back from her teeth in a pasted-on smile. Her parents adored Erik. They didn't know about Chloe's companies and financial success, or about Erik blowing his inheritance on bad land deals, gambling and lousy, high-risk investments and Chloe paying his way for five years before putting her foot down, giving him $1 million and telling him to make or break himself. They did know Erik had hooked up with Ryan Greene and was supposedly doing great.

If Boy Wonder fell off his pedestal, her parents would blame Chloe—his screw-ups were *always* her fault—but when they did, she was going to deny blame and, by God, be telling the truth. But she could chew on that later.

Now, she needed a lie. "Being arrested is a status symbol for royals, Tatiana." Scratching that vanity should dull the kitty's claws a bit. "Of course, I've got a record. Possession of marijuana. I got photographed, fingerprinted and even placed in a cell—maximum royal treatment." Chloe suppressed a cringe at the memory, and her heartbreak at Erik's sacrificing her. Why hadn't he confessed the truth and taken responsibility for having the marijuana?

Renee had offered her comfort. *We all pay for our mistakes, Chloe. Sometimes it shows, and sometimes it doesn't. But no one escapes their conscience.*

Chloe had believed her then, and did now. Still, the experience had been bloody awful. It had cost Chloe Harvard and earned her more of her mother's disgust. She regretted that, though she wasn't foolish enough to believe anything would change it. Tilting her head, she looked at Tatiana in the mirror. "You lack a record, I take it."

Tatiana hesitated, unsure if her proverbial chain was being

yanked, but just for a second, thanks to Emma biting a smile from her lips. That smile was a dead giveaway to Tatiana's internal lie detector. "Don't even try to mess with my head, Chloe St. John," she said. "You're not in my league."

For which Chloe would forever be grateful. "Of course not, darling." She gave her a broad smile. "I'm the It girl princess with a record." *Stuff that hairball, Ms. Superiority.*

Tatiana's tanned face flushed. She clamped her jaw and squared off at Chloe's back. "Emma, I'm pissed at you."

"Me?" Emma turned on her. "What did I do?"

"You stole my appointment at LaBella."

"Sorry," Emma said, doing her demure demeanor stuff. "I *really* needed a peppermint foot treatment, and I knew you wouldn't mind."

"I mind."

Chloe sighed. "If you mind, then you shouldn't have stolen her appointment last week."

Tatiana glared at Chloe, then lifted her coral lips in a thinly disguised smirk. "*You're* advising *me?* You can't even do pot without getting caught—and you couldn't even talk your way out of it! The royals had to love that." Tatiana looked down her nose at Chloe and sniffed. "Not that I'm surprised. You've always lacked flair and style."

Bent on giving Tatiana a swift kick that'd acquaint her backside with the heel of Chloe's Jimmy Choo, she tried to spin around, but Kristi grabbed the front of her skirt and Emma locked down on her shoulder. Chloe couldn't move.

"Don't do it!" Emma whispered. "She's pissed because Renee gave you this assignment."

"No blood on this skirt, Chloe St. John," Kristi muttered from between her teeth. "I mean it."

It took a long minute, but Chloe managed to bury her anger. "All right." When the others let go, she turned toward Tatiana.

"Actually, the royals were overwhelmed." They had been, and ticked off to their blue-blooded gills. "I made international news for three days. My story, darling, had legs." Chloe dropped the hand planted at her hip to her side and softened her voice. "As for being bright—well, I guess it only matters that I'm bright enough to have your number, Tatiana, and I do. So long as tearing me down makes you feel better about yourself, you just go right ahead. I can carry anything you need to throw my way." Her mother had been the master of this kind of destruction. Compared to her, Tatiana was on training wheels. "Now, do you want something, or are you just hanging around because it's what you do best?"

Tatiana blew off the insult and smoothed a hand down her marmalade Dior sheath at her slender hip. It suited her exotic skin tone. "And Renee thinks *you* can handle my assignment."

Such a predictable kitty. Chloe put a bite in her tone. "If you have a problem with Renee or her assignments, then take it up with her."

That got Tatiana's attention, but her sense won out. "You're not even out of the G.R.C. and you're already screwing up. The job is as an escort. You're dressed like a hooker."

"Excellent observation." Freshening her lipstick, Emma answered first. "We're going to one of your old haunts."

Tatiana's slanted eyes narrowed. "Which one?"

"Hollow Hill Hotel, in the Meatpacking district." Flustered, Kristi reeled off the hotel bar and threw up her hands. "That's where they're going, okay?" Kristi turned to Chloe. "Now will you *please* be still. If I stick myself one more time because you're wiggling, I'm going to stab you right in the ass with this needle."

Tatiana laughed and walked off. Her singsong voice carried back to them. "The It girl princess is going slumming."

Chloe frowned at Emma. "Shoot her."

"First thing tomorrow." Emma crossed her heart with a pastel pink fingertip. "She's analyzing my finances tonight."

"I'll shoot her," Samantha volunteered, taking a bite of apple. "She's already done mine."

"Don't you dare, Sami," Emma said. "We have to wait until my investments are secure." She shot Chloe an apologetic look. "My loyalties are divided. You're excellent with money, but Tatiana is pure Midas. I'm protecting my retirement."

"You're not even forty."

"But a gazillion years from now I will be, Chloe. Besides, I don't feel like cleaning my gun tonight."

Renee's law. If you fire it today, you clean it today. Chloe sniffed and looked down at Kristi. "It's always something."

"Always." Kristi took a last stitch, cut the thread, then checked the skirt hem with a critical eye. "Perfect."

Chloe turned to the mirror and gasped at the scrap of black leather. "Good grief. I don't mind showing a little leg, but if this skirt was any shorter, my ass would be hanging out."

Kristi let out an exaggerated sigh. "It's always something."

Alan Burke walked in and over to Chloe and Emma, carrying a small plastic vial and a pair of tweezers. "And today, that something is this."

Chloe met his eyes in the mirror. "What is *this,* exactly?"

"Your secret weapon, angel face. Wipe off the lipstick." He stepped in front of her, unscrewed the cap, and waited.

She swiped at her lips with a tissue.

He pulled a thin film out of the vial with the tweezers and pressed it against her lips. "If you get into a jam, this will allow you to leave Hollow Hill tonight with your hide intact."

"I'm all for that," she said. "Is it lethal?"

"Not lethal, not legal." Alan's eyes twinkled. "But kiss a man and it will knock him on his ass for hours. He'll wake up with a hell of a headache and little memory, but he will wake up." Alan moved to Emma and repeated the process. "It produces short-term amnesia, like when you have surgery."

Emma grunted. "Sounds like a roofie."

"Oh, it's much better." He pinned a small gold rose on each of their tops.

"What are these?"

"Tracking devices," Alan said. "We'll know where you are at all times. He backed up and checked his work. "Excellent. Now reapply your lipstick and you're good to go."

"You're a wizard," Emma said, smiling.

"Don't you know it?" Alan winked. "You two make remarkable redheads." He looked at his sister. "Not bad, Kristi."

"Why are we redheads?" Chloe asked. The three Russian women had all been brunettes.

"I told you. Renee's orders," Kristi said. "The name of the service is Special Reserves Escorts. Harvey Walker manages the escorts and sets up the interviews. There are eight offices in the metropolitan area. Hollow Hill is the home office. It's on the lobby level. Emma, you're Kira. Garrett is your interviewer. Chloe, you're Oksana, and you meet with Warren. You two are smart, vulnerable, sophisticated, broke and Russian. Okay, great." She shot Alan a look. "We all agree, brother dearest, that you're a genius *and* you have excellent taste." Kristi shoved the crystal-studded glasses onto Chloe's nose. "Now, go. Jimmy's got the limo waiting in the alley—and for goodness' sake, be careful."

"We'll be fine," Emma said. "Don't worry, Kristi."

"I'm not worried." She hung the measuring tape around her neck. "You two can handle this or you wouldn't be assigned."

"She's wringing her hands, Emma." Chloe pointed. "She knows I'm going to bomb."

"You're not going to bomb." Emma slid Chloe a wicked

grin. "Look at it this way. You get to be a virgin again. How many women get that chance?"

"Glenda Huntsberger's been one three times," Samantha interjected, then wiggled her eyebrows. "Just ask her exes."

"Stupid men don't count." Chloe stretched over to a chair and grabbed her handbag, then swung her gaze to Emma. "Explain."

"You're a rookie escort, right? Rookie. Virgin. See the connection?" Emma snapped the top on her lipstick tube, then lifted her hand. "Fake it 'til you make it, baby."

"Right." Faking it was daily life. But this kind of faking it? "Hanging with you is going to get me killed."

Emma turned serious. "If this investigation takes us to the top and the Duke's sitting in the chair, it might."

More afraid than she cared to admit, Chloe dipped her chin and looked at Kristi over the rim of the glasses. "For the record, on the off-chance I live—"

Kristi lifted her eyebrows in an unspoken question.

"I'm really not bulletproof, and I hate fricking crystals." Chloe tapped the frame at the bridge of her nose and strolled out the door.

Well, Warren wasn't older than God and he wasn't a dog, even if he was wearing a knock-off Ralph Lauren suit in a low-quality fabric Ralph would *never* approve of. Somewhere in his thirties, the man who'd opened the hotel door at her knock had blond hair, blue eyes, a face with a little character and a small paunch that suited him. Maybe she wouldn't throw up. Maybe she could even get through this interview stone sober.

"Kira?" he asked.

That was supposed to be Emma's name. Chloe was supposed to be Oksana. *Damn it.* It was too late to make a switch now, so Chloe nodded. Did that mean he was Garrett?

He stared at Chloe's red wig and frowned. "I specifically told Harvey to send me only brunettes." Stepping back, he slammed the door in her face.

Rude jerk. As she stood in the hallway of Hollow Hill Hotel's fifth floor, an alarm in her mind strung her nerves even tighter. If he called Harvey or Warren, she and Emma both would be out on their asses and the Russian women, if here, would be screwed. Why had Renee ordered them to wear red wigs, anyway? She knew the women being abducted were brunettes.

Later. Now you need a plan!

A last-ditch effort gelled and Chloe knocked on the door. "Garrett," she took a chance. "Please, I will dye my hair. I will do whatever I must. I'm desperate." She put a plea in her voice and hoped it didn't botch her Russian dialect. "I have no one. Nothing. If you'll please just give me a chance…"

The door cracked open. He switched to Russian, too. "Come in, then. I can at least look at you."

She smiled and stepped inside.

He looked her over, then twirled a finger. "Turn around."

Turn. She could do that. No problem. She'd learned turning in the best damn finishing school in Sweden. Her heart raced and she hoped it didn't explode. She did a slow turn.

He let out a little groan. "Take off your coat."

She removed it, draped it over her arm, then turned again.

He nodded. "How far did you get in school?"

Chloe paused just a second. His tie tack was a knock-off, too. Brooks Brothers would not be caught dead selling it. "I'm self-taught," she said with a little shrug. "I lacked money for university, but I am well read."

Doubt riddled his eyes and he rubbed the back of his neck. "That could be a problem."

She smiled to soften a challenge in her tone. "Test me."

He fired off half a dozen questions about everything from wine to world politics. Clearly surprised by her answers, he then tried yet another. "Name two art museums."

She dipped her chin. "Any specific place?"

He smiled. "New York?"

"The Museum of Modern Art, Whitney Museum of American Art, the New Museum of Contemporary Art, the Museum for African Art, Guggenheim Museum…"

He was surprised, but not impressed. "And in Paris?"

"Louvre Museum, Musée Rodin, Musée National Picasso…"

"Rome?" His eyes glittered.

"Gallery of the National Academy of St. Luca."

"Another?"

She paused only a second, then added, "Museum of Galleria Borghese."

"Frankfurt?"

She decided to trick him. "Deutsches Architekturmuseum."

"That's not art." He frowned.

She gave him a slow, sexy smile. "It is if you're an architect."

"I'm impressed," Garrett admitted, a new appreciation for her sparkling in his eyes. "Do you speak languages other than Russian?"

"French, German and Spanish."

He hiked his brows. "And you're self-taught, you said?"

"Largely," she said, thinking fast. "I had a mentor who was appalled by ignorance." She lowered her lashes. "He was very good to me."

Understanding lightened Garrett's expression and his doubt disappeared. "Ah, I see." He paced between a table and the door. "So with all these skills, why are you unemployed?"

"Honestly?"

"Always," he insisted.

"I have no papers to be here," she confessed. "I can find work, but to build a career, I need papers. That takes money," she said earnestly. "And I have a tiny problem there."

"What kind of problem?"

She dipped her chin and looked him right in the eye. "I prefer champagne, gourmet meals and intelligent company over time clocks and chains to a desk."

"I see your point." He nodded, a smile teasing his full lips. "Have you ever modeled?"

She let out a delicate laugh. "I'm built like a woman, not a stick."

"True." Garrett smiled, appreciating the difference. "You have a certain charm, Kira."

"Thank you." She feigned licking at her lips, careful not to actually touch the film.

"I'm willing to give you a try."

"Really?" She forced herself to beam.

"Yes," he said. "Special Reserves Escorts is hosting an event this coming weekend. If you do well there, then we'll make the arrangement permanent."

"Fabulous." She widened her eyes. "Will I be paid for this event? I need money now."

He frowned. "For drugs?"

"For food and shelter. I have no place to stay."

A new interest lighted in his eyes. "So you just arrived in the U.S.?"

She nodded.

Pleased, he pulled out his wallet and passed her five hundred-dollar bills. "Come back here Friday at noon—and dye your hair brown."

Chloe took the money and walked to the door. "Thank you."

"Kira?" He cocked his head, and when she looked back,

he added, "Don't be late, and don't even think about taking my money and not showing up. I won't take that kindly."

"I'll be here," she promised, suppressing a cold chill. "I've nowhere else to go."

He patted her on the shoulder and spoke softly. "I'm sure you'll find a home with Special Reserves."

Her skin crawled. "Wonderful." She walked out and closed the door. Her part of tonight's assignment was a success. But should she celebrate or mourn?

Riding the elevator down, she replayed his questions in her mind. The interview confirmed the situation being exactly as the Governess and Renee predicted, and that had Chloe trembling head to foot.

She walked into the bar to wait for Emma, certain it'd take at least a double—maybe two—to get calm enough to stop shaking. Garrett almost definitely had marked her for slave trade.

Chapter 4

The bar was crowded and the din of voices nearly drowned out the soft music from the piano. Chloe scanned the dimly lit room for a table, sat down and looked to see what people were drinking. Most sipped at beer. Wanting to feel close to Jack, she ordered a mojito then demanded her insides stop shivering and settled in to listen to the music.

Half an hour later, Emma came in. Chloe caught her eye, and Emma nodded, surprised but clearly pleased to see Chloe already there.

She rushed over and sat down beside her. "What happened?"

"I come back Friday for an event they're hosting." She touched a fingertip to her red wig. "He took one look at me and got spooked. He specifically told Harvey send only brunettes."

"They switched us," Emma said. "Warren thought I was Oksana, and I was supposed to be a brunette, too."

Chloe's stomach clutched and her shoulders tensed. "Think the switch was deliberate?" The red wigs definitely had been.

"No. Harvey would have interceded. It had to be a clerical error on their end," Emma said. "I come back Friday, too, so we're set."

"Did he put you through the paces?"

She nodded. "Music." Fortunately, mostly due to her love of piano, she was well versed. "I got orders to dye my hair."

"Me, too." Chloe sipped at her drink.

"Well, at least now you can ditch the confidence crisis and relax." Emma blew out a relieved sigh.

She had old-money confidence and the personal esteem that came from being raised by non-neurotic, disgustingly healthy parents. If Chloe named one Gotham Rose *the* It girl, it'd be Emma.

Dropping her voice, Emma leaned forward on the table. "Very interesting scenery." She held her gaze on a guy just sitting down two tables over.

Chloe looked at him and did a double take, her breath catching in her throat. He was gorgeous. Great shoulders, square jaw, strong face and classic navy Brooks Brothers suit. His tie sucked and the black-frame glasses were a little heavy, obscuring his eyes, but he was definitely yummy. Her interest piqued, she smiled at him.

He smiled back, and a little ripple of pleasure tiptoed through her chest to her belly.

"Put your glasses on," Emma said softly. "Do it now."

"Oh, hell." Who here would recognize her, for pity's sake? Between the wig and the leather, she looked nothing like herself. Still, she fumbled in her coat pocket and shoved on the fricking glasses.

"Chloe, listen to me."

She turned to Emma, her skin between her brows wrinkling.

"My bones were right."

"Shut up." Chloe grunted. "Really?"

Emma nodded. "Warren confirmed it."

Chloe went rigid. "I don't believe it."

"Believe it." Emma motioned the waitress. "Unintentional, of course. But confirmed."

"Marcus?" Chloe's heart sank.

"No."

The slave trade. Chloe considered it confirmed, too. Intel's identified pattern was consistent with her experience. "Yeah, same here."

A petite blonde with one ear quadruple-pierced and a black skirt nearly as short as Chloe's walked over, carrying a tray. "May I help you?"

Emma smiled. "What kind of champagne do you have?"

"Dom Perignon 1996, Veuve du Vernay, Champagne Mumm, Korbel, Perrier Jouet, Grande Cuvee, and Roderer Cristol."

"Grande Cuvee," Emma said.

"Glass or bottle?"

Emma looked shocked. "One can buy champagne by the glass?"

The waitress grinned. "One can here."

Emma still hadn't recovered, so Chloe said, "We'll take the bottle." Kristi could just get over it. Chloe needed a drink.

The waitress nodded and then walked over to the bar. Scant minutes later, she returned with the champagne in a silver-bucketed stand and set it beside the table. The cork had been popped. She filled two glasses, then seated the bottle back in the crunching ice. "Enjoy." She walked away.

"Thanks." Chloe curled her fingers around the glass stem.

Emma sipped at her champagne and spoke softly. "I'll be happy when we're out of this."

"We'll have to strengthen the connections when we come

back on Friday." Resigned, Chloe swallowed two draws on her drink. "How did you find out about the slave trade?" She frowned. "Are you sure Warren wasn't jerking you around?"

"I'm sure. I beat the hell out of him."

"You *what?*" Chloe whispered a shout.

"No, no. It's okay," Emma said. "Seriously. It was part of the interview. Zero tolerance policy on sex, but lots of leeway in other areas."

Chloe shuddered. "Well, at least it worked." She sneaked in another appreciative glance at Mr. Brooks Brothers, and again felt the ripple. Her eye candy was moving toward the door. Following him with her gaze, Chloe spotted a man she instinctively recognized. She froze. The light had to be playing tricks on her. He was on a plane to London. He turned toward her, and she gasped. "Jack!"

"I thought he was in—" Catching Chloe's expression, Emma looked back and saw him. "Son of a bitch. Who's the brunette?"

Anger replaced shock and burned in Chloe's belly. "I don't know. But unless she can teleport him to London, it doesn't much matter. Let's go." She slid off her chair, grabbed her coat and purse, so furious she was shaking.

"You're going to confront him?" Emma scrambled to catch up. "Bad idea, honey. Remember where you are. Remember why!"

Too angry to listen, Chloe walked up to his table and just stood there until he stopped talking and looked up at her. His eyes widened in shock.

"This is London?" Chloe ignored the woman with him.

Regret washed through his eyes. "Oh, no."

"Sorry to interrupt. This will take just a second." She spared the woman a glance, then bent low and whispered in Jack's ear. "I trusted you, you lying son of a bitch."

"I can—"

"Save it, *darling*." She smiled. "It was enlightening to see you again." She kissed him, activating the film on her lips and hoping when he went lights out, he broke his damn nose.

He slumped forward, dropped face-first onto the table, and hit it with a thud.

Feigning a surprised look, she turned a cool gaze on the woman. "Apparently, he still can't hold his liquor."

Emma grabbed her sleeve. "Let's go."

"He loves me, eh?" Chloe turned toward the door.

A camera flash blinded her.

Oh, hell. This was *not* good. This was really *not* good.

Emma swerved, seeking an alternate exit. Chloe started to follow, keeping her back to the camera—and recognizing the woman standing behind it. That bitch of a reporter, Rubi Cho. Chloe's stomach knotted. *Damn it.*

"Renee is going to kill us." Emma groaned.

"This way," a man said.

Chloe looked up and saw her eye candy. Emma started to turn away, but Chloe grabbed her sleeve and followed him. He shielded them from Rubi all the way to the street, preventing any more photos.

Jimmy stood curbside at the limo with the door open. Emma got inside. Chloe hesitated and turned to the guy. "Thanks."

He didn't smile. "You're welcome."

She couldn't move. He had the most unusual eyes she'd ever seen, a haunted gray that mirrored how she felt inside. Jack had lied to her. She'd dared to trust him and he'd lied. And these eyes understood the pain of that betrayal…

"Hurry, Chloe," he said. "Rubi is almost here."

She stilled. "How do you know—?"

He coaxed her, nudging her shoulder for her to get in the limo. "Next time." Bending, he reached for the hem of her coat and tucked it inside.

She turned her head to thank him and her lips collided with his. Shock widened his eyes. His knees folded. He collapsed toward her, half in and out of the limo.

"Oh, God!" Emma shrieked. "What did you do?"

"It was an accident." Chloe pulled and tugged at the man, trying to get him into the car. "Jimmy, help me!"

He rushed out and around, heaved the man in and slammed the door, then slid back behind the wheel. Before his own door shut, he punched on the gas.

"Oh, God. I can't believe this!" The unflappable Emma wailed. "Do something. His head's in my crotch."

Chloe tugged at his shoulders, sliding him off Emma and trying to get him onto the opposite seat. "Could you stop screeching and help me here?"

"Help you?" Emma positioned her knee under his stomach, got her arms against his chest and shoved. His head banged against the door.

"Damn. That had to hurt." Chloe winced.

Emma glared at her.

"It was an accident," Chloe repeated, earning herself another glare. Finally, they got him situated on the seat.

"He's out cold." Flustered, Emma swiped at her hair. "Damn it, Chloe. Five minutes ago you see Jack with another woman, and now you kiss this guy? Don't you think you're moving a little quick on a pickup?"

"Don't be stupid. I'm crushed. I didn't mean to kiss *him*."

"Ladies, stop. Stop."

"I *didn't* kiss him." Ignoring Jimmy, Chloe defended herself. "We just bumped mouths."

"Well, you'd better just bump into a plan. What the hell do we do with him for the next few hours?"

"I don't know." Chloe pressed a hand to her fluttering

stomach. "I couldn't leave him on the street. He knew my name." He'd helped her.

Emma looked at her as if she were dense. "Of course he knew your name."

Chloe rounded on her. "Do you know him?"

"I've seen him, sure. But I don't know him."

"Where have you seen him?"

"At the G.R.C. He comes to see Renee once in a while."

"I've seen him, too." Jimmy chimed in. "He's one of the Governess's representatives. Never heard his name, though."

"Whoa." Chloe couldn't believe it. "What's he doing at Hollow Hill?"

Emma glared at Chloe again and swiped at the wrinkles in her skirt. "I expect the Governess sent him as our backup." Her bracelet caught on her sleeve and she worked it loose. "We've got to do *something* with him."

"We could take him to the G.R.C.," Chloe suggested.

"Won't that look good?" Emma challenged her. "Renee will report it to the Governess. She'll fire him *and* us."

"Oh, no." Jimmy's voice carried back to them. "Rubi Cho's tagging us. She definitely recognized you two."

"Can this nightmare get any worse?" Emma half-turned to look out the rear window. "Lose her, Jimmy." She looked at Chloe. "You know, the Rose agents should form a strategic business alliance, buy that damn paper and fire her."

"I've thought the same thing," Chloe confessed. "But she'd follow us anyway, just to annoy us."

Jimmy sped up, made a couple quick turns, and then opened up the engine on the straightaway. Chloe looked back, but didn't spot Rubi's car in the traffic. "What happened?"

"See the black SUV?"

She spotted it four cars back in the right lane. "Yeah."

"I don't know who's driving it, but they've got Rubi boxed in, and it's deliberate," Jimmy said. "Jack maybe?"

"No," Chloe said, remembering Jack thudding nose down on the table. "It's definitely not Jack." The lying son of a bitch. Another woman. After that call to Chloe about missing her already and their *incredible* morning?

Emma looked back again. "It's Erik. I saw him in the lobby."

Chloe nearly choked. "What was Erik doing at Hollow Hill? He never goes there, it isn't trendy enough for him." This was beyond bizarre. Jack *and* Erik *and* the Governess's representative all in a place none of them would normally be?

"Good question," Emma said. "And I'd be asking it right after I dealt with Mr. Brooks Brothers here, if I were you."

"We have to figure out what to do with this guy." She motioned with a wave. "We can't leave him in the car for two hours."

"Why not?" Emma asked.

"He's vulnerable, Emma. He helped us." Chloe smacked her lips. "Do you have a loyal bone in your body?"

"You know better than that. Just because you're devastated about Jack being a two-timing ass, don't get pissy with me."

"Call Renee. She or the Governess can tell us how to handle it," Jimmy said, trying to get them back to the matter at hand.

"No way." Chloe wasn't having any part of that. "She'll report this and the Governess will be all over him for letting me drop him. He was helping us and I bumped him. It's totally my fault he's out—even if it was an accident—and I'm not letting him get busted for it."

"She's right about that, Jimmy," Emma said. "The Governess will bust him—and likely us, too."

She definitely would if she heard about Jack. Dropping *him* hadn't been an accident. "I'm taking him home with me," Chloe announced. "Damage control. Frank's at home and the fewer who know about this debacle, the better." If Tatiana caught wind of it, she would gloat until they died of old age.

"Agreed. That's safe."

"Whatever," Jimmy said, "but you should tell Renee."

"No," Chloe vetoed that. "When he wakes up, I can explain what happened, and he can just go…wherever it is that the Governess's representatives go when they're not around us."

"If he doesn't shoot you first." Emma pulled the film off her lips and then retrieved her lipstick and little gold mirror from her purse. "Okay, that's settled." Emma painted her lips with the tip of the tube. "On to another matter."

"What?"

"Tatiana must have tipped off Rubi. How else could she know we'd be at Hollow Hill?"

Tatiana and Rubi had gone clubbing a few times, and Tatiana was totally ticked about Renee replacing her with Chloe. Odds ran high Tatiana had tipped off Rubi, but they had no proof of it. Yet. "This wouldn't have happened if you'd listened to me but no, you were too worried about your money."

"Noted, but academic now." Emma snapped her mirror closed. "It probably was Tatiana, but since Mr. Brooks Brothers was on site, obviously people outside the G.R.C. knew we'd be there, too."

And there were a fair number of people between the Governess and the Roses. The Governess coordinated the Roses' assignments and issued her orders through Renee, but there were consultants, representatives and who knew who else gathering the intel she passed along.

"Wonder how many Roses knew where we'd be tonight?" Chloe asked. "Kristi lost it and shouted our plan at Tatiana."

"Sub-levels are soundproof," Jimmy reminded her.

"Bug heard it, for sure," Emma said, using her nickname

for her best friend, Porsche Rothschild. "Samantha, too. Could have been others."

Likely many others. There were always women around. Tonight had gone south in a hurry. Considering the mission, that was worrisome. But honestly, all the missions carried significant risks to the Rose, to her standing in society, and sometimes—as in Madison's case—to her family. Yet the risks hadn't produced a shortage of willing heiresses, even though no one, not even family, could know of their activities. Which was why Chloe couldn't ask Erik why he'd been at Hollow Hill tonight. She'd expose herself.

Sometimes this secret life was hard.

"I can't see Porsche or any Rose agent saying a thing, much less calling Rubi. Besides, they wouldn't have a clue what they were reporting, because only Tatiana knew what we were doing."

Chloe thought about that. "The Rose agents are bright women, Emma. The way we're dressed, where we were going… They'll figure out more than you think—and far more than they should. Hell, they're agents. That's worth remembering."

Emma worried her lip with her teeth. "It was probably Tatiana." Sparks shot through Emma's eyes. "We'd better consider her the leak. We have too much to lose to risk not believing it."

And Tatiana would know it, and she would know she was risking exposure of all the Roses, including herself—which was why she might *not* have done it. "She's a social-status, power-hungry slut, but she's not stupid. Assuming she's guilty isn't really fair to her, either, Emma."

"For God's sake, think of the mess we're in. I'm sure enough to know we wouldn't be in it without her interference." Emma shook her head, worried her lip with her teeth. "Screw being fair. I should've shot her."

"What?" That from Jimmy. "Emma, you can't shoot another agent. What's wrong with you?" He glanced back at Chloe. "Just how much did she drink in the bar?"

"She's talking virtual, Jimmy." Chloe hoped she was right.

Emma's expression sobered then grew more serious and she frowned. "You sound so blasé about this. Do you truly understand what just happened?" Fear flickered in her eyes.

Chloe stiffened. Emma was the most courageous woman she had ever met in her life. If she was afraid, Chloe should be terrified. "What?" Chloe asked. "So Rubi got a photo. In tomorrow's column, she'll write that I've been drinking and partying too much again, and as short as this skirt is, I'll probably be staring at my red thong in the photo—" when the flash went off, she'd been stretching "—but that's not seriously atypical. It does mean—"

Out of patience, Emma interrupted. "Your mother is destined to lay another lecture from hell on you about what an embarrassment you are and what a waste you're making of your life, living off your inheritance and yada yada. You should really blow her mind and tell her the truth about what you do."

"Never." Chloe flatly refused. She'd ruin it. "The point is, it'll just be the usual irritation, and then it'll be over."

"No, it won't." Emma glared at her. "This isn't going to cause the usual upheaval or reactions. You haven't scraped the surface of all the hell that's coming because of this."

Chloe changed perspective to see the situation through Renee's eyes, and the truth sank in. Then came the fear, and her stomach flipped over and soured. "Oh no." She turned on the seat toward Emma, grasped her arm and squeezed. "Our covers have been blown."

Emma groaned. "Finally, she sees the light!"

Frowning, Chloe followed the linear thought. "We know

we're after the Duke now, but we still don't know his identity—"

Emma nodded, lifted a hand, palm upward. "However, with Rubi's column..."

"Good grief." The fear turned to terror and ripped through Chloe's chest, up into her throat and burst out in a gasp. "The Duke will know ours."

Chapter 5

"Chloe St. John, get your hand out of that man's pants." Frank, who'd gotten up to help Jimmy carry Chloe's casualty inside, looked totally beside himself. "He can't do nothing for you, Princess. He's out cold."

Bent over a sprawled-on-her-sofa Mr. Brooks Brothers, she rolled her gaze heavenward. "I'm trying to get his wallet."

"What for?" Frank walked into the living room and stopped beside her.

"So I can find out who he is."

Frank's jaw dropped. "You got your hand down the pants of a man on your sofa and you don't know who he is?"

"No," she said, out of patience and realizing she looked like a fool. "I know who he is, I just don't know his name."

"Well, if you'd put your mind to what you're doing and not on getting into the man's pants, you'd likely figure out his wallet's in the inside pocket of his suit jacket."

Chloe jerked her hand back and stared at Frank.

He frowned, reached over and tapped the bulk outline of the wallet. "Right there."

"Oh, hell." She reached in and pulled out the wallet.

"Might I ask you one more question?"

"What?" Chloe asked, seriously considering kissing Frank, too. But she'd already removed the lip film.

"What's Jack gonna think about you fritzing around with another man?" Frank nodded down at Mr. Brooks Brothers.

Betrayal stung deep. "I don't expect it much matters, considering I caught him with another woman tonight." Chloe opened the wallet and saw a government ID card. *Senior Special Agent Harrison Howell.* No agency was mentioned, which seemed in keeping with a Governess representative.

"Jack was with another woman?" Shock rippled through Frank's voice. "I don't believe it."

"Believe it," Chloe said, sparing him a deadpan look. "I confronted him myself."

"Well, what did he say?"

A little embarrassed about giving in to her temper and knocking Jack out, she shrugged. "Nothing." She thought again. "Actually, I think it was, 'Oh, God.'"

"I expect he had a reason for not being honest with you, Princess." Frank nodded to add weight to his claim. "If he was cheating, I'd be happy to shoot him for you. But I think you should give him the benefit of doubt."

She frowned. "There is no reason for not being honest."

Getting her message, Frank turned the topic. "So who's this one. Why'd you knock him out?"

"I didn't." Chloe frowned. "Well, I guess I did, but I didn't do it on purpose."

"Uh-huh." Frank rubbed his chin and crossed his chest.

"I really didn't." She turned a weary look on Frank. "Can you just believe me and let it go? I swear it's all okay."

He stared at her a long second. "I can and will. But he's gonna wake up madder than a wet hornet."

"Damn right," she borrowed Frank's favorite phrase.

"Best take his gun." Frank walked to the door, heading for his own apartment on the floor below Chloe's. "Or at least steal his bullets."

Harrison had a gun? She looked down at his chest and peeking out from beneath his jacket she saw the holster. "Probably should—just until he cools off." She put the gun on the mantel, a safe distance away. Then she covered Harrison up with a soft velvet throw and turned out the light.

Chloe changed into a pair of gray velvet Ralph Lauren slacks and top—the closest thing to sweats she owned. Wanting to be close by when Senior Special Agent Harrison Howell came to, she sat with her second cup of tea and a box of tissues in a chair in the corner of the living room and cried her heart out. How could Jack do this? Why would he do it to them? Things had been so good…

He was just like the rest of them. Couldn't trust him any farther than she could throw him. She'd been an idiot to do it. How many times would it take for her to get it through her head that no man who seemed to be romantically interested in her could be trusted?

By the time she'd gone through half a box of tissues and started on the second pot of tea, she wondered if Harrison Howell was ever going to wake up. She got up to check on him—maybe he'd had an adverse reaction to the drug or something. He had his arm thrown over his head, half-hiding his face, but his light snore was steady enough. He was sleeping, not dead.

The doorbell rang.

Chloe went rigid. The night security guard hadn't phoned up, which meant it had to be someone on her approved list. Erik maybe? Wondering why she'd been at Hollow Hill?

Possible. She walked to the door, depressed a button under a small screen and saw Jack standing outside. First thing tomorrow, she'd take him off her damn approved list.

Chloe unlocked the door and cracked it open. "What?"

He looked unsteady. The effect of the drug? "I can explain." His words slurred.

"Go ahead." Explain? How could he explain lying to her?

"Can I come in?"

She debated, then saw Mrs. Granger stick her head out her door across the hall and decided it'd probably be best. Stepping back, she allowed him space to come through the door.

He stumbled into the living room and his eyes widened at the sight of Brooks Brothers. "What is he doing here?"

"I'm not in the mood to answer your questions, Jack. You explain why you're not in London and why you were with another woman at Hollow Hill. That, I'm ready to hear."

"No, Chloe," he whispered, tugging her back to the entryway, his usual grace absent. "You don't understand. That man—"

"I understand plenty." She swallowed tears. "It's okay for you to be with another woman, but not for me to be with a man." She lifted a hand. "Screw that double standard, Jack."

"No." He reached for her, but she backed up. "Listen. Would you just listen?"

She crossed her arms, glared at him.

"Chloe, I want you to stay away from that man."

"Why?" He worked for the Governess. He was a Senior Special Agent. Next to Frank, he was the safest man on the planet—apparently, far safer than Jack.

Jack paused, closed his eyes and shook his head, then looked at her. "I can't tell you. But it's important, Chloe."

"Why were you at Hollow Hill?"

His expression soured. "I can't tell you that, either."

Anger surged through her stomach. "You can't tell me much of anything, can you?"

Jack looked her right in the eye. "I can tell you that you didn't see what you thought. That you need to stay away from that man. I can tell you he might be dangerous."

"Dangerous?" She scoffed. "Come on, Jack. Are you that desperate to get rid of him because he's shown interest in me?" A lie, but a safe one.

"Chloe, I'm nearly positive he's connected to an underground ring selling women into slavery."

Stunned, she couldn't move.

"Did you hear me?"

Struggling to calm down, she gave him a perplexed look. How did he know about this? How had he gotten involved? Why had he said he'd be in London when he was here, investigating this? "What are you talking about?"

Exasperated, Jack nudged her. "This is no time for games. I know why you were at Hollow Hill. I know Erik was there."

Chloe lifted her chin. "You know a lot of things, none of which make sense to me." True, as far as it went. Who'd turned him onto this story?

"Fine, then just listen to me." Jack dragged a hand through his hair. "Honey, I am concerned about everything that has anything to do with you. I care about you—and you care about me."

"You care? You lied to me, Jack. I suppose you care about the brunette you were with, too, right?"

"Well, yes—but not in the way you think."

Outraged, Chloe jerked open the door. "Go home, Jack."

"Will you be reasonable? I trusted you about Marcus, didn't I? Can't you afford me the same—"

"I never lied to you about Marcus. I never claimed I was leaving the country when I wasn't." Steamed, she elevated her voice. "I told you I couldn't tell you why I was pretending to be engaged to him. I didn't lie." She pointed out the door. "Go home, Jack. Go lie to someone else."

"Fine." He walked out into the hallway. "Call me when you get over your snit and get reasonable."

"Don't hold your breath." She started to close the door.

He blocked it with his foot, and looked at her through the crack. "One last thing."

She waited.

"I think that man on your sofa is working for the Duke."

"So what did you do?" Emma asked over the phone.

"I slammed the door." Chloe paced a path between the marbled countertops in her sleek kitchen.

"You didn't ask how he knew about the Duke?" Shock riddled Emma's voice.

Chloe pulled the phone away from her ear. "Now how the hell could I do that without admitting *I* knew who the Duke was?"

That took the wind out of Emma's sails. "I suppose you couldn't. He can't know Harrison works for the Governess."

"Obviously not."

"Chloe, what are you thinking?"

"I'm thinking Jack was there," she said on a swallowed sob. "I'm thinking he was with a brunette. I'm thinking he knows about the Duke, and he says he knew why we were there."

Emma gasped. "You think Jack's the Duke?"

God help her, she'd considered it. "It's possible. How else would he know all these things?"

"Oh, God," Emma said. "We need to talk to Renee."

"I've already phoned Olivia and set a meeting for first thing in the morning. Meet me at the G.R.C. at nine."

"It's two now," Emma said. "Is Mr. Brooks Brothers back from the dead?"

"Not yet." Why was that? He'd been out a lot longer than two hours.

"Is he breathing?"

"He's snoring." Chloe walked to the end of the room where she could see into the living room and confirmed it.

"Must be extremely sensitive to drugs. He's been out a lot longer than Jack was."

"Or Alan was worried I'd screw up and get into trouble. Maybe he fixed it so the dose of drugs on the film gets stronger with every freaking kiss."

"Either's possible," Emma conceded.

"Thanks for the vote of confidence."

"If you'd make your damn training meetings, they wouldn't be worried."

She was right. "I'll see you at nine."

At 7:25 a.m., Harrison was still lights-out. Probably had gone from knocked out to sleeping naturally. Chloe sat bleary-eyed at the kitchen bar on a stool with the telephone at her ear and the newspaper opened to Rubi Cho's column, wondering if she could bribe Frank to put on the lip film and keep Rubi knocked on her ass for about a year. If he was willing to shoot Jack, surely he'd kiss Rubi. He liked Jack.

The photo was awful, but the comments were atrocious—and uncannily reminiscent of Tatiana's remarks at Gotham Rose Club last night. "What *It girl* princess was seen in the once-popular but now slightly seedy Hollow Hill last night, dressed in a black leather skirt that almost wasn't there?"

Chloe could cut Rubi's tongue out. And not one mention of Emma. Why was that?

Tatiana.

She turned her attention to her phone conversation as Adele

Phillips, Chloe's partner in Adelphio, caught her up on their recent fabric acquisitions. Adele had paused for a response. Chloe said, "That sounds great—and we got the silks?" The supplier had been giving Adele fits for a week.

"We did—and at the reduced rate."

"Music to my ears." The phone beeped, signaling another call coming in. "Let me run, Adele."

"Okay, but don't forget to pick up your gown for the Halloween Ball. Or do you want me to just have it delivered?"

"Better deliver it."

"You've got it."

Chloe checked the caller ID. It was her mother calling. "It's going to be one of those days."

Chloe took a sip of steaming coffee—tea had ceased keeping her awake at about 4:00 a.m.—steeled herself, then clicked the flash button. "Good morning, Mother. How are you?"

"How do you think I am, Chloe?"

Oh, hell. Here it came. "I don't know. That's why I asked." *Please don't let her know Erik was there, too.*

"Don't be trite. I know you've seen Rubi's article. What are you doing to this family? Single-handedly destroying it?"

"No, Mother. I assure you, the destruction of anything is not my objective."

"Then what is?"

Oh, but she'd like to tell her. In graphic, vivid detail. But she couldn't. Not that her mother would believe her, anyway. "Is that it?"

"I beg your pardon?"

Chloe thumbed the rim of her cup. "If the only reason you called was to tell me I'd embarrassed the family again, then we can consider it done and get on with our day."

"Chloe, do not take that attitude with me. I am your mother."

"So what do you want, Mother?"

"I want you to stop doing thoughtless things that publicly reflect on the rest of this family, including your brother. He deserves better from you."

Erik deserved nothing from her. Less than nothing.

"I want you to do something constructive with your life. The only thing you do that is worthy of your crown is your charity work with Renee, and apparently you're failing at that, as well."

"I beg your pardon?" Chloe set her cup down. Hard.

"You certainly should. You do nothing else—nothing else, Chloe—and yet you raise a mere $2 million for the Women's Shelter? I sincerely hope that this date auction you're sponsoring tonight increases that to a respectable sum."

Anger churned in Chloe's throat, but she swallowed it. "Then I suggest you bring your checkbook, Mother. Father, too." Her mother was a successful designer and nearly as wealthy as Chloe. Her father had done well for himself, too, in antiquities. They could afford to be extra generous, and she was just angry enough to encourage it.

"We will be attending, of course. And we'll certainly make the Halloween Ball at the end of the month."

"Wonderful. I'll see you—"

"I noticed that Ryan Greene was mentioned in Rubi's column as well."

He was Manhattan's most eligible and gorgeous bachelor, according to Rubi. She clearly had a crush on him, not that Chloe could blame her. He was charming.

"Why can't you get involved with someone like him, Chloe? Look at the stabilizing influence he's had on Erik."

"I'm stable enough alone, thank you." Chloe sighed, bone weary of battling her mother. "I've got to go. Busy day."

She hung up the phone before her mother could say anything else to upset her—she had a stomach full of upset already thanks to Jack—and leaned over and pressed her forehead against the bar, then groaned. "God, I don't need this."

The phone rang again. "Hello."

"Chloe, it's me." Emma sounded urgent. "Duck your mother's calls. Rubi got art and her forked tongue is firmly in her cheek. Olivia called. Renee has an appointment. We're to meet her for tea at 10:30 instead of 9:00. There's been a development."

"Too late on my mother. I've seen the art—it sucks—and what development?" God, hadn't enough crises hit them already?

"She thinks someone in the club has betrayed us."

"So do we. Tatiana." That was pretty much a certainty and they both knew it. "You weren't identified. That's pretty much a dead giveaway it's her."

"No, Chloe. Directly to the enemy, on the assignment."

"Oh, no." This was worse. The G.R.C. could be exposed.

"Use the alley," Emma said. "The press is camped out front, determined to find out the truth about Marcus's death, your kidnapping and now this ordeal at Hollow Hill. Renee doesn't want us talking to the media until after we talk with her."

The honchos knew it all. *Damn it.* "Okay." Chloe rubbed her forehead, which was now throbbing.

She caught a flicker of movement out of the corner of her eye and glanced over at the sofa. "Um, I need to go, Emma. Harrison's awake."

"It's about time," she said, mirroring Chloe's thoughts. "Don't be late."

"I won't." Chloe hung up the phone, went to the kitchen and retrieved a cup of coffee, then brought it to Harrison, who was now sitting upright and rubbing his temples. "Coffee?"

He took the cup. "Chloe, why in hell am I on your sofa?"

Angry. And in pain. "Can I get you a couple aspirin or something?"

He glared at her. "You can answer my damn question."

"I'm so sorry. I didn't know what to do with you."

"Excuse me?"

"You fainted—"

"I do *not* faint."

"Okay, then." Frank was right, as usual. Harrison Howell was thoroughly and totally furious. "You passed out. I brought you here. You slept, and now you're awake."

He reached for his gun.

"It's on the mantel." The bullets were on the kitchen bar.

He sipped at the coffee. "I bent down to get your coat inside the car, and we bumped heads."

"Actually, we bumped mouths."

He slanted her a sidelong look. "And that knocks men out?"

"Um, no, not usually. Not exactly." She really didn't want to admit this, but there was no help for it. She stood out of his reach but near the sofa. "Do you know Alan Burke?"

Harrison sipped from his cup. "The Gotham Rose Club's resident genius."

She nodded. "It was his lip film. I had it on, and when we bumped mouths—*pow*—you were lights-out."

Harrison grunted. "You should have called Renee."

"You might have gone up on report." She shrugged. "It was totally my fault, and I didn't want you to get into trouble. After all, you were helping me, so it wouldn't have been right."

He sent her an indecipherable look—maybe appreciation or disbelief, maybe censure. "How did we bump mouths?"

Heat rushed up her neck to her face, and she shrugged. "It was an accidental thing."

"I see." He stared hard at her, but didn't challenge her response. "May I use your bathroom?"

Relieved, she let go of some of the tension. "Of course." She motioned. "Third door on the left."

Harrison stood up and swayed, shook his head to clear it, and then disappeared down the hallway.

Chloe slipped into a pair of black Valentino slacks and a crisp white Adelphio blouse with a standup collar, hastily smeared on some lip-gloss and ran a brush through her hair, then returned to the living room, glad her housekeeper was away.

Harrison sat on the sofa, holding a hot coffee cup against his forehead. "If the offer stands, I'll take those aspirin."

She glanced at the mantel. He'd retrieved his gun…and his bullets from the counter. "Sure." She poured him a glass of orange juice and snagged the bottle of aspirin. "Here you go."

"Thanks." He wolfed down three of them then set the bottle on the glass-top coffee table. "So tell me something."

He wasn't going to shoot her. Feeling certain of it now, she sat down in a chair beside the sofa. "If I can, I will."

"You can, but I seriously doubt that you will." He forked his fingers through his hair, ruffling more than smoothing it. "Why do you take that flack from your mother?"

That was one question she hadn't expected. Obviously, he'd been awake longer than she'd realized, and he'd overheard her and her mother arguing on the phone. *Great.* Chloe pasted on a smile, but answered by rote. "What would she do without me to be disappointed in?" Tossing out the canned response she'd used successfully so often should make her comfortable, but it didn't. For some reason, it sounded flat. "I'm her fodder."

He looked at her through cool, gray eyes. "She has no idea who you are or what you do—I mean, outside of the agency."

"None," Chloe said. "And I intend to keep it that way."

He frowned and reached for his glasses, then seated them on the bridge of his nose. "Why?"

Something in the timbre of his voice told her the inquiry was more than idle curiosity, so Chloe told him. "She ruins everything, Harrison. She doesn't mean to do it, she just does. I've worked really hard to build my companies, and many, like Adelphio, involve other people. I won't have her ruining them."

"So you're not hiding from her." He softened his voice but the look in his eyes remained unyielding. "If you're hiding from her, Chloe, then she's controlling you."

"I'm not hiding." And if she was, she couldn't admit that even to herself much less to one of the Governess's representatives. "She's going to be nose-in to someone's business. If not mine, then whose?"

"Your service to mankind is appreciated—at least, by me. But it wouldn't hurt for her to nose-in on Erik for a while."

"Erik?" What did Harrison know about her brother?

"He's keeping fast company these days. Someone needs to take an honest look at what he's doing."

"What is he doing? And what fast company?"

"Ryan Greene, Brit Carouthers, and until he was killed, Marcus Abbot Sterling, III."

A bit of a surprise there. "Who is Brit Carouthers?"

"Caulfield Carouthers's brother. When Caulfield got arrested, someone took over his illegal activities. Brit may have been elected."

Chloe frowned. She knew Caulfield Carouthers had been busted for running a drug ring. Fellow Rose agent Vanessa Dawson had been part of bringing him down. "Erik was friends with Marcus?"

"In a way." Harrison reached for his cup and took a sip. The steam curled up into the air. "Marcus helped your brother lose a great deal of his fortune. Now Erik is in business with Greene and Carouthers."

Chloe's jaw dropped. "I had no idea."

"No one did, except us," Harrison said.

Marcus hadn't been the Duke. His death hadn't led

Harrison to the Duke, either, since the Roses were still searching for him. Disappointing for all of them. "So what are you saying? That Ryan and Brit are a bad influence on Erik?"

"I'm saying Prince Erik is just as bad as Ryan and Brit. They're all overindulged, spoiled and self-destructive."

Harrison's opinion startled her. "Maybe Brit is corrupt. But Ryan is a darling. Everyone loves him."

"He's a Rose slut, Chloe, doing his damnedest to sleep with every one of you."

Blunt again. "I guess he is," she agreed, being equally honest. "But it's typical for a man in his position to date women in mine. And he's a huge champion of women's causes, Harrison. Is that what you don't like about him?"

"Of course not." Harrison frowned, looking truly affronted.

"What is it then?"

"His damn veneer teeth."

That left her reeling. "Excuse me?"

"His teeth." Harrison bared his own and tapped them. "Veneers are okay, if there's substance under them. With Ryan, there's only blind ambition behind his porcelain-whites."

Well, she couldn't dispute him on that. Not after some of the real estate deals she'd seen him and Madison Taylor-Pruitt compete for. Ryan consistently went for the jugular. But so did Madison, and more often than not, she won. "Is that how you see Erik, too?" Chloe asked Harrison.

"I know you're protective of him, but your first loyalty has to be to the Governess now, and to your mission."

"I'm well aware of my responsibilities—and that you didn't answer my damn question."

"Erik's ambition isn't blind," he said. "He sees it very clearly, and you can keep protecting him, as you have, provided there's no collision of loyalties. If there is, the Governess wins, regardless of who gets hurt. That's not negotiable."

The truth hit Chloe hard. "You saw Erik last night at Hollow Hill, too."

Harrison nodded. "Do you know why he was there?"

"No, I don't." But she'd wondered a lot since learning it.

"And you can't ask him without revealing that you know he was there, too." Harrison grimaced. "Perfect."

Harrison knew too much, knew her too well, and his assessments made her nervous as hell. Erik had always pushed the edge and done as much as he could get away with doing. He had a string of successes at getting away with things for which he should have been punished—her fault. Had her covering for him and making his mistakes and indiscretions disappear encouraged him to risk bigger mistakes and indiscretions? What if *he* was the Duke?

Her chest went tight and she couldn't breathe. It would kill her mother. Humiliate her father—and he'd worked so hard to become a worthy man in his own right, without his crown. And if Chloe was forced to expose Erik... *Oh, God.*

She thought it through. It'd be bloody awful. Her mother couldn't be any more disappointed in her than she was already. But she could alienate Chloe—and she likely would. No one damaged her baby boy.

"I'm sorry," Harrison said. He stood and walked over to her chair. "And I'm sorry about Jack, too."

"Who is he—really?"

Harrison cocked his head. "A reporter, Chloe."

"No," she said. "Harrison, he thinks you might be connected to the Duke. He knows far too much for a reporter."

"Me?" Harrison looked shocked.

"I know." She touched his sleeve. "He obviously doesn't know that you work for the Governess. But what I want to know is how he knows about the Duke at all?"

"You didn't tell him?" Harrison asked without censure. "Pillow talk?"

"Of course not. I'd never put him in jeopardy."

"Calm down, Princess. Just asking a legitimate question."

"He betrayed me, Harrison." She let him see her pain in her eyes. "I trusted him, and he lied to me."

He returned her gaze with that haunted look she'd first noticed in his own. "I'm sorry."

Her stomach clenched. She stood, looked up into his face and saw his regret shining in his eyes. He really was sorry. "Harrison, am I going to lose my family over this mission?" Her family wasn't perfect, but it was hers, and the idea of losing it was almost more than she could bear.

"I don't know." He clasped her shoulders. "But if you do, I'll be here to help you. It's not much, Chloe, but it's the best I can do."

Tears burned the backs of her eyes. She blinked hard. "Thank you." She didn't trust him, would never again trust any man, but they weren't all lying scum. "You seem like a good person, Harrison." One with a kind heart.

"Actually, I'm a man with an agenda."

Uneasy, Chloe tried to back away but the chair was against her calves. "What agenda?"

The look in his eyes warmed. "I know last night was an accident—that mouth bump—but I want to see if your kiss knocks me to my knees as much today."

"It won't," she said, with a little smile. "No lip film."

"Unless you object." He dipped his chin and spoke against her mouth. "I think I'll judge that for myself."

"I shouldn't. Jack broke my heart."

"Is there a time when a woman needs tenderness more?"

Tears filmed her eyes. "No, there isn't." On a breathy sigh, she tiptoed and pressed her mouth to his—and while his knees seemed fine, hers went a little weak.

Chapter 6

At 10:32 a.m., Chloe entered the Gotham Rose Club through the private parking garage. Olivia met her at the back door and sent her straight to the sunroom, where Renee and Emma sat waiting.

Chloe held up a hand. "I know I'm two minutes off, but Frank had to circle to escape the paparazzi."

Renee stood and pointedly checked her watch. "I have 10:30, straight up and down. Emma?"

She didn't even look. "10:30."

"Ah, you made it then," Renee said. "Sit down and I'll pour you a cup of tea." She was already reaching for the pot.

Chloe dragged in a steadying breath. "So how bad is it?"

Emma's expression was sour, which told Chloe all she really needed to know.

"Drink your tea, and both of you listen well," Renee said. "We're going to go out and meet with the press. Do not open your mouths until I've finished with my statement. When I do and they ask questions, turn every answer into a commercial for the date auction tonight, which will benefit the women I'll be discussing." She dipped her chin. "The Governess and I have consulted and we—and Intel—are certain someone inside Gotham Rose Club betrayed you last night."

"Tatiana is the obvious choice," Emma said baldly.

"We have no hard evidence of that, Emma."

"Screw hard evidence, Chloe. Sometimes you go with common sense." Emma sat up straighter. "She was replaced and angry. She goes clubbing with Rubi. Rubi used almost the exact verbiage in her column that Tatiana used in the dressing room. You were mentioned, I wasn't. It was definitely Tatiana."

Renee took all that in, thought a moment and then added, "Yet Tatiana has been undercover on four assignments in the last year and she knows exposing Chloe could get her killed."

"That'd be a bonus," Emma added. "Tatiana hates her."

"She envies her, darling. There's a difference."

Chloe was unsure there was that much difference to Tatiana.

"It isn't that simple." Renee set down her cup, her hand trembling. "Keep your eyes open and watch your backs." Fear burned in her eyes. "I—I can't do this."

"Do what?" Chloe asked.

"This assignment." Renee looked from Emma to her. "As of now, this assignment no longer exists. I'm shutting it down."

"Renee, no!" Emma insisted loudly. "We're so close."

"I know that." Renee's face twisted. "But I can't risk the lives and reputations of the women here, and thanks to Rubi, your covers are blown. There's nothing to be done for it except cover it up. Still, the Duke will know the cover up is just smoke and mirrors. He'll figure out why you were there, and he'll retaliate. I feel it."

The hair on Chloe's neck stood on end. "I guess that's it then. We meet with the press, then close the case." She had to tell Renee. "You know what happened last night?"

"Emma filled me in, yes."

"You know Jack came to my apartment before dawn, too?"

"No, that I didn't know."

Figures. She couldn't catch a break with both hands and a net. "He's investigating this, Renee. He knew about the Duke. Actually, he's on the wrong track—he thinks Harrison Howell could be working for the Duke—but how does he know anything about the Duke at all?"

Renee stiffened but showed no other signs of alarm. "I suppose I'll have to find out."

A chill started at the base of her spine and swept up to the base of her neck. "You'll be asking the Governess, then?"

"Of course, my dear." She sighed. "There's no choice." She lifted a hand. "If Jack is investigating the same thing we are, then that gives more weight to it being true."

"By the questions we were asked last night, Renee, there's no doubt about that. I don't know where the women are being taken, but I expect Chloe and I would have found out on Friday."

"That is *not* going to happen. Not now." Renee looked from one of them to the other. "There's been too much exposure to risk any more. We can't jeopardize the entire G.R.C."

Chloe understood that rationale, and felt guilty because she was relieved.

Emma looked rebellious. "But Renee—"

She raised a hand. "My mind is made up. Alan has modified the design on the Rose pin to gain greater distance range."

"We got one last night. He's updated them since then?"

"Yes," Renee said. "I want all of the Roses to wear the new ones so your locations can be pinpointed at any time. You two are particularly vulnerable. Alan will distribute them after we meet with the press." She stood up. "Ready?"

Chloe nodded. Emma fell into step beside her and they walked outside. Cameras flashed, reporters shouted. Renee stepped up to a podium and was nearly obscured by the number of microphones. She waited for the reporters to get quiet and then spoke. "You're all interested in the latest flutter created by columnist Rubi Cho, so I'll address that topic immediately."

The bitch stood front row, center. Chloe smiled at her.

"Last night," Renee said, "two of the Roses were at Hollow Hill. Princess Chloe St. John and Miss Emma Bosworth and, yes, they were photographed there." Renee smiled at the cluster of faces, eagerly awaiting her every word. "These two women are renowned in this city for their dedicated service to charity. As those of you who will be joining us for the date auction tonight at 8:00 in Perrini's Grande Ballroom already know, the members of Gotham Rose Club are dedicated to helping women who are struggling, including those trying to hold together life and limb and have nothing left with which to barter except their bodies. To understand those challenges and provide assistance to these women, we must closely examine them in their lives. That is what Princess Chloe and Miss Emma Bosworth were doing last night at Hollow Hill. I do hope to see many of you at the fund-raiser tonight—or at the Halloween Ball. Thank you."

Renee stepped back from the microphone, and the shouted questions started in earnest. Most of them were about Marcus and directed at Chloe. Chloe and Emma stuck strictly to the script, which frustrated the press.

"Come on, Princess. Tell us what happened."

Chloe stared down at the ground for a long moment, substituting in her mind Jack's betrayal for Marcus's. "I lost my fiancé," she said, a tear rolling down her cheek. "Forever."

"That's enough." Olivia cut off questions. "I'm sure you understand that Princess Chloe needs privacy to grieve."

Renee slid an arm around Chloe and led her back inside.

Olivia shut the door then turned a worried gaze on Renee. "You need to call the Governess as soon as you possibly can."

When the hallway cleared, Chloe stepped near the fire, trying to let her nerves untangle and her heart rate slow down.

Emma joined her, then looked around to make sure no one was within hearing distance. "Something's wrong, Chloe."

"What do you mean?" She whispered because Emma had, though there wasn't another person in sight.

"Renee called off the mission too easily with us being this close to the Duke." Emma held up her fingers, pinched them together. "That's a big warning that something is way off."

"Whatever it is, it isn't our problem anymore." True, but Renee ordering them to wear red wigs when the missing women were brunettes still didn't sit well with Chloe. For some reason, Renee didn't want them inside that operation. "Regardless, she's shut down the assignment. We're done, Emma."

"And don't you find that odd when just yesterday she dumped every guilt trip known to woman and beast to get us to take on the assignment? Now today she's pulling the plug?"

"A lot's happened. Rubi blew our covers. Renee has to protect the G.R.C. so the Rose agents can continue to function."

Emma warmed her hands at the fire. "I'm not backing off."

"Emma, the assignment is over." Fear swirled in Chloe's stomach. "You have your orders. You have no choice."

Emma slowly turned her head and looked Chloe right in the eye. "I always have a choice."

Chloe's stomach sank. "Aren't you afraid?"

"Terrified. But I'm not backing off, knowing he's selling women, Chloe. I became a Rose agent to stop crime. I'm not turning a blind eye to it. I can't."

Chloe prayed for divine intervention to get Emma to come to her senses and stay safe. She prayed for the FBI to rescue the missing Russian women. And then she prayed for herself, because she was such a coward she'd settle for *anyone* fixing this, so long as it didn't have to be her.

"Those three women are still out there, Chloe. They're still being exported and *sold*. And there have to be others."

There it was. The truth in bald light. No shadows and nowhere to hide and not see it. "You're going after them."

"Damn right."

"I realize it won't do a bit of good to object, but this isn't a smart move, Emma."

"Maybe not," she said, then thought again. "Okay, it's not a smart move, but it's the right move. And the one I'm making."

She was right. And no amount of debate would change that. "Damn it, I have to go with you."

"No, you don't. Not if you're opposed."

Chloe laid a glare on Emma meant to drop her to her knees. "You're my friend and my partner—even when you're suicidal. I can't leave your back wide open. Someone else could kill you."

Emma turned dead earnest. "Someone might kill us both."

Fear ricocheted through Chloe's heart and its bitterness coated her tongue. She willed Emma to change her mind, but she was too hardheaded to do it.

"The odds are in their favor." Chloe stared into Emma's eyes a long, unblinking moment.

If she didn't do this, she wouldn't ever again in her life be able to meet her own eyes in the mirror. Emma had acknowledged that, while Chloe had tried to ignore it out of fear. But even fear didn't alter the truth. "Damn right."

Chloe rode down 72nd Street to Central Park West, then south to Perrini's, *the* place in the city for ultra-glamorous black-tie affairs.

Normally, booking the Grande Ballroom required a minimum two-year notice as well as a sum affordable only to the very rich, but when Chloe had been in her "building her companies" phase, Lucas Perrini had fallen on hard times, as had so many business owners after the 9/11 crisis. He was a proud man, old school, and would never borrow or ask anyone for money. And he was smart. Very, very smart.

Seeing all of his assets, Chloe had gone to him. But she hadn't offered to lend him money—he surely would have refused. Instead, she bent his sixty-year-old ear about her wanting to do something worthy with her life and needing a mentor to guide her. Being the consummate chivalrous gentleman, as well as a damn smart businessman, Lucas had agreed to assist the fair Princess Chloe by taking her money and making her a silent partner he could teach to do business wisely.

Both were far richer for it.

Of course, Chloe got preferential treatment at Perrini's, which impressed even Renee, and having a vested interest, of course Chloe booked events there at every opportunity. It was guerilla-warfare marketing, learned from Lucas Perrini, after learning Smart Business 101 at the knee of Renee Dalton-Sinclair.

"How much longer, Frank?" Chloe freshened her lipstick, the same shade of bold red as her slinky Vera Wang.

"Line's moving pretty slow," he said from the driver's seat. "We're only three back now, though."

Chloe adjusted her tiara. "Is this sucker straight?" She hated wearing it, but her parents would be here, and so she deferred to please her mother. Why Chloe bothered, she had no idea, and she was in no mood to think about it now.

Frank cranked his neck to look back through the lowered glass. "It's straight." His eyes warmed. "You're a pretty princess, Chloe." Frank inched the limo up. "Harrison's eyes are gonna bug right out of his head when he sees you."

"How do you know Harrison will be here?" Her heart beat faster. He hadn't mentioned coming tonight. Of course, they hadn't talked. They'd kissed, he'd stared at her and then left without a word.

"I met him in the garage this morning when he left. He mentioned it." Frank eased the car closer to the curb. "Your turn." Again, he looked back. "Have fun—and ignore your mother. She can't help it if she's goofy."

Leave it to Frank to put everything in his own unique perspective. "I will. You stay warm."

"Princess, if Jack's here, you might hear what he has to say. He did trust you about being engaged to Marcus. That's worth remembering."

He had. She hadn't explained that the engagement had been a survival measure forced on her. And Jack had trusted her, cared for her, even acted lovingly toward her.

Then, he'd broken her heart.

"I tried giving him a chance to explain, Frank. He didn't."

"Maybe he couldn't."

"He's a reporter, not a secret agent. What could possibly keep him from telling me the truth?"

"Well, now. I'd say that's a good question. I can't answer it. But before you give him the boot and take up with that Harrison fellow, maybe you should."

"Maybe." Her car door opened and Chloe stepped out.

Lucas Perrini greeted her, wearing black tails and a broad smile. "Princess Chloe." He looped her arm through his and moved to the door. "You're too beautiful to arrive alone."

Chloe smiled, loving this man who was as blunt as Frank and thought it was high time Chloe married some nice Italian man and settled down. "I'm looking for a man exactly like you," she said. "He's hard to find."

"You can do far better than me, my dear." He patted her arm and delivered her to the grand ballroom.

She kissed his soft cheek. "There is no one better than you, Lucas."

"Oh, but that I were thirty years younger." He let out a sigh. "However, I did meet with your new young man today, and he's good. Not Italian, but otherwise, he's good."

Fear trickled through her. "Whom are you talking about?"

"Harrison Howell." He looked at Chloe as if shocked she had to ask, and then suspicion filled his eyes. "Did this man lie to me? He said he was to watch over you and insisted on checking the security here."

"Oh, no. He didn't lie." She covered for him but wondered what he'd been doing. "He's worried. I got a few nasty notes."

"That idiot Rubi and her silly column." Lucas's expression turned to stone, but his voice stayed soft and he absently patted her arm. "Say the word and I will ban her."

"No. No, thank you. It'd just make her worse."

"As you wish." He dropped his voice. "If you need protection, you need only let me know. I have friends who would be honored to protect you."

"Oh, no," she said, unsure she wanted to get involved with those friends. "These are just the usual threats."

He nodded. "If you need anything, I'll be here for you."

"Thank you." She pressed a second kiss to his cheek, then walked into the ballroom. The first person to greet her was Ryan Greene. Tatiana had dated him, too.

"Chloe, you look—" he paused and his gaze drifted down her body "—amazing."

The silky red fabric clinging to her curves heated. "Thank you, Ryan." She looked past him to the two men with him, recognizing the elder as his father, though they'd never formally met. The other man, in a wheelchair, she had never before seen.

Ryan handled the introductions. "May I present Princess Chloe?" He smiled. "Chloe, this is my father, Franklin Greene, and my brother, Julio."

She greeted them warmly, wondering how Julio, who looked Latino, had become part of Ryan's family. Both of his legs and his left hand lay useless. How difficult it must be to live restricted inside a body that wouldn't work for you. Imagining it put an ache for him in Chloe's heart, but after they'd talked for a few minutes, Julio's charisma was so strong, she forgot that he had physical limitations—and she bet that was an enormous asset to him in his practice of international law.

Chloe moved on and checked in with Renee.

Renee cut her gaze to Franklin and Julio and visibly tensed. "Everything is in order. Senator Richardson and Mayor Siegal have arrived," Renee said. "The auctioneer is here, too, and he's set to start the date auction promptly at 9:00."

"Good." What was wrong with Renee? "Are you okay?"

Her gaze went again to Julio, and she didn't answer.

Chloe moved to block her vision. "Do you know him?"

"Yes," she said, drawing in a sharp breath and turning her gaze to Chloe. "I don't wish to discuss it, darling. That was a sad time and this is a happy one. Let's enjoy it."

"All right." Chloe agreed, but she'd never seen Renee ill at ease, and it rattled Chloe in a way she hadn't realized it could. Why did seeing this man affect Renee so deeply?

The mayor stepped up to the podium and made a few opening jokes. "My daughter Leah is one of the Roses being auctioned off tonight." His voice turned stern. "Remember, men. *All* we're auctioning is dinner."

The crowd laughed as it was supposed to, and the mayor went on. "Of course, I have to thank Renee Dalton-Sinclair for the charitable efforts of the Gotham Rose Club, and Princess Chloe, New York's own royal Rose, who sponsored this event. Ladies, your dedication to making life better for the women in this city is admirable, and the City of New York is grateful."

After a polite round of applause, the mayor introduced Renee's oldest friend, Senator Ellie Richardson, who gave a brief but moving speech about domestic violence and crimes against women that ended with, "We've come a long way, but we have a long way yet to go. So, please, be generous tonight."

More applause and laughter, and the auctioneer began auctioning dinners with the Roses. Chloe glanced around the crowded ballroom, hoping for a glimpse of Harrison, but didn't see him. She did, however, spot Erik talking with Julio and Ryan, and then a fair distance away, her mother, who was deep in conversation with the mayor's wife.

Someone touched her on the shoulder.

Chloe turned around, saw Harrison and smiled. He had been gorgeous in his Brooks Brothers suit, but in a Hugo Boss tux, he was breathtaking. "Hi." Her voice didn't want to work.

He smiled, stared at her mouth. "Hello, Chloe."

"Lucas told me you were here." Damn it, she sounded like a kid. What the hell was wrong with her?

Harrison nodded. "You look beautiful."

"So do you."

He chuckled. "Was this date auction your idea?"

She nodded, though after learning that other women were really being sold into slavery, what had seemed like a fun idea had lost its enchanting gleam. "It's a good way to meet new people." God, that sounded lame, even to her.

"Chelsea Adair," the auctioneer said.

Chloe turned to watch. Chelsea stepped forward on the

stage, looking gorgeous in a shocking purple Narciso Rodriguez creation. She pivoted and her black hair floated down her bare back. "I want to see who wins her," Chloe whispered to Harrison. "Erik's had a thing for her for a couple months."

"Five thousand dollars," Erik shouted.

"Ten." Ryan one-upped him.

"Fifteen," Erik fired back.

"That's a lot of money for the pleasure of a woman's company for dinner," Harrison whispered to Chloe.

"It's all relative," she said. "And for charity." Erik got Chelsea for $15,000, and they both positively glowed.

"True." Harrison watched as Ashley Thompson was auctioned off to the eldest son of a fast-food dynasty.

Glenda Huntsberger was next in line, signaling she was single again, and available.

Porsche Rothschild sidled up to Chloe, her infamous pet ferret, Marlena, dangling mischievously from one arm. "If she convinces her buyer she's a virgin, I'm going to permanently give up on all men."

Harrison lifted a questioning brow at Chloe.

"Don't ask," she whispered.

Brit Carouthers bid on Glenda. "Seven thousand."

"He's gorgeous," Porsche whispered.

"Don't even think about it, Bug," Emma said, joining them in a crème silk Chanel.

"You know I'm just looking. He can't compete with Sam," she said of the handsome man she met on her first mission, guarding a movie star in California. Porsche had only recently become a Rose agent. She frowned at Emma. "Who is he?"

"Brit Carouthers." Emma lowered her voice. "He's a publishing heir with a gambling habit and a racy lifestyle."

"Monaco has its perks," Porsche insisted. "And what's wrong with a racy lifestyle?" Absently she stroked Marlena.

Emma frowned. "Ask Vanessa," she said, talking about Vanessa Dawson, a sister Rose who'd recently had a run-in with Caulfield Carouthers in Florida on the drug-mule case.

"Well, look," Samantha said, joining them. "He's friends with Ryan."

"So is half the world," Emma said, totally out of patience. "Listen," she dropped her voice lower still, assuring that only Porsche and Samantha could hear her. "Vanessa thinks he's seriously bad."

"Silly woman." Porsche wiggled her eyebrows. "Don't you know bad can be delicious?"

"Or deadly," Emma said dryly.

"Deadly?" That got Samantha's attention.

"He just tried to buy his brother's way out of trouble."

"What kind of trouble?"

"Drugs, suspicion of murder, attempted murder, blackmail."

"No way." Porsche didn't believe it. "And he's here?"

"Way. A witness and evidence disappeared. The D.A. had to reduce several of the charges."

"Wow," Samantha said. "That's a lot to lose, you know?"

"Exactly."

"What a waste." Samantha grunted. "He lost the bid, too."

The insufficient evidence portion of that conversation was privileged, and them having it in Perrini's Grande Ballroom had Harrison's jaw tight enough to crack. Chloe shushed them.

"Are you being auctioned?" Harrison asked Chloe.

"Yes, I am."

"I'm on duty or I'd buy you."

"Bid on me," she corrected him. "For dinner."

"That's all that's being sold?" He gave her a smile so seductive it melted her down to her toes.

"You're next, Chloe." Renee's assistant Olivia tapped her on the shoulder, then turned to Emma. "Have you seen Alexa?"

"She's over there." Emma nodded to where Julio Greene was seated in his wheelchair.

Alexa Cheltingham, a Rose who'd been with the agency for four years, stood next to Julio, chatting. She'd lost her right leg as a teen, and Chloe had had no idea until Alexa had taken on a mission that had required her to go undercover as a stable hand. It had been hell on Alexa, but she'd done it, and finally she'd opened up to the other Roses about her leg. Chloe admired Alexa all the more for the extra effort it took for her to do her work in the agency. With her attitude and Julio's charisma, they'd be quite the couple. Of course, Alexa was pretty well taken now, by Ross Hardel of Hardel Industries.

Chloe stepped onto the stage and saw Madison Taylor-Pruitt with the love of her life, John, plus her father and her newly recovered uncle William, who'd been kidnapped as a child and only recently had found his family again. She positively glowed. Love and happiness looked good on her—and released a longing ache for both in Chloe.

"Princess Chloe St. John," the auctioneer said.

Chloe's stomach fluttered. What if no one bid on her? What if someone did, and he turned out to be a jerk she couldn't stand?

If no one "bought" her, perhaps she could steal a few minutes here and there with Harrison. The man could definitely get under her skin. And if she noticed that Jack wasn't here and felt just the tiniest bit empty because of it, well, that was normal. She'd been crazy about him for years. She couldn't get over him in a piddling day. Hopefully, she wouldn't be saying that about a piddling lifetime…

"Twenty-five thousand." Ryan Greene's voice rang out.

Chloe groaned, covered it with a delicate laugh. "Oh, he's

such a charmer." *Dang it.* She'd turned him down for dates at least a dozen times in the last two months. The man just considered "no" a challenge. But okay. Okay. Three hours. Maybe four. For the Women's Center, she could stand being with the Rose slut for three or four hours.

"Thirty." Ryan's father, Franklin, put in that bid.

Surprised, Chloe smiled. Now why would he bid on her?

Ryan jumped onto the stage and stole the microphone from the auctioneer. "Fifty thousand dollars." Ryan lifted a hand. "And, Dad, I'll warn you, no matter what you bid, I'm going to raise it. I'm having dinner tonight with Princess Chloe, regardless of the cost."

That earned the man a collective sigh from an adoring audience. Ryan stood his ground and the auctioneer closed the bid. The room erupted in applause, and Chloe smiled.

Out of the corner of her eye, she spied Renee.

She was not smiling.

Chapter 7

Rubi Cho snapped a photo of Ryan and Chloe. So did Ashley Thompson. "This is going to make a great feature," she told Chloe, talking about a future issue of *Chic*. "Father and son compete for princess and royal dinner."

Chloe tried her best not to snarl.

Ryan offered her his hand. She glanced again at Renee, who stood stone-faced. Had Chloe done something wrong? But she realized Renee wasn't looking at her; she was looking at Ryan. And at that moment, Chloe felt down to her bones that Renee hated him. But why?

"Come on, Chloe," Ryan said. "Unless I'm mistaken, Rubi wants a few words with us."

Chloe stepped down and the auction continued with the sleek and sophisticated Becca Whitmore, fellow Rose agent and master gemologist, who'd only returned this afternoon from Africa. She noticed the blond, blue-eyed man who bought Becca wasn't part of the usual crowd. Interesting.

Rubi took several photos of Chloe and Ryan.

"You and Julio must be close," Chloe said to Ryan. "He seems to adore you."

"He does." Ryan smiled.

"Are you two really brothers?"

"He's adopted." Ryan turned on a mega-watt smile for Rubi. "You Roses aren't the only philanthropists around."

"May I ask a few questions?" Rubi offered them her most charming smile.

After last night and her fricking column this morning, Chloe was tempted to knock it off her face.

Ryan smiled back. "Anything for you, sweetheart."

"I see you're both wearing Rose pins tonight. Ryan, why do you have one?"

Chloe hadn't noticed his and looked. Of course, it was different from the ones Alan had passed to the Roses. Its diamond winked in the light.

"I'm a Rose fan." He chuckled. "Which surprises no one."

It didn't. Harrison was right. Ryan was doing his best to sleep his way through them all. Fortunately, he wasn't enjoying as much success as it appeared to outsiders.

"Princess Chloe." Rubi turned to her, and the warmth in her eyes faded under the glitter of suspicion. "I was at the G.R.C. today when Renee revealed the reason you and Emma Bosworth were at Hollow Hill last night. Why did you run from me?"

Ryan's grasp on her arm stiffened, and Chloe winced. "If you knew I was running, Rubi, why did you print the column?"

She shrugged. "News is news."

"There was no news, as you now know. Will you be printing a correction tomorrow?"

"No."

"Predictable." Chloe stared her down. "Who told you I would be there?"

Rubi hesitated, and then gave her an exaggerated blink. "I never reveal my sources."

Chloe smiled sweetly. "I'll remember that and phone the *Post* the next time I have a juicy tidbit to report." She walked away, leaving Ryan standing there.

He caught up to her. "What happened at Hollow Hill?"

"Don't worry, Ryan. Nothing that will impact you. Rubi still thinks you're perfect—right in line behind Adonis."

"I asked what happened, Chloe."

His charm dissipated, confusing Chloe. "I can't believe you didn't hear about it. It's been a hot news item all day."

"I've been out of pocket with Julio. Tell me."

"It's nothing really." Chloe shrugged. "Emma and I were doing some research down there for the Women's Center, to help get prostitutes off the streets. We—umm—dressed for the part. Rubi showed up and this morning, we were in her column."

"Good cause." Ryan cleared his throat, darted his gaze as if looking for someone. Within seconds, he added, "Chloe, I'm suddenly not feeling well. Would you forgive me if I asked for a rain check on dinner?"

Thrilled to be off the hook, she had to temper her reaction. "Why no, of course not."

"Thanks." He lightly kissed her cheek. "I'll call and we can set up something next week."

"I hope you feel better." She squeezed his arm, and let go, grateful beyond belief to be rid of him.

He walked to the door, saw Tatiana and stopped to speak.

"She doesn't look happy with the conversation, does she?" Harrison spoke from beside Chloe.

Smiling, Chloe looked at him. "No, she doesn't." Tatiana

stood ramrod straight and her jaw was tight enough to be wired. Now what was up with that?

"I never liked her much," Harrison whispered.

"She doesn't like me much, either," Chloe confessed, glad he wasn't taken in by Tatiana's lush, sultry looks.

"Ryan's departing the fix," he said, using lingo from the agency. "Does that mean you're free for dinner after all?"

Chloe smiled up at him. "It does."

His eyes twinkled. "Will you join me?"

Her heart rate kicked up a notch. It shouldn't, considering Jack, but he'd wounded her pride and hurt her heart, and both reacted warmly to a gorgeous, appreciative man. "I thought you had to work."

"Even I get time off to eat."

"In that case, I'd love to." Chloe walked to the ballroom door with an improved attitude. Jack could make all the accusations he liked. Harrison worked for the Governess. He'd passed the most rigorous security check known to God and man. Chloe didn't have to trust him; the Governess did. And clearly he hadn't hated Chloe's kiss or he wouldn't be interested in dinner. That was a fringe benefit. Minutes ago she'd dreaded dinner. Now she was looking forward to it. She could relax.

Lucas had set up a private dining room for her and her date, and if he was surprised that she wasn't with Ryan Greene, he didn't show it as he escorted them to their table.

"I hope you don't mind," she told Harrison. "Since I'm the function's sponsor, I have to stay on the premises—in case there's a challenge."

"Not at all." He walked at her side. "I eat here often."

Expensive tux, expensive food. Harrison couldn't be living on his agent's pay. The Governess might pay him well, but she was a government employee herself. She couldn't possibly pay him that well. Who was this man?

Lucas stepped aside. "I hope this room will be satisfactory, Princess Chloe."

She looked around. The walls were covered with antique tapestries that well might have hung on medieval castle walls. The candlelit table and its matching two chairs were hand-carved, the wood rich and gleaming. An opulent chandelier hung in each corner of the room, and a night-sky painting covered the ceiling. "It's beautiful, Lucas."

"I know you love the tapestries. I thought you'd enjoy them." His smile grew broad. "Of course, at the time, I worried you'd be bored to death with one of those silly men. I didn't know you'd be dining with Mr. Howell."

"Neither did I, Lucas." So he knew and liked Jack and Harrison. "My good fortune."

Lucas chuckled softly. "Michael and Andre will be taking care of you tonight. If you need me, they'll let me know."

"Thank you." Harrison seated Chloe then took his chair.

Dinner was relaxed and the conversation was warm and friendly and strictly personal, which was an unexpected treat. When the Perrini's specialty dessert of chocolate fudge cake with raspberry sauce was served with piping hot cups of coffee, Harrison introduced an unexpected topic.

He lifted his cup, seeming somewhat pensive. "Did you notice that Renee seems really upset tonight?"

It was a test. There wasn't a doubt in Chloe's mind. "Yes, I did," she confessed. "But she didn't wish to discuss it." Should Chloe disclose what she'd noticed? She debated and decided she should. After all, she and Harrison were on the same team. "She grew particularly upset when looking at Julio Greene." Turnabout was fair play. "Do you have any idea why?"

"Probably an emotional reaction to his injuries. She's a very compassionate woman."

Renee was extremely compassionate. Yet something undefined niggled at Chloe. "Do you know anything about him?"

"A little," Harrison said. "His injuries were caused by a drunk driver in Colombia. His father was killed."

"How horrible."

"He was really young at the time."

"How did he end up with Franklin Greene?" she asked, trying to fit the pieces together.

"He and Julio's father were friends and business partners in an emerald mine. Franklin was Julio's godfather." Harrison removed a cake crumb from the table and put it inside his napkin. "After the accident, Franklin took over Julio's care and eventually adopted him."

"Medical care is so much more advanced in the States."

Harrison mumbled his agreement.

"But what about his mother?"

"She disappeared. Franklin spent a fortune looking for her, but…"

How terrible. "Did they get the drunk driver?"

Harrison scanned his memory. "I don't believe they did."

Chloe frowned. Colombia supplied seventy-five percent of the world with cocaine. Drug lords, not law enforcement, meted out justice. Of course they hadn't gotten the driver. "That must have been hard on Julio and his family."

Harrison stared across the candlelit table at Chloe, an odd expression in his eyes.

"What?" Had she dripped raspberry sauce on her chin? She dabbed at it with the napkin.

"You constantly surprise me, Chloe." The timbre of his voice said that the surprise was in a good way, not a bad one. "You're not what I expected."

"What did you expect?" she asked, but she wasn't at all sure she really wanted the answer.

"Honestly?"

She nodded.

"A partying rich bitch, living off her inheritance and playing off her title."

Not very flattering, but it's what most people expected from her—and what most people, including her mother, believed she was doing. "I do love to party," she confessed. "But I love to dabble in businesses, too."

"Dabble?" He chuckled. "Chloe, don't peddle that nonsense to me, okay? I've read your dossier." The teasing light left his eyes. "Why do you buy property?"

"Madison is very good at it. I learned from her."

"Yet other than Eleanor Towers, you don't buy in New York."

"No, I don't." She shifted on her seat, uneasy. "It wouldn't be right to become Madison's competitor. Pruitt & Pruitt is extremely active here."

"Pruitt & Pruitt owns the local market," Harrison said, "but that's not why you don't buy here."

"Isn't it?" She hiked her chin, challenging him.

"You don't want your mother to know you're not living off your inheritance," he said softly. "You have no partners in your property ventures. My guess is that you don't want her to know anything about your business life."

He had intuited far more than he'd read in her dossier or heard at her apartment that morning, and that had been too much. Feeling uncomfortably vulnerable, Chloe schooled her breathing, slowed it down. "I buy properties, improve them and then sell them." Largely to single mothers, trying to build lives for themselves and their kids. "It's fun, productive and profitable."

"What other businesses are you involved in?"

He already knew. This was yet another honesty test, and while she was growing weary of the grilling, she understood his need to know the character of the woman with whom he was dealing. "I own a line of skin care products and, as you already know, I'm a silent partner in Adelphio, and elsewhere in a business I'm not at liberty to disclose."

"Perrini's," Harrison said.

Chloe looked him right in the eye and said nothing.

"What possessed you to support the Adelphio label?"

"I don't. I support Adele Phillips," Chloe said. "When I met her, she was a gifted designer with amazing vision and talent, no money and an abusive ex-husband. She divorced him without a dime, without a roof over her head and with two children to support. I figured if she was willing to take that kind of leap of faith on herself, then she deserved someone to believe in her."

"So you did."

"I did, and I do." Chloe smiled, still thrilled for Adele and the boys. "Now she has a house on Long Island that is solely hers, a restraining order against the jerk and a very good lawyer on retainer in case he acts up, and we both have a great deal more money."

"There you go again." Harrison guffawed. "Surprising me." He rested a hand on the table. "That was a significant leap of faith for you."

"Adele has two little boys, and she's a very devoted mother."

"Unlike yours."

That hurt. It shouldn't; it was true. But it did. "My mother is devoted," Chloe said, trying to hide how deeply that comment had cut. "Only it's about what *she* wants for me, not about what I want for me."

"It was a good thing—what you did for Adele."

Chloe shifted the topic. "So, now that I've spilled my secrets, tell me yours. Who are you, Harrison Howell?"

"Just a representative of the Governess," he said. "That's about all there is to me."

"You have on a Hugo Boss tux, Italian leather shoes that cost more than a government employee's monthly salary, and you frequently dine at Perrini's." She didn't have to mention that prices weren't printed on Perrini's menus. If you had to ask, you couldn't afford to dine there. "You're not *just* anything. Now, be fair."

"Okay." Harrison removed his glasses, tucked them in the inside pocket of his jacket. "Like you, I inherited. And like you, I invested. I got lucky."

"How lucky?"

He frowned. "I didn't start out with as much money as you, but I've caught up."

"Really?" Well, well. He surprised her, too.

He nodded.

"But you're not involved—socially, I mean."

"No, I'm not." Harrison looked her straight in the eye. "My blood isn't blue, and I'm not interested in the games these people play, Chloe. Life is serious business, and I mean to make mine matter."

"So you want to make a difference." Many in her circle did, too, but there was a disproportionate share of superficial people, and she couldn't honestly deny it.

"As do you," he said, "or you wouldn't do what you do."

She'd been working up the courage to ask him something since that morning. It had taken all day, and she wasn't sure her voice wouldn't crack even now. "Are you married, Harrison?"

"I divorced about two years ago." He sighed. "The job takes everything, you know? And considering the secrecy issue, being involved with someone outside the loop is just too complicated."

"That's true." Becca Whitmore had broken an engagement

to a man she cared about to protect him from her job. He'd come dangerously close to discovering that she was an agent. Of course, he now thought she was a snobby rich bitch, and Becca had chosen to let him.

Chloe recalled the man who'd bought Becca at the date auction. There'd been something about the way he scanned the room…perhaps Becca had found a man who understood secrets.

Harrison sipped from his wineglass, ignoring his coffee. "You know we're going to have to look at all the Roses to expose the leak to Rubi."

"I know." What else had been leaked? And about whom? Chloe frowned. "But I don't have to like it."

"Considering many of them are people you call your friends, I'd be disappointed if you did." He looked at her and his expression softened. "I like you, Chloe. I know relationships don't work, but I swear, you make me wish they could."

She smiled from the heart out. "Every once in a while there's an anomaly. Who knows? Maybe you'll be part of one."

"With you?"

Her breath caught. "Tough odds," she admitted. "I have a broken heart, remember?"

"Ah, Jack," Harrison said. "The reporter who's deduced that I'm connected to the Duke."

She shrugged. "He has more information than he should."

"Apparently, just enough to really get things screwed up."

"Yeah, but his heart's in the right place."

Harrison frowned. "I'm not so sure, Chloe."

She stared at him, afraid enough of saying the wrong thing to say nothing.

"How does he know so much?"

He was questioning her about breaching security? She tried not to be angry. It was a legitimate question. "I don't know."

"Well," Harrison paused, thoughtful. "If he isn't on our side, then it stands to reason…"

Surprise rippled up her back and set her skin to crawling. "You think *he's* working for the Duke?"

Harrison looked her right in the eye. "It's possible."

"No," she denied it. "Jack is a good man, Harrison."

"You love him," he said. "You're not objective."

There was truth in that. She couldn't dispute it.

Her cell phone rang. Two rings, and then it stopped. Immediately, it rang again. Two rings, and again it stopped.

"Oh, God." Chloe stood up.

"What's wrong?" Harrison pushed back his chair.

"Emma's in trouble." Chloe snatched up her purse, tossed her napkin onto the table.

"What kind of trouble?" Harrison asked. "The I-broke-a-nail kind of trouble, or the—"

"Stop it!" Chloe shouted. "Someone is trying to kill her!"

Chloe rushed outside. It was dark, except for some of the neon signs and the streetlights, shining down on the pavement and reflecting off the cars. She scanned up and down the line of limos parked at the curb. It was nearly impossible to tell them apart in the darkness. Finally, she spotted Emma's driver, Perry, leaning against the fender of Emma's gray Rolls. "There he is."

Chloe rushed over. "Perry, where's Emma?" she asked on a gushed breath. Harrison stopped at her side.

Perry set his magazine on the hood of the car. "She's gone to dinner. Is something wrong?"

"With whom did she go?" Chloe asked, ignoring his question.

"Give me your cell phone," Harrison told Chloe.

She passed it over just as Frank touched her shoulder. "What's wrong, Princess?"

"I need to find Emma, Frank." Panic threaded her voice.

"She went to dinner with Brit Carouthers," Perry said.

Chloe couldn't believe it. Emma was the one who'd warned everyone about him. Why would she agree to have dinner with him?

"He came back ten minutes ago," Frank added. "Alone."

"Find him, Frank," Chloe said, hearing Harrison speaking softly into her phone. "See where he left Emma."

Chloe's stomach knotted. Her chest tightened, and she couldn't seem to drag in enough air. She and Emma had worked out the phone signal four years ago. It had never been used.

Until tonight.

Frank came back outside. A worried Lucas Perrini was with him, but it was Frank who had Chloe's answer. "She got ticked off at Carouthers at the restaurant and doubled his date auction bid for him to leave. She'd just been served dinner."

"What restaurant?" Chloe asked.

"Lagniappe." Lucas responded. "What's wrong, Princess?"

Waves of fear washed over Chloe. "Emma is in trouble."

"Carouthers is no good, like his brother," Lucas told Frank. "When he won her dinner date, I warned her not to leave the building with him."

"Did they leave here alone?" Harrison asked.

"No, Prince Erik and Chelsea Adair were with them," Frank said. "They were all in Ryan Greene's car. Ryan told the driver to drop him off at home and to take care of his friends for the night."

"Ryan. Again. Erik. Again." Chloe turned to Harrison. "Call Lagniappe and see if she's still there."

"I'm on with them now," Lucas said, his phone at his ear.

Frank locked gazes with Chloe, clearly worried sick about his girl. "Miss Emma's hurt, isn't she, Princess?"

"I don't know, Frank," Chloe admitted, fear filling her. "I just don't know."

"She's not there," Lucas said. "The doorman thinks she left in a black limo."

Chloe went numb with fear. "There are hundreds of black limos in this city. Whose was it? Did anyone hear where she was going? Was anyone with her?"

Lucas asked the question, and they waited for the answers, but no one seemed to have any.

"Frank," Chloe whispered. "Call Alan. Tell him to activate Emma's tracker."

Frank nodded and stepped away to make the call. But when he returned to Chloe, his face was drawn and pasty white. "It's in the middle of the river, Princess. That's where the pin says she is right now."

Chloe felt raw. As if the skin and flesh had been seared off her bones. "No. No, that can't be. It can't be, Frank."

Harrison's cell phone rang. He answered, listened briefly, then said, "Got it. Thanks." He looked at Chloe. "The pin might be in the river, but Emma's not. Let's go, Chloe."

Frank took off like a shot to the car and opened the back door. Chloe rushed to it, and to her surprise, Lucas followed her. "Where's Emma? Where are we going?"

"I traced the location of the incoming call. It wasn't made from the river, Chloe. She did not drown, okay?"

Okay. Okay. Emma had *not* been killed and her body had *not* been dumped in the river. Her Rose pin was in the river. That was all. Just the Rose pin. Chloe schooled her breathing, forced herself to calm down. "Where was she when she called?"

Harrison winced. "The Meatpacking district."

Chloe's lungs seemed to collapse. Oh, no. Oh, God, no. The Russian women. *The Duke.* "Frank, hurry!"

On the way, Lucas and Harrison pieced together what little they knew. According to the doorman, Emma left in a black limo.

According to a female witness, Emma had left on foot.

And, according to a guy sitting on the steps two doors down from Lagniappe drinking out of a bottle wrapped in a brown paper bag, she'd hailed a cab.

More and more frantic at what could be happening to Emma, Chloe took the lead when they reached 14th Street.

Harrison grabbed her arm. "Where are you going?"

She gritted her teeth, steeled herself to fight him. He'd definitely object. "Hollow Hill. I'm doing a room check."

Harrison frowned. "You can't do that."

"Hell, yes, I can." The sense of urgency in her doubled. Emma needed her *now*. Her stomach clutched. The hair on her neck stood on edge. "There's no added risk. Our cover is blown. They know us." She spared him a glance and sped up. "You know what? I don't want to hear any objections, Harrison."

"Chloe, listen to me. You could be walking into a trap."

"I'm going," Chloe insisted, striding down the sidewalk in that direction. "I know she's there. I feel it in my bones." Emma's pet expression had never felt so right.

"Okay. Okay," he conceded. "We'll go in together."

"Flash your badge," she said, heading up to the lobby door. "I'm not leaving until I inspect every damn room." She turned to Frank and Lucas. "Would you two please cover the front and rear exits?" At their nods, she and Harrison went into the lobby.

The man behind the sleek desk was about Chloe's age, had black hair, a broad flat nose and a bored expression. He wore a steel-gray suit and a name tag. "Harvey Walker, Manager."

The escort handler managing the hotel? There had to be a prostitution contingent at Special Reserves Escorts, after all. Chloe's skin crawled.

"Good evening." Harrison flashed his badge.

Harvey's boredom disappeared and wariness replaced it. "What do you need, sir?"

"To search the premises."

"Um, don't you need a search warrant for that?"

"Your permission works, too," Harrison said, steady and calm, not frazzled.

Harvey frowned. "I would need a warrant."

"No problem." Harrison smiled, but it was frozen and didn't touch his eyes. He pulled out his cell. "Mr. Walker, before I make this call, I'm giving you a chance to reconsider. If you slow me down to get a warrant, you'd better be ready for a visit by every inspector in the city."

Harvey stroked at a little scar on his left cheek, then nodded. "We always cooperate with authorities, sir."

"And we always appreciate your cooperation," Harrison replied. "We'll start on the bottom floor and work our way up."

"I'll have to notify the guests," Marcus insisted. "You can't just burst into their rooms. There are privacy issues."

"Fine." Harrison pulled out his cell phone again. "Let me just get a couple dozen officers here to assist."

"Wait." Harvey's face bleached white. "Perhaps house-keeping can help."

"That sounds promising." Harrison clipped his phone.

"Rosalita," Harvey said, announcing the housekeeper's arrival.

Dressed in a gray housekeeping uniform, Rosalita left her cleaning cart parked against the wall and came to them. She looked worried, and Chloe smiled to put her at ease.

Harvey issued her instructions on what to do, and she, Chloe, Harrison and Harvey began checking the rooms.

By the third floor, Chloe was questioning her bones. By the fourth, she was certain she'd been dead wrong. On the sixth floor, she swore if they found nothing, she was going to ignore her intuition and doubt her judgment for the rest of her life.

Rosalita knocked on the third door. "Housekeeping."

No answer.

She keyed the lock, shoved the door open—and screamed.

Harrison shoved past her into the room. Chloe followed.

Emma lay battered and unconscious on the floor.

Beside her lay Jack.

A man appeared outside the window, then drew back.

"Get down!" Chloe jerked Harrison's sleeve, dropped belly down on the floor. He landed beside her with a thud.

The glass shattered.

She covered her head with her arms. A bullet had entered the wall, chest high where she'd been standing.

Harrison pulled his weapon from his shoulder holster, slid on his stomach around the foot of the bed, working his way to the window. Rosalita had shoved Harvey into the bathroom; they stayed put. Chloe pulled her gun, positioned herself above Emma and Jack at the side of the bed and aimed at the window, her heart beating so hard it blocked out her hearing.

Harrison was still crawling when a gun appeared, and then the arm of the man holding it.

Chloe fired. The gun flew out of his hand and fell to the street below. "Disarmed," she said to Harrison.

He jumped to his feet, looked out the window, stretched and scanned, but didn't fire his weapon. "He's gone."

Chloe caught her breath. "I know him," she said. "I mean, I've seen him. He's targeted me before."

Harrison looked at her, waited for her to explain.

Jack had a pulse. *Thank God.* She moved to Emma. The pulse at her throat beat at Chloe's fingertip, but it was weak and thready. "Call 911. Hurry!"

Harrison pulled out his phone and dialed 911. "Two ambulances. STAT." He turned to Chloe. "Who was the shooter?"

"One of Marcus's men at the church—when he kidnapped me."

Chloe sniffed. Was the mob still intent on killing her to tie up loose ends? Or were Marcus's partners in the white-slave trade venture after her now? Her and Emma?

Either way, it appeared someone wanted them both dead.

Chapter 8

The doctor who had cared for Chloe and Emma for the past decade came out into the ICU waiting room.

Chloe jumped to her feet. "Dr. Scoffield, are they okay?"

He swiped a hand on his pale blue scrubs, and his weary eyes turned gentle. "Emma's arm is broken again, she has multiple contusions, lacerations and severe bruises. So far, we've found no evidence of internal bleeding or damage to her vital organs, but we're still running tests."

"Her face?" Shaking like a wind-tossed leaf, Chloe swallowed hard. Emma had been so swollen and bloody…

"Will heal completely, though I'm afraid the news won't be as positive about her arm." Sadness filled his eyes. "Between the old injuries and these, she's suffered irreparable damage, Chloe. It pains me to say that her time as a professional pianist is over."

"Oh, no." Tears burned in Chloe's eyes. Emma had worked so hard to play again, after the car explosion injury in California. She'd had three surgeries and months of intense physical therapy, trying to correct and repair the damage. It had only been in the last few weeks that she'd dared to be hopeful about playing again. And now this.

"This injury will be difficult for her to accept," Dr. Scofield said slowly, giving them time to absorb the news. "But I'm afraid there's a more immediate challenge for Emma, Chloe, and it's significant."

"What? Was she…?" She let the question hang, unable to make herself say *raped.*

"No," he said. "She wasn't sexually assaulted." His expression, already grim, turned more solemn. "She's in a coma."

Chloe gasped, felt Harrison stiffen beside her and Renee's arm circle her back. "A coma?" She'd thought Emma had passed out from the pain of the beating. But this news was staggering.

"I'm afraid so," he said. "It's a deep coma, which means we have no idea how long it will be before she wakes up. It could be hours or days, or even…longer." He forced himself to add, "Her condition is critical, Chloe. Be prepared."

Chloe couldn't respond. Couldn't move. Couldn't think.

Renee cleared her throat. "Can we see her?"

"Not now, Renee. We're still working on her." He touched a consoling hand to her arm. "As soon as we can, okay?"

She nodded, strain lining her face.

Dr. Scoffield rubbed at the back of his neck. The stethoscope dangling from it swayed on his chest. "Have you notified her parents?"

"They're on the way," Chloe said. "Her mother called a few minutes ago. Traffic is backed up. They've summoned a helicopter and should be here soon."

"Good." He gave them an empathetic look.

He hadn't mentioned Jack. Not once. Chloe could barely breathe. God, she couldn't lose him. Couldn't face life knowing he was no longer living it. They might not be together, but they could never be apart. Not so long as he had her heart. "What about Jack?" she asked, terrified of the answer.

"No injuries," Dr. Scoffield said. "He was drugged, Chloe. We're not sure with what, but his vital signs are stable."

Relief twisted inside her. "I need to see him."

"As soon as he wakes up." Dr. Scoffield patted her shoulder. "I'd better get back."

Chloe couldn't speak, didn't move, just watched the doctor walk back through the double doors and disappear.

Renee and Harrison stood with her. "No injuries?" Chloe asked them, incredulous. "I *know* he didn't just stand there and let them brutalize Emma and inject him with some drug."

Harrison whispered but his calm tone chilled her. "He might have ordered it, Chloe."

Renee scoffed. "Uh, no. That's not possible."

Hopeful, Chloe darted her gaze to Renee. "Harrison thinks Jack might be the Duke."

Rene's eyes widened in shock. She stared at Harrison, who nodded, then frowned.

"That's ridiculous," Renee said. "Jack works with the FBI."

"It's possible," Harrison countered. "Although if he is affiliated with the FBI, his actions may well have honorable explanations."

Renee turned to Chloe, whose mouth was open. FBI? "The assignment was supposed to be over. What were you two doing?" Renee flipped from frightened to furious to frightened again. "Never mind. Whatever it was, it ends now. This assignment is sealed. Drum-tight. What was Emma doing at Hollow Hill?"

"I don't know," Chloe said. "She was supposed to be at dinner with Brit Carouthers, but she paid him off to get rid of him. He came back to Perrini's alone. She had dinner alone, then left. How she left is in dispute, but all reports cite she left alone."

"What the hell was she doing dining with Brit Carouthers?"

Chloe shrugged. "He won her at the date auction."

Renee murmured, "Why didn't she buy him off at Perrini's?"

"I don't know." Chloe wished she did. Had her anger at Brit triggered her beating? If he was like his brother, he wasn't above having someone beat her. Or had the Duke attacked her, retaliating? He knew she and Chloe had been at Hollow Hill. Her being there, could be a message to the Roses that he could and would take them down. Or was the beating by someone else, for some other reason entirely?

"Do you know why Jack was there?" Renee asked.

"No." That terrified her. Could Harrison be right about Jack? Chloe's heart didn't want to believe it, but she had to try to make judgments based on fact not emotion. "Why didn't you tell me Jack was FBI?"

"I thought he would have told you. Perhaps he was ordered not to. Regardless, you're done with this assignment," Renee said. "That's a direct order, Chloe. No exceptions."

Rubi walked out of the elevator and headed into the ICU waiting room. Figuring she'd either picked up the news on the police scanner, or received a call about Emma from Tatiana, Chloe stepped away so Renee could intercept her.

"Are you okay?" Harrison asked Chloe.

She walked over to a row of empty burgundy seats, sat down and stared sightlessly at the gray wall. "No, I'm not okay," she admitted. How the hell could she be okay? "I'm on the edge of hysteria about Emma and Jack, and I'm just as relieved that it wasn't me." She clasped her head with her hands. "Isn't that awful?" Blowing out a deep breath, she shook herself. "Oh, God, ignore me. I know it's awful." *Coward. Coward. Coward.* "Worse, I'm so thankful that

Renee issued me a direct order to drop the assignment—and I'm sickeningly ashamed of myself because I am." She laced her hands in her lap, squeezed, and looked at him. "So no, Harrison. I am *not* okay. I am far from okay."

He sat down beside her. "Tell me all of it."

At this point, he was the only person in the world she could talk to, because it seemed everyone else in her damn life had suddenly become a suspect. Including her brother. Striving for control, she didn't hesitate. "I should be determined to find out who did this to Emma and why—in spite of Renee's orders. Emma is one of my oldest friends, and I should be just as determined to prove the truth about Jack."

"Because…"

"I love him, Harrison. I've always loved him." Tears welled in Chloe's throat. "But… Oh, God, I'm such a coward."

Harrison covered her hand. "You're not a coward."

She shot him an angry look. Couldn't he see the truth right in front of his face? What kind of spy was he? "I am."

"Chloe, you charged into Hollow Hill. A coward couldn't have been dragged in there at gunpoint."

"But that was different." She sniffed. "We didn't know then. Now we know, and I just want to hide."

"Listen, you've had a really bad shock. Seeing Emma beaten, Jack unconscious, a jerk shooting at you—hell, Chloe, any one of those things would knock a person to their knees, but all of them at once? Of course you're afraid. You'd lack sense if you weren't scared stiff. Give yourself some time to get your emotions off the roller coaster and lick your wounds. Everyone needs time to heal, including you."

He wasn't placating her. "Okay. Okay, I will. Thanks."

His cell phone rang. He answered it, then moved around the corner and then walked outside to talk. Chloe watched him through the long windows, moving in and out of the streaks of light spilling onto the concrete walkway from the streetlamps.

Emma's parents arrived, harried, worried, and Chloe hugged them, consoled them, tried to reassure them. When Ryan Greene and Erik walked in, she turned them over to Renee.

Erik carried a bouquet of roses. Flowers weren't allowed in ICU, but Chloe didn't have the heart to tell him; his thinking of others was too rare.

He planted a kiss on her cheek. Rarely serious, his expression was solemn, his tone hushed. "How is she, Chloe?"

Chloe glimpsed inside her brother, remembered that he'd grown up with Emma, too, and he was afraid for her. "She's in a coma." Chloe's voice cracked.

"I'm sorry." Ryan gently squeezed Chloe's arm. "Do they have a prognosis?"

"It's too early." She should smell Erik's coral roses, but her scattered senses noted peppermint instead, triggering Emma's explaining to Tatiana why she'd stolen her LaBella appointment. *I really needed a peppermint foot treatment, and I knew you wouldn't mind.* Suspicion flooded Chloe.

Erik moved to speak to Samantha and Becca, sitting at the far end of the waiting room on a soft, leather sofa. Madison paced behind it, wanting more information and wanting it now, and Porsche sat on a chair looking like a freaked-out zombie, wired and set to trigger. Chloe noticed immediately that Marlena the ferret was not with her, and guessed that the hospital had stood firm on allowing no animals through the door. Alexa and Vanessa flanked her, standing by silently, there for Porsche, if needed.

Every Rose agent was terrified for Emma.

Every Rose agent believed the attack was related to the assignment. That Marcus and the Duke were engaged in white-slave trade. And Chloe and Renee suspected that Tatiana had leaked dangerous information to Rubi. Tatiana's absence from the hospital was conspicuous.

Ryan still wore his tux, Chloe noted. "Weren't you sick?"

"Yes. But I had to check on Emma." He smiled warmly, and shifted topics. "Did you have dinner? Should I have Perrini's bring something over?"

"No, thank you. I've eaten." Good grief, it was nearly 2:00 a.m. and he didn't look at all ill. Why had he lied? Couldn't anyone tell the truth anymore?

Ryan stepped closer, crowding her in an utterly charming way that annoyed her. "We could have dessert. I'm feeling *much* better now."

He had to be kidding. That he'd be sexually suggestive now knocked him down a dozen rungs on her "charm and sex appeal" ladder. Gorgeous? Indisputably. But way too self-absorbed, and apparently clueless about where her mind was at the moment. "You're not getting laid, Ryan. Not by me. Not now, not ever."

He smiled. "That almost sounds like a challenge."

"It's not," she promised. "It's fact."

His smile faded and he grumbled. "Why?"

"Listen, you're adorable, Ryan, but it just doesn't work between you and me."

He seemed genuinely surprised. "Why not?"

She sighed. "Because you're a Rose slut, sweetheart," she said without heat. "But mostly because I'm not just another Rose. I've got thorns."

"God, I love saucy Roses," he said in a deep-throated growl, touching a light fingertip to her Rose pin.

"Sure you do." Chloe smiled, seeing Harrison return. His expression grim, he motioned for her to join him away from the others. She caught Samantha's eye, gave her a subtle signal to take Ryan off her hands by brushing a hair behind her ear.

"Ryan, so glad you're feeling better." Samantha snagged

him by the arm. "I'm frantic and need consoling. You know I think the world of Emma." She shuffled him over to where the other Roses had gathered, sat down beside him on the sofa and rested her head on his shoulder.

Ryan Greene was down until Samantha chose to let him get up, and that was that. Chloe had to give it to Sami. When she meant for a man to stay put, she set him up so that he'd have to detach himself from her to move.

Admiring her, Chloe walked over to Harrison. He led her back around the corner until they were out of sight, then she asked, "What is it, Harrison?"

"Your wound-licking time is over," he said softly. "That was the Governess calling. She's reclassified this assignment top priority, and she wants you to stay on it."

The Governess thought all the incidents were connected. So did Chloe. "Stay on what, specifically?" Renee had closed and sealed the investigation before and after Emma's attack. "The white slavery assignment? The Gotham Rose Club leak?" Definitely Tatiana. "Or Emma's attack?"

His eyes searched hers. "All of it."

Her stomach threatened to revolt, and she leaned back against the wall.

Harrison slid a hand into his pocket. "She also wants you to answer only to her—through me, of course."

The Governess had cut Renee out of the loop? Shock pumped through Chloe and she sought valid reasons for the order, but there could be only one. "She thinks Renee is involved?"

"That's for you to find out."

Renee rushed past them, heading for the door.

"Renee?" Chloe called out after her. "What's wrong?"

"Walk with me," she said. When Chloe caught up, she went on. "Haley's throwing a fit, and I need to get home. Preston is just beside himself."

"What's wrong with her?" Renee's daughter was a handful.

She shrugged, seemingly undone. "She's not adjusting well to her father's return home. It's been just the two of us for such a long time, and her friends were such bitches about Preston being in prison. I keep telling her he was innocent and his damn family was responsible, but she won't hear any of it." Renee stepped outside. "It's like a war zone, Chloe."

The valet drove up in Renee's silver Mercedes. "Here you go, Mrs. Dalton-Sinclair."

"Thank you." Renee slid in behind the wheel. "Keep me posted on Emma. I'll be back as soon as I negotiate a peace accord at home." She stomped the gas.

She hadn't slowed down long enough to do what she should. "Seat belt," Chloe called out.

Renee waved and kept driving.

Chloe turned and saw Franklin with Julio near the valet's desk. Franklin looked furious.

"It's all right. Don't be upset," Julio said so softly Chloe barely heard him.

"Bitch."

Chloe turned to Harrison in shock. "What's that about?" she whispered.

"I don't know. But I suggest you phone Renee and ask her."

Franklin's driver pulled up and he and Julio got into a dark-green limo. When the driver put Julio's wheelchair in the trunk, got in and closed the door, Chloe dialed her cell phone.

"Yes?" Renee sounded really harried.

"It's me, Renee," Chloe said as she made her way back to the waiting room. "Did you know Franklin and Julio Greene were at the hospital?"

"I saw them not long after Emma's ambulance arrived. Why?"

"What were they doing here?" Chloe asked.

"I heard Julio was having severe muscle spasms. It happens whenever he gets too tense."

He hadn't seemed tense, but Franklin had. "Renee, have you and Franklin had some kind of falling out?"

"It's impossible to argue when you never speak, darling."

Disappointment washed through Chloe. She knew Renee far too well to deny knowing she wasn't telling the full story. "Why would he call you a bitch behind your back?"

"I don't wish to discuss it." Sadness crept into her tone. "There's nothing to be done for it now. Believe me on this."

"I see." Even more disappointed, Chloe tried to hide it. "Well, I just thought you'd want to know."

"Thank you, darling." The phone clicked in Chloe's ear, and she turned to Harrison. "She won't discuss it."

"Not good news." He looked out into the darkness, quiet, still and thoughtful. The streetlamps splashed amber light on the cars parked in the lot.

"I don't want to do this, Harrison." Chloe tucked her phone into her Gucci handbag. "Renee, the Roses—these women are my friends. Renee's treated me better than my own mother. I don't want to pry into their lives like some paparazzi zealot."

"They have to be investigated. There's a leak, Chloe."

She lifted a hand. "It's Tatiana."

"Can you prove it?"

"She's not here." In Chloe's book, that said it all.

"That's not proof." He sighed. "Don't you realize that not knowing for fact jeopardizes every Rose agent and every assignment? These people—your friends—could be killed."

With Emma clinging to life by a thread and Jack drugged to the rafters, how in hell could Chloe not realize it? But, damn it. Why her? Why did she always get the dirty work? With Erik, who appeared to be involved in this up to his royal neck, and Jack and Renee—people she loved? It wasn't right or fair, and she was so tired of her life not working out right or fair.

"Whether or not you realize it doesn't matter," Harrison said. "You can't let more women end up like Emma. You have to investigate. You've got no choice really."

Chloe let out a frustrated breath. "Emma's in a fricking coma, Harrison. Don't you see that I'll be next?" Chloe shook. "She was good at this. I'm not."

"You are good, and you have a good partner."

"Who?" If he said Tatiana, Chloe would just shoot herself here and now and call it done.

"The Governess has ordered me to assist you," he said. "Not as your handler, but as your partner."

That news made her feel surprisingly better, but she still hated the situation. Staring out into the night, she scowled.

"Rein in your enthusiasm, okay?" His voice reeked of sarcasm. "I can take your lip bumps and your sweet charm, but these bursts of wild joy at partnering with me just deflate me."

"I'm sorry. It's not you, it's the situation," she said. "Be honest. You could care less whether I'm glad or sad to be partnered with you. Keep it real, Harrison." She needed real.

He pressed a hand over his heart. "That's not true, Princess. I'm delighted to put my ass on the line when the woman watching my back doesn't want to be there."

"Oh, lighten up. I won't let anyone hurt you." She'd already disarmed one guy who'd fired on them. Well, fired on her.

"Glad to hear it." Harrison's sarcasm faded and his tone turned dead serious. "Because I've got a bad feeling in my gut about this assignment."

She lifted her chin to look him in the eyes. "Why?"

"I don't know." He cupped her face. "But I'm afraid that before it's all over, you're going to wish you really were the bulletproof princess."

Icy chills shot up her back, and she feared he was right.

"Come on," Harrison said. "Frank is waiting outside to take you home."

Chloe protested. "I can't leave."

"Emma's protected, Chloe," Harrison said. "Her family is here, and there's a police guard at her door. They'll call if you're needed."

"But Jack…"

He stilled. "Oh, I see."

"No, you clearly don't," she countered, walking back to the waiting room. "This is professional. I want to hear what he says happened."

The head nurse for the ICU unit came out through the double swinging doors into the waiting room. Conversation ceased.

"Dr. Scoffield asked me to tell you that Emma is critical but stable. He wants all of you, except Emma's parents, to go home and not return until noon tomorrow. If there's a radical change, we'll call one of you and you phone tree the others."

The nurse then walked over to Chloe. "Mr. Quaid is awake, Princess Chloe. He wants to speak with you."

"I'm coming in, too." Harrison stood up.

"No." Chloe looked up at him. "I need to do this alone."

"You're not objective."

"Harrison, I'm going in there alone."

The nurse ended the debate. "Only one visitor at a time."

Harrison didn't look happy about that, but he stopped arguing and sat back down.

"Let's go," Chloe said.

The nurse led her through the double doors into the unit. They swished closed behind her, and she went into a small glassed-in room. Jack lay against the sheets, watching her.

Her heart thudding, she stopped beside his bed, fighting the need to touch him, hold him, feel his heartbeat against hers. "You okay?"

He nodded. "They're keeping me overnight for observation."

"In intensive care?"

"It's easier to guard Emma and me if we're together," he said. "She needs ICU."

Chloe checked to ensure their privacy, then turned back to him. "Jack, Renee said you're FBI. Why didn't you tell me?"

"It was too dangerous. I would have told you once this case was over. I'm sorry."

"What happened in that hotel room?"

He rubbed at his forehead. "When I got there, Emma and Tatiana were out on the floor. They'd both been beaten."

Surprise ripped through Chloe. "Tatiana was there?"

He nodded. "Emma wasn't breathing, Chloe." Fear flickered through his eyes. "I tried mouth-to-mouth and got a pulse. The next thing I knew, I was waking up here."

Lip film. "Where did Tatiana go?"

"I don't know," he said. "She was breathing, but out cold. Emma looked bad, Chloe." His voice caught. "But Tatiana looked even worse."

Clearly, they'd discovered something and were following it up. But the only way they'd go to that room is if someone lured them there. "Why did you go there, Jack? Were you with them?"

"No. They were out when I got there. The door was open, and I walked in and found them." He shuddered. "I got a tip from Rubi Cho. She said if I went to that room, I'd find three missing women. I asked how she knew that, and she said she'd gotten an anonymous call. She'd go herself, but they told her they'd have people watching. If anyone but me showed up, the women would be moved and never found. So I went."

Force is the only way Rubi would turn over a hot tip, but

she could also verify part of Jack's story. Chloe dipped her chin. "And the brunette in the bar? Who was she?"

"The sister of one of the missing women," he said. "The bar at Hollow Hill was the last place she knew her sister had been. She'd met a man there for a job interview, so we were checking it out."

Oh, no. Too familiar. Way too familiar. "What kind of job interview?"

"An escort. No prostitution—her sister was adamant about that. Just straight escort work."

Chloe's heart beat harder, faster, and she tilted her head. "Why did you lie to me about going to London?"

He looked directly into her eyes. "I had no choice."

Surprised, she asked, "Who took the choice from you?"

His eyes plead with her. "I can't tell you that."

Still, she pushed. "How do you know about the Duke?"

"Rubi Cho told me about him," he said.

Another surprise. "How does Rubi know about him?"

"Tatiana told her the Duke was going to kill her. Kill Tatiana, that is."

Oh, God. Chloe couldn't begin to think of all the challenges that implied. Not here and now. "Why?"

"Because she knows who he is."

"Does Rubi know his identity, too?"

"No."

"Do you?"

He sipped from a glass of water at his bedside. "I can't prove it, Chloe. But I've come to believe that Harrison isn't working for the Duke—he could *be* the Duke."

"Why?"

"He makes sense," Jack said, setting his glass down. "Unfortunately so do a few other people."

"Like who?"

"Ryan Greene, Brit Carouthers, and…" Noting her expression, Jack let his voice trail.

With the citing of each name, the fissure of fear in her opened wider. He knew too much to just be FBI. "Who the hell are you, Jack? Who subcontracted you? Renee?" She'd known him and been friends with his parents for years.

He flatly denied it. "No."

He had the perfect career, the perfect background and bloodline and family. Renee probably groomed him just as she had Chloe. "I don't believe you."

"I swear it, Chloe."

The truth dawned. "Oh, God." It fit perfectly. Made sense—and it explained why, back when Marcus had sacrificed her to the mob, Renee had turned to Jack to get Chloe out of the assassin's line of fire. "You're not the Duke."

"No." He frowned, angry that she'd even think he could be.

"You work for the Governess." *Just like Harrison.*

Jack reached for her hand, held it in his and squeezed. "Trust me, Chloe," he whispered. "Please. I don't want to lose you."

Trust him? Now? After he'd lied to her? True, she'd not told him everything, including that she was a Rose agent, but she'd never lied to him. She'd not disclosed things, but he'd known it. On those, she'd asked for his trust. He'd lied to her deliberately, and only when she'd caught him red-handed at it had he asked for her trust. "I wish I could, Jack." Tears welled in her throat. She'd wanted this man and cared about him for most of her life. "Haven't we already lost each other?"

He didn't answer.

A tear rolled down her cheek. She ignored it. "You know trust is an issue with me, and you know why." After Marcus, Jack couldn't not know it. "I love you, Jack." The truth in that terrified her. "But if I forgive you for breaking my trust, then

I also forfeit my self-respect. That's what forgiving you costs me." She stroked his hand, lifted it to her lips, her tears flowing freely down her face to his knuckles. "Ask me," she whispered against his hand. "If you ask me, I'll do it."

Pain lashed his face. He stilled for a long, tense moment, then brought her hand to his lips, kissed it and let go.

She waited, watching him, and he closed his eyes.

Her heart shattered. Partly in gratitude, and partly in mourning, she swallowed silent sobs and walked out of ICU and then out of the hospital.

Frank waited at the curb, and she got into the car. "How did you know I was coming out?"

"Jack called," he said, his voice gruff. "You all right?"

"I will be, Frank. I need to go home and sleep awhile, I think." She sniffed. "Pass me a tissue, please." She reached through the window between them.

Frank slapped his flask into her hand. "Have a toddy, Princess. It'll help you sleep."

Until she got some rest, her mind was going to stay mush. So she removed the top and took a swallow. It burned going down her throat. She took another. "What is this?"

"Whiskey, girl."

"Whiskey. Okay, then." The third swallow didn't burn anymore, but she had a little buzz going. "Strong stuff."

"Yep, pretty much."

She leaned back on her seat and thought through her situation. Jack had done the right thing. Whether or not he'd done it for the right reason, she had no idea, but letting her go was hell for him. His pain was raw and honest; no one was that good an actor.

The thing was, she could love or hate this new world of deception, but it was her world now. It lacked safety nets and mentors. It lacked everything familiar to her, and fear of it kept her nearly numb. Never before had she not known what to wish for. But this time, her success meant that someone she personally knew and likely cared about was guilty of horrific crimes. And her failure meant the Duke could murder her and Emma and all the Rose agents, one by one.

He wasn't the kind to settle for an eye for an eye. The Duke would demand the lives of all the Roses—and likely those that the Rose agents loved. There was no doubt in Chloe's mind that the black-hearted bastard would claim the lives of those for whom the Rose agents worked…all the way up to the Governess.

Chloe's muscles contracted all at once. And she, a mere coward, who was neither brave nor strong nor smart, was supposed to stop him.

Oh, please don't let me fail. Please, don't let me fail…

Chapter 9

At nearly 4:00 a.m. Chloe retrieved her ringing cell from her handbag. It was Harrison. Damn tired of being confused, she ignored the call, and dialed the direct line for the Governess.

"Hello, Chloe." The metallic, disguised voice offered no clue as to the Governess's true identity.

She traced incoming calls. No surprise there. "I'm sorry to bother you so late, but accusations are flying, and I'm getting whiplash. I need clarity."

"What is the problem?"

What wasn't? "Harrison briefed you on Emma and Jack Quaid, correct?"

"Of course."

"Tatiana was reportedly in the room and in a similar condition to Emma." Chloe then relayed what Jack had said about Rubi and her tips, then bluntly asked, "Does Jack work for you?"

No answer.

Not an admission, but not a denial. Taking that as a "yes" settled a lot of her upset with Jack and put some of her doubts to rest.

"Jack thinks Harrison could be working for the Duke. Is it possible?"

The Governess hesitated. "I'd say you should consider anything possible, but make your own determinations. There are things Jack doesn't know."

"Renee took the Roses off the case," Chloe said.

"I've been made aware of this."

Harrison had told Chloe the truth. *Good. Better.* "Harrison says you want me to stay active on it, anyway."

"Yes, I do. Chloe, we're closer than we've ever been to the Duke, and we have to stop this slave trade."

"I agree." She needed to know who had beaten Emma to a pulp and drugged Jack. "If those are your orders, then why direct me to keep Renee out of the loop?"

"Excuse me?" She sounded surprised. "What do you mean?"

"Harrison said we were partners. I was to report directly to him and you wanted Renee left out of the loop."

"I did *not* issue that order, Chloe." She sounded ticked. Ticked and uneasy.

"Those were the explicit instructions he gave me in your name." So what did this mean? That Jack was right and Harrison was the Duke? That Harrison had doubts about Jack *and* Renee and pushed them on Chloe? Did he intend for the order to be protective or did he have a personal agenda?

"I did not authorize that, but Harrison is known for adjusting orders if he feels the situation warrants it. I'll take it up with him." The Governess paused. "Chloe, here are my explicit instructions. From this moment on, you're on your own. You report directly to me. While I confer with my consultants, I want you to go home and get some rest. You're going to need it. I'll phone you there with further orders."

"Yes, ma'am." Chloe hung up the phone, her stomach queasy and her hands unsteady. If Jack didn't work for her, she'd have said so in a second. But did Chloe make the leap from that to Jack being right and Harrison being the Duke?

Chloe had a hard time making that leap, but it wasn't impossible, and one of Frank's lectures came to mind. *Divide and conquer.* Harrison had deliberately insinuated doubts about Jack in Chloe. And then doubts about Renee. And Emma's influence over Chloe had been neutralized by her attack. Had he made a concerted effort to do that?

Separate her from the aid and advice of those she trusted, and she was weaker. Then he would become the favored one, aiding her, comforting her, working closely with her—and he would know exactly where she was in the investigation *and* exactly what she was going to do next. And if he was the Duke, then he would know all he needed to know to stay one step ahead of her.

Possible. Plausible. But not proof.

So Chloe would work with him, but separately. And she'd tell him only what she wanted him to know—unless the Governess called back with conflicting orders.

Frank turned into the private parking garage at Eleanor Towers. "I'm going to play a little cards with Carmine and Craig, Princess."

Carmine owned the deli on the corner and Craig was her parking garage supervisor, and they often had wee-hours poker games. "Have fun, Frank." She stepped into the elevator, pushed the button and watched Frank park the car.

The butterflies in her stomach had turned into dragonflies. Hopefully, the Governess would call back soon. At least then, Chloe would have explicit orders straight from the top. That would cut out a lot of the confusion.

* * *

The phone rang.

Groaning, Chloe ignored it and buried her head under her pillow, but it persisted, and she remembered. *Emma! The Governess!* She snatched up the receiver. "Yes." She'd croaked. Clearing her throat, and tried again. "Hello."

"Oh, hell. I'm sorry, Sis. I should have realized you'd sleep in today."

Erik. Unsure whether to feel relieved or more stressed, Chloe dragged her sleep-deprived brain into functioning, cranked open an eye and checked the clock—8:40 a.m.? "It's okay." Erik never got up that early. "Are *you* all right?"

"Never better. I was worried about you, because of Emma."

No mention of Jack. Erik knew how important Jack was to her. Why neglect to mention him?

"I know this has to be scary," he went on. "How is she?"

Chloe stared at the phone. She was either dreaming or an alien had invaded her brother's body. Erik worried about Erik. And he had no idea how scared Chloe was about any of this. He couldn't know—or could he? He had been at Hollow Hill…

Suspicious as sin, she threw back the luxurious covers, walked to her bath then splashed her face with cold water. Something had prompted this call, and she needed to be fully awake to grasp what. "Emma's critical but stable. I got an update at 5:30." Right before she'd finally gone to sleep.

"You were awake until then?"

"Yes," she confessed. It was strange, the bargains she struck with herself when someone she loved was clinging to life—especially in the darkest hours before dawn. *If I just stay awake, she can't die. If I pray hard, she'll live. If I do nothing wrong, she'll wake up from the coma and be fine.*

Whether or not those bargains worked, Chloe had no idea.

Until now, no one close to her ever had been gravely ill. But she wasn't taking any chances. Not with Emma.

"Mother is still inconsolable about you being seen at Hollow Hill."

Ah. An update on Emma, and their mother: the real reasons Erik called. "We discussed it." Chloe slung on a silk robe and hit the kitchen. Coffee was definitely needed. Lots of coffee.

"Well, apparently she doesn't consider the discussion satisfactorily concluded because I spent thirty minutes on the phone with her last night, hearing all about it."

Why was Mother calling Erik about Chloe's business? He wasn't involved. "Emma thought she saw you there—at Hollow Hill the other night."

"I was there."

An admission? Did that translate to innocence? "Why?"

"Slumming with Brit and Ryan."

"Slumming?" Surprise streaked through her.

Erik laughed. "Guys do that, Chloe."

"What for?" She filled the coffeepot with water.

"For fun." He laughed deeper. "Just for fun. Things have been busy lately. We needed a break."

Slumming? Fun? What was wrong with him? She'd love to scorch his ears about this, but she couldn't push without alienating him. When Erik got angry, he got distant, and she needed him close to see what he was doing.

"What's keeping you so busy?" Remembering Harrison's warning, Chloe scooped out the coffee and then flipped the switch. Erik usually had tons of free time. He actually lived the life their mother believed Chloe lived.

"Ryan and I have been keeping odd hours lately."

Harrison's warning returned with a vengeance, but since he, too, had been dishonest with her, she tempered it and relied more on her own instincts. "Erik, be careful around Ryan, okay? The last thing you want is his reputation."

"Hell, Chloe." Erik guffawed. "He's adored by women, feared by men and respected in the world of business. I'd love his reputation."

She frowned into the receiver, hoping he could sense it. "I like to think that you have more substance." She prayed every day he would acquire it. For him and their parents.

"Substance is a flaw I've been working hard to correct. It's a liability in the business world." He sounded serious.

"Have you lost your mind?" He meant it. She knew he did.

A forced laugh crackled through the phone. "Just teasing."

He hadn't been teasing. Chloe knew it as well as she knew Renee had an issue with Franklin Greene. "Listen to me, okay? I'm your sister and I love you, and I'm telling you that Ryan can be a bad influence. Be careful, Erik. If you swim with sharks, you're going to either get bitten or become one of them. Either way, you're scarred." Advice she'd picked up from Lucas Perrini that had served her well.

"Oh, hell, Chloe. Half the world would love to be like Ryan Greene. Swimming with him would be fantastic for my bottom line. Do you realize how successful he is?"

"Half the world might love to be like him, but you're Prince Erik, and that carries other responsibilities that half the world doesn't have—including Ryan Greene." The coffee had brewed and the smell filled the kitchen. Inhaling deeply, Chloe reached into a glass-front cabinet for her favorite cup. "Don't get me wrong. Ryan seems like a good man, but he's picked up some questionable friends lately, and that's worth noticing."

"Like who?" Erik challenged her.

"Brit Carouthers," she said. "The man is unsavory."

"The man's a successful media giant, Chloe."

"With a brother who has a horrible gambling addiction and an arrest record for some extremely serious crimes."

"Most of those charges were dropped," Erik countered. "Besides, his brother's arrest doesn't make Brit a bad man. You were arrested, and that doesn't make me a bad man."

She could have choked him. She'd been arrested because Erik had let her hang for his crime. That he'd use it against her like this appalled her, but giving him hell wouldn't serve her immediate objective.

She returned to the topic of Brit. "You might want to read up on his brother's case and see why those charges were dropped." She didn't dare go further, though she could tell him the D.A. dropped them due to a dead witness and "lost" evidence that someone pilfered from the evidence room. No doubt for a fee Brit paid them. Florida had Sunshine Laws. Erik could look it up, but through her channels, that information remained classified, damn it. "Just stay away from him, okay?"

"Why?" Rebellion etched his tone.

"Because I asked you to, Erik. Do it for me." Whether or not he would, she had no idea. She'd never before asked him for anything. But nearly everyone in her life was suspect, and she'd love to remove her brother from that list. "Please."

The line went quiet. Chloe's heart thudded hard and her nerves snapped tight, sizzled up her back. *Come on, Erik. Come through for me. You know the lengths I've gone to, helping you.*

Finally, he answered. "I'll try to avoid Brit, but I can't promise. He's a member of the business cartel I've joined, and we have contracted agreements in joint ventures. I can't just ignore my business."

A cartel? With Ryan and Brit? And he had refused her. A lump formed in the back of her throat. She couldn't talk around it. Her eyes stung, but he'd broken her heart too many times for it to break again. "Fine."

"Don't be mad, Chloe. If I could do it, I would. But I have important business with these guys. I can't drop it just to avoid Brit. It's business, you know?"

"I understand." What was left to say? She'd asked, and he'd chosen. She couldn't take him off her suspect list. "Good-bye, Erik."

"Damn it, Chloe. I said I'd try and—"

She hung up the phone.

Chloe showered, did her makeup and, feeling the effects of missed sleep, had a second cup of coffee. She dropped her mascara wand twice, and bent to pick it up when the phone rang.

Startled, she jerked and bumped her head on the vanity's curved front. "Ouch." She rubbed the spot and reached for the phone. "Hello?"

"Chloe, it's me."

The Governess. "Good morning."

"I have instructions for you. Run your investigation and continue reporting to Renee for the time being, but simultaneously report directly to me."

"Dual reports. Got it."

"I'll have further instructions for you later today. Until then, be especially reserved with everyone." The metallic voice sounded slightly tense.

"I will." Chloe ended the call, then dialed Tatiana.

No answer.

She finished her makeup and tried again.

Still no answer—at home or on her cell.

Another fifteen minutes, and Chloe tried again. This time, when she still didn't get even Tatiana's voice mail, Chloe called the G.R.C. Olivia put her through to Renee, who was already at her desk. "Good morning."

"Is it?" Renee asked.

"Not really," Chloe confessed. "I can't reach Tatiana. Have you had any luck?"

"None. Olivia and I have scoured her haunts, contacted all the Roses, and no one has seen her."

"Jack says she was beaten and left in a condition like Emma in that hotel room, Renee."

"He told me."

He had? That was reassuring news. "What about her Rose pin?"

"Alan checked it. It's not transmitting."

Damn it. Chloe played a hunch. "Have you tried Rubi Cho?"

"No," she said. "Why would I?"

Apparently Jack hadn't told Renee about Rubi and her tip that led him to that hotel room. "They go clubbing together. She might know something."

"I'll call her now," Renee said. "If we have any luck, I'll let you know. Will you be at home or on your cell?"

Emma had stolen Tatiana's LaBella appointment. If she and Tatiana had hooked up there, the owner, Jacques, would know it. "On the cell. I've got an appointment."

"Anything I need to know?"

"Not yet." Chloe hung up, then dressed in a sporty green Adelphio sweater and slacks, switched handbags, Gucci to Hermès, and splashed on a little *Remember Me*, her Dior signature fragrance. Blowing it dry on her wrists, she pulled out her car keys. Frank had left a text message that he'd returned to the hospital, so she walked downstairs to take her green Jag.

In the garage, she phoned Frank, and they talked on her drive over to LaBella. "How's Emma?" Chloe tapped her left turn signal. The Jag was running a little rough.

"Still critical, Princess," Frank said. "No change, Doc Scoffield says. Lucas Perrini just brought lunch up to her folks. They're holding up all right."

"Any of the Roses there?"

"Porsche and Ryan Greene were here at straight up noon. Not together, they just arrived at the same time and tried to get in to see Miss Emma, but Doc Scoffield nixed that."

The nurse had made it clear only immediate family would be allowed. Porsche was Emma's best friend, but it was odd that Ryan would try. "Brit Carouthers hasn't shown up there, has he?"

"No, and I'm hoping he doesn't," Frank said, gruff as Chloe ever had heard him. "If he hadn't left her at that damn restaurant by herself, she wouldn't be here now."

Chloe didn't agree with that. She'd like to, but she couldn't because she believed this had everything to do with their blown cover and nothing to do with a random attack, which is what the police claimed had happened. "I've got some work to do, Frank, but you stay with Emma and if Brit, Ryan or Erik shows up, you let me know."

She thought back a second, remembered Franklin and his reaction to Renee at the hospital last night. "And Franklin Greene. Let me know if he tries to see her." Something niggled at Chloe. Something she should be getting that was significant but she couldn't quite grasp.

"Haven't seen Franklin, but Julio came up with Ryan. He looked like he'd rather be anywhere else and didn't say much."

"Did he try to see Emma, too?" Chloe braked for a red light, ignored a cab's horn and smiled at a mime pretending to wash windshields as he crossed the street.

"No. He talked to Miss Emma's parents. That was it. Only Ryan and Porsche tried to get inside the ICU unit."

Chloe's mouth went dry. Until she knew what was putting knots in her belly, she was taking no chances. "Frank, talk to Dr. Scoffield and make sure that order stands. Have him limit visitors to her parents, you and me. I've got to talk to her. Tell him it's important to discovering who attacked her. We can't take any chances."

"Damn right." Frank sounded worried. "Princess, is there something about this you want to tell me?"

"I can't. Trust me, Frank." Chloe took in a deep breath, swearing if he refused to trust her on the same day Erik had, she'd just call it quits on living a life with substance and become what her mother thought she was: rich and useless.

"Of course," Frank said.

Relief and gratitude restored her spirits. "And hire the best security guard you can get to watch over Emma—the sooner, the better."

"Ain't one of them enough?"

Chloe slid into a parking space three stores down from La-Bella. "She has a guard?" Off-duty police had been there last night, but that had been a stopgap measure.

"Sure does."

"Who sent him?" Oh God, what if the Duke did? What if—

"Harrison brought him up this morning and introduced him to Miss Emma's folks. His name is Mac Dayton. Seems like a good man," Frank said, interjecting his opinion, which considering this was about Emma, was expected. "Harrison says he'll be guarding her until the person responsible is behind bars."

Harrison. The Governess was behind this, of course. Chloe could halfway breathe again. The Governess hadn't condemned Harrison for issuing additional orders in her name, although she hadn't given him a pass yet, either. She would advise Chloe with her next call. "Good. But no one gets into her room alone."

"The nurse stays put." Frank frowned. "You worried about Jack and Harrison?"

Chloe sighed. "Until I know who hurt her, I'm worried about everyone but you and me."

"I'll be parking myself bedside, then."

For his girls... "Good. I'll check in later. Call me if—"

"If there's any change in Miss Emma's condition, if anyone named Greene shows up, if anyone tries to get in to see Miss Emma, and—" Frank paused to catch his breath. "How about I just call you if anything at all happens?"

Chloe smiled into the phone. "That'll work. Bless you, Frank. I adore you!"

"Damn right."

Half an hour later, Chloe departed the salon. According to Jacques, on the day Emma had taken Tatiana's appointment, Tatiana had come in and been taken as a walk-in, filling in a cancellation. They'd left the salon together, deciding where to have lunch. Which made the discussion at the G.R.C. about Emma stealing the appointment totally bizarre.

By the time Chloe locked herself in her car, she realized that for the first time since finding Emma, she wasn't numb with fear. She was confused about what the hell was really going on, but she was not numb with fear.

It had to be because she was *doing something* and not just waiting to become the Duke's next victim. She put her purse on the passenger seat. Maybe that was the key to dealing with fear constructively: to do something, even if it wasn't totally right. She no longer felt helpless.

Pondering on that epiphany, she keyed the ignition and then phoned Ryan Greene at his Manhattan office.

When he answered, she said, "Ryan, I'm terribly sorry to bother you, but I'm trying to find Brit and not having much luck." Okay, it was a lie. She hadn't tried anywhere else. But it couldn't hurt to know where Ryan was, either. "Any idea where he might be?"

"He and Erik are having lunch at Perrini's. I'd be with them, but Tatiana and I had to review some documents and—"

"Tatiana is there?" Shock, laced with disappointment. Jack had lied to her. Again. *Damn it.* "May I speak with her? It's important."

"I'm sorry, but she just left," Ryan said.

Oh. Had she been there, or was this yet another lie? "Did she happen to say where she was going?"

"Gotham Rose Club to do something for the Halloween Ball."

No way. Definitely a lie. The ball was on Chloe's turf. Tatiana wasn't involved except as a guest. "Thanks, Ryan."

"Of course," he said. "I still owe you dinner. When do you want to collect?"

Twelfth of never. Chloe grimaced. "Can I get back to you on that? I'm *so* tied up with preparations for the ball."

He poured on the charm. "Don't make me wait too long."

"I won't." Chloe hit End then speed-dialed the G.R.C. When Olivia answered, she asked, "Has Tatiana showed up there?"

"No. We've been scouring the state for her. So far, it's as if she doesn't want to be found."

"Rubi didn't know anything?"

"Not a thing," Olivia said.

Disappointed, Chloe stopped at a red light and watched a young mother push a stroller with twins in it across the street. "What about her Rose pin?"

"It was found in the hotel room with Emma and Jack, Chloe."

"So she *was* there." Jack *had* told the truth. But Ryan had just lied.

"Her pin was, anyway," Olivia said. "Renee is terrified that something has happened to Tatiana. I know you two aren't the best of friends, but you won't let that get in the way—"

"Of course not." The light turned green. Chloe pressed down on the gas pedal. "What does Renee think happened to her?"

"The same thing that happened to the three Russian women."

"Ryan Greene just told me that Tatiana was with him until a few minutes ago and she was on her way to the G.R.C."

"That's impossible." Olivia was emphatic.

"Why?" Chloe hooked a left and stopped for another light. Traffic was a bear, but with luck, she'd get to Perrini's before Erik and Brit departed.

"Because Samantha's been watching him since he left home this morning and Tatiana hasn't been anywhere near him."

Proof. Ryan lied. "I'm all over it, Olivia." Chloe ended the call then glanced at her watch—nearly two o'clock. She pulled up to Perrini's curb. Her stomach growled; she'd missed lunch.

The valet notified Lucas of her arrival, and he met her at the door. "How is Emma, my dear?"

"There's been no change." Chloe pressed a light kiss to Lucas's cheek. "That was thoughtful of you, bringing lunch to her parents at the hospital."

"They won't leave her even to eat decent food," he said. "I'll see to it that they are fed well while they wait with their daughter. They have to keep up their strength."

"Thank you, Lucas." Chloe squeezed his arm.

"Are you hungry? I was just about to sample a new dish."

She was, but first things first. "Starving. Can we eat in a bit—in your kitchen?" For Chloe, eating in the kitchen with Lucas was a wonderful, comforting event. In her parents' home, she'd never been allowed to eat anywhere but in the formal dining room, and at her apartment, she had rebelled by never eating at the table. But in Lucas's kitchen, the intimacy and warmth that should be in a home at the kitchen table surrounded her. Chloe loved that feeling.

"Of course, my dear." Clearly pleased, he smiled and his eyes twinkled. "You have something to do first, I take it?"

"Erik is here with Brit. I want to talk to him."

"I wish Prince Erik was not associating with that man." The lines alongside Lucas's mouth deepened to grooves. "He should never have left Emma alone. Most assuredly, not there."

"She paid him to go," Chloe reminded Lucas, though he was old world and that wouldn't relieve Brit of responsibility for Emma's safety. Not in Lucas's eyes, or in Frank's. Necessary or not, it was kind of nice, noble, that protective chivalry.

"Come," Lucas said. "Take care of the nasty business so that we can progress to the pleasant." He clasped her arm and patted it as they walked through the corridor to the main dining room. "Shall I ask Luigi to make you linguini with white clam sauce?"

Her favorite. "I'd love it, but whatever you're tasting today will be wonderful." Luigi couldn't make a bad meal. He was incapable of it.

Lucas escorted her to the table where Erik and Brit sat, then walked away. "I'm sorry to interrupt," Chloe said.

Erik and Brit stood up. "Sis," Erik said, clearly surprised to see her. His throat flushed and the bright color crept up over his face. No doubt, he was remembering the promise he wouldn't make to her that morning.

Brit smiled. "You're welcome to interrupt anytime."

"Thank you, Mr. Carouthers," she said, keeping it formal.

"Call me Brit, please."

She nodded and sat down. The men returned to their seats. There was no alcohol on the table. Erik resolutely refused to drink during negotiations. "I see this is a business lunch," she said. "I'll try not to keep you long."

"It's no problem," Brit said. "We've concluded that portion of our meeting."

Chloe glanced at Erik, who looked away. "Actually, I came to talk to you about Emma. I'm hoping you can give me some insight on what happened last night."

"There isn't much to tell, really," Brit said with a slight shrug. "I won her date at the auction, Ryan dropped us off for dinner at Lagniappe. She asked a question I refused to answer, and she doubled my bid to get me to leave—so I did. That's about it."

"What was the question?" Emma was direct, but typically she was subtler than Brit had described—unless she was angry or afraid. Then, all bets were off on what she would say or do.

The look in his eyes turned molten. He was angry and not bothering to hide it. "She asked how much it had cost me to buy down the bulk of my brother's charges in Florida."

Chloe fought to keep her shock from showing and smiled. "Vintage Emma," Chloe lied. "Subtle as mud."

"Damn, Brit," Erik said. "You had to be furious. How did you answer that?"

Glad Erik had asked so Chloe didn't have to, she waited for the response. When it came, it wasn't what she had expected.

"A dead witness doesn't charge a dime." He smiled but it didn't touch his eyes. "It was absurd. Who would I pay?"

Erik laughed, thinking Brit was joking, but Chloe knew better. He'd left a witness dead—officially, due to natural causes, of course. *Not bloody likely.* "That's quite an answer," Chloe said, straddling the line.

"I thought so." He smiled, clearly pleased with himself.

"So you left Emma at Lagniappe and returned to Perrini's."

He nodded. "I didn't leave here until after midnight." He turned serious. "Once your brother's been arrested, when anything happens, you're the first suspect on everyone's lists—even if you've never committed a crime. For the record, I haven't," he said. "Not in Florida, and not last night. Emma was fine the last time I saw her. I'm sorry she's hurt, but I have no idea what happened to her."

He had a point Chloe understood well since her own arrest. And believe him or not, she recognized an exit line when she heard one. As far as Brit was concerned, this discussion was over. Considering what she'd learned, that was just as well.

Emma didn't frighten easily, but she clearly had feared him. That was the only time she went straight for the jugular. So what had he said or done to trigger fear in her?

"Thank you for talking to me." Chloe stood up. "I'll leave you two to your business." She avoided meeting Erik's gaze, left the table and headed for Lucas's kitchen.

She walked through the single swinging door. "Luigi, I'm starving," she called out.

It thrilled Lucas's chef. He laughed hard and deep, his round stomach jiggling. "Ah, good. Luigi appreciates a woman who knows good food. Come to my table, Princess."

Eager to do just that, she smiled and walked around a lattice partition.

Jack was sitting at Lucas's kitchen table.

Chapter 10

Chloe stopped in her tracks and stared.

Lucas clasped her arm and guided her to her chair. "You listen to Jack, Princess Chloe," he whispered that advice "with your ears and your heart, eh?"

She looked from Lucas to Jack.

"I hear you've been dodging bullets again." Jack took a bite of ravioli.

Lucas flushed guiltily. "I told him about the gunman shooting at you when you found him and Emma." He held up a staying hand. "Harrison did not shoot, Princess. The man who fired on you stood on a ledge on the outer wall of the building, and Harrison did not fire his weapon." Lucas paused and let that sink in. "I beg you. Just listen to Jack."

Chloe had realized that about Harrison, of course. Couple it with his lie about the Governess's orders, and all his motives were suspect. "You look fine. Are you?"

Jack nodded. "I expect I'd feel nothing if you hadn't shown up when you did."

She hadn't dared to think of that. But the gunman…

His eyes held a lot of hurt and a little challenge. "Has it occurred to you that the only time you're getting shot at is when you're with Harrison Howell?"

Jack sipped from his wineglass. "Think for a second, Chloe. We're doing great. Then you find me in a compromising situation just as Howell shows up, plants absurd suspicions in your mind that you should know better than to believe, and we're alienated." The censure in that remark was clear. "Then he turns on Renee and makes you doubt her." Bitterness put an edge on Jack's tone. "*Then* Emma's attacked and left in a coma, Tatiana disappears—no insight available from either of them— I'm drugged and out of commission, and then you're shot at— again." He lifted his eyebrows. "Are you seeing a pattern, here?"

An idiot would see the pattern. Chloe rubbed at her forehead. "There are things you don't understand and I'm not free to explain, Jack."

"Ditto." He put down his fork. "Which brings us to a new bottom line."

She didn't track that shift. "What new bottom line?"

"We can work together and maybe survive this, or not and…"

"And what?"

He looked directly into her eyes. "Die."

Chloe absorbed that, then looked at Lucas and asked a question that abused their friendship. She could but hope he'd forgive her. "Are your friends' friends still pursuing that contract on me because of Marcus?"

Lucas spoke with no hesitation and no doubt. "No friend of my friends would dare to touch you. There is no Mafioso contract, my dear. There never was."

That left her reeling. "Then who tried to assassinate me to prove to Marcus he should do what the mob told him?"

Lucas didn't answer.

Jack did. "It wasn't the mob that wanted Marcus to lose evidence. It was Marcus's associate—the Duke."

When Lucas agreed, Chloe asked, "Who *is* the Duke?"

Jack spared Lucas a glance. "On that, we have a difference of opinion. I believe he's Harrison Howell."

Chloe looked at Lucas. "Ryan Greene," he said. "Marcus went to him for help. He's part of the business cartel with Brit Carouthers. And he knows too much, and has too great an interest, where he should have little—namely, in the Roses."

She looked back at Jack. "Harrison could be working for Ryan. Or vice versa."

"If Ryan is guilty," Jack said, "one person knows it."

"Tatiana." She would have guessed from seeing his financial records. "And she's missing."

"Not missing," Jack corrected her. "Kidnapped."

Chloe's skin crawled. "It appears so."

Jack wasn't happy to not be taken at his word, but that was just too bad. He had given Chloe valid reason to doubt him and to verify what he told her. She met his gaze without apology.

He drank from his glass. "So do we work together, Chloe?"

She didn't want to end up dead, and she did feel he had told her the truth as he believed it to be. He'd also made some very astute observations. "Yes, we work together."

Leaving Jack in Lucas's kitchen, Chloe tried repeatedly to contact the Governess for those further instructions—no luck—and spoke with those who'd attended the date auction. Three of them verified that Brit Carouthers had danced in the grand ballroom until well past midnight. He couldn't have attacked Emma.

But did he know who had? That remained possible.

Chloe returned to the kitchen, to Jack. "Any luck?"

"No one has seen Tatiana. Her family sounded very nervous. Not afraid, just nervous."

He thought a second. "What if she faked it, Chloe?"

"Why would she fake it?" Chloe had her own opinion on that, but wanted to hear his.

He lifted a shoulder. "Maybe she tipped her hand, and the Duke's decided she has become a liability."

"Could be, if he's discovered that she knows his identity." He'd protect himself at any costs. Chloe was convinced of that.

Jack stood and came out from behind the table. "I need to run down a couple things. I'll call you shortly." He didn't touch her. The hurt was still in his eyes, but so was concern. "Be careful, Chloe."

"You, too." She watched him leave. Her heart felt wrung out and she mourned all they'd lost. Would they ever get back to where they'd been before he'd lied to her about London?

Lucas circled her with an arm. "Give it time, my dear."

Blinking hard, Chloe looked up at him. "I don't think there is that much time, Lucas."

"Of course there is. The heart has an impressive ability to heal, Princess. One must only let in that which restores."

Once broken, trust was just...broken. "What restores?"

He gave her a tender smile. "Forgiveness."

It was nearly five o'clock before Chloe got back in her car and left Perrini's. She buckled her safety belt, then dialed Harrison's cell. He'd find it odd if she didn't check in with him.

On the third ring, he answered. "Howell."

Uneasiness rippled through her. "It's me, Chloe."

"Ah, the princess awakens."

"The princess hasn't been to sleep, she's been gathering information, which is in short supply, and she's hoping her partner's had better luck."

"A little. Can we talk, or do you want to meet?"

She definitely didn't want to see him without first hearing from the Governess, and even then, not unless she was wearing a Kevlar vest or Frank's suit of armor. She'd dodged enough bullets already, thank you very much. "Phone works for me."

"You first, then."

Chloe relayed events between Emma and Brit. "I verified that he was on the dance floor when Emma was attacked." Chloe swallowed hard. "Thanks for having Mac Dayton guard Emma."

"The Governess considered it prudent."

So did Chloe. Yet if she didn't completely trust Harrison, could she trust Mac Dayton? No. But Frank was there.

"You okay, Chloe?"

She wasn't. But for the first time since she'd seen Emma battered and bruised on the floor and Jack unconscious, Chloe felt more angry than scared. Confused and lost, too, but more angry than scared. Maybe she wasn't a coward. Maybe she was just almost a coward. "I'm fine."

His line clicked. "Damn. Let me call you back. The Governess is phoning."

"Sure." Suspicious, Chloe quickly dialed the Governess.

The phone rang and rang, but neither her voice mail nor her answering service answered. The Governess was not in her office, and that set off an alarm in Chloe. At the next red light, she dialed Renee. "Have you heard from the Governess?"

"No," she said, agitated. "I've been phoning her since early this morning and have yet to reach her."

"She was supposed to call me this morning, but I haven't heard from her, either." Chloe was worried. Especially now that Harrison *and* Ryan had claimed contact with women Chloe couldn't reach. "Still nothing on Tatiana, right?"

"Right. We've searched all day. I did phone Rubi, but all she knew was that Tatiana had gone to Hollow Hill to meet the man she's been dating."

"Who is he?" Chloe asked.

"Warren," Renee said. "Rubi didn't know his last name."

"Emma's interviewer." Was that significant?

"Yes," Renee said, a tremor in her voice. "That's why I believe Tatiana is missing woman number four."

Chloe pulled into a drugstore parking lot and stopped to give the call her full focus. "I need help on this, Renee."

"Didn't the Governess assign Harrison to work with you?"

"Yes, but I have reason to doubt him. That's what the Governess was going to call me about." Chloe sighed. "I need Jack."

No answer.

"Did you recruit Jack to work for the Governess?"

"No, I did not."

Chloe clenched the steering wheel. Maybe she'd asked the wrong question. "Did the Governess recruit him?"

No answer.

Irritated as hell, Chloe sighed. "Look, I understand the need for secrecy, but I'm warning you that if I don't have help I trust, I will fail. You know what that means to these women."

"Jack lied to you, and you still trust him?"

"I do." It wasn't unqualified trust, but it was trust. "He had his reasons. He protected them in the wrong way, but he hasn't had as much experience at it as the rest of us."

"I'm glad you've taken a leap of faith on him, darling. Jack is a good man, and he loves you."

That was as close to an admission as she was going to get. "I don't know if he loves me, but I can rely on him."

"You do know that Harrison believes Jack is the Duke."

"Yes." So Harrison had shared his suspicion with Renee. "Have you proven conclusively that he isn't?"

"Do I have hard evidence? No. But I don't have to be bulletproof when I'm with Jack. I do with Harrison."

"I noted that trend. Do you believe he's the Duke, Chloe?"

"I don't know," she said honestly. "But I can't dismiss its merit. He has access to the Governess and her consultants. That makes his staying ahead of the Roses much easier."

"Until we know, let's keep him on the fringes."

"I'm already there." Chloe rubbed at her forehead. With so many people proving unreliable, that should just be her motto. *Keep everyone on the fringes until all is unraveled.* "If you contact the Governess, or hear from Tatiana, let me know."

"I will, darling. Be very careful."

"I'm trying." Chloe dropped her phone into her purse, dragged her lip between her teeth, thinking through events, and hit on an oddity that had occurred in the dressing room just before she and Emma went to Hollow Hill. An oddity in Emma and Tatiana's exchange. She dialed Jack.

"Quaid."

"Got a second? Something strange happened yesterday. I'm not sure what to make of it. Can we talk it over?"

"Sure."

"I need to ask two questions first. I'll answer, too."

"Will you trust my answers?"

More faith required. "Yes, I will." Chloe meant it.

"Okay."

"Do you work for the Governess?"

"Yes."

"Are *you* the Duke?"

"No."

"Okay, your turn," Chloe said, risking relief.

"Are you the Duke?"

"No, I'm not." She waited, but he didn't ask anything more. "Is that it?"

"One more."

"Okay."

"Are you still crazy about me?"

Her heart beat hard and fast. "I'm stuck with it."

"Okay. I'm done," he said. "What's strange?"

He didn't sound a bit different. Was he happy about that, or did he see her caring as a liability? She wanted to know, but couldn't bring herself to ask. "When Emma and I were at G.R.C., dressing to go to Hollow Hill, Tatiana made a big deal out of Emma stealing her appointment for a peppermint foot treatment at LaBella."

"Okay." He sounded lost.

He couldn't understand yet. "Emma responded as if Tatiana were bitching her out about it for the first time."

"I'm trying, but this is like a special code for women, and I'm not tracking."

"Be patient. I'm getting there. I went to the salon and Jacques, the owner, told me Emma had taken Tatiana's appointment, but that Tatiana had come in, too. Fortunately, they'd had a cancellation. So Tatiana got her peppermint foot treatment."

"Chloe, I'm sure that in some twisted way this makes sense to you, but that they both got a peppermint foot treatment isn't striking me as a significant discovery."

"They left LaBella together, discussing where to go for lunch, Jack. Now if they both already knew Emma had stolen the appointment and Tatiana had wrangled an appointment anyway—"

"Then why bring it up at the G.R.C.?"

"Exactly." Chloe cranked her engine and adjusted her shoulder harness on her chest. The damn thing was trying to do serious injury to her right boob. "The issue had been resolved at the salon."

"Then it had to be a message—to someone."

"That's my thinking," Chloe said. "But I'm not sure wha the message was, or for whom it was intended."

"Who else was there?" he asked.

"Kristi, Samantha and me." Chloe checked the clock Nearly nine o'clock. Samantha was now tagging Ryan Greene under Renee's orders.

"That leaves you and Kristi. Why would Tatiana pass a message to Kristi?"

"I can't imagine."

"Think back. Anything else unusual happen there?"

Chloe remembered the fricking rhinestone glasses, the skimpy black skirt—and the red wigs. She debated mention ing them, and decided to err in favor of Emma. "I know thi was intentional, but I don't know the rationale."

"Go ahead."

"You know the three missing Russian women are all bru nettes, right?"

"Yes, I do." Now he sounded wary and charged.

"Emma and I were ordered to wear red wigs for the inter views, Jack."

"Red?" He sounded incredulous. "I didn't notice that."

"Poor lighting in the bar," she said. "Definitely red."

"Damn it, why? Harvey wanted brunettes. Regal, sophis ticated brunettes. Kristi must have screwed up."

"No, she didn't." Chloe hoped this revelation didn't pu Renee in a bad spot, or reveal that she was already in one "Renee specifically ordered it. When we got there, we wer sent to the wrong men for interviews, as well. We thought tha was a clerical error and went with it, but now I wonder. Could that have been Renee's added insurance?"

Jack went silent. Chloe waited, but when he didn't sa anything, she prodded him. "Jack?"

"I'm here. Just absorbing."

"What are you absorbing?" She cranked her engine and turned her lights on. The twin beams shot out in front of the car and down onto the parking lot.

"The objective was to get you two on the inside, and two discrepancies is no mistake. Renee guaranteed you and Emma wouldn't be tagged for sale, which puts all her actions into question. Why would she deliberately sabotage an assignment?"

"Protecting us?" Chloe suggested, at least half-certain she was right. "She's a second mother to all the Roses. But, in her own sophisticated way, she strong-armed us into taking the assignment and putting ourselves at risk in the first place."

"Then something happened between the strong-arming and you going to Hollow Hill. Something that made her pull back." Jack grunted. "Chloe, was she protecting you and Emma, or herself?"

Chloe was *not* going there. "Renee isn't on the wrong side of this." Chloe had lost Erik; she couldn't lose Renee, too. "Maybe she had to get us to accept the assignment, but she wanted us to fail so we'd be safe." That made perfect sense. Renee couldn't very well ignore orders from the Governess.

"Maybe." Jack warned her. "But you'd better be prepared for a more complex reason than that."

"That's as far as I'm willing to go, Jack." Renee had not been open with her, but that didn't mean she had changed sides.

"I understand." His voice softened. "You okay?"

"No, Jack. I'm not okay." Of all the times he'd asked, she hadn't been okay even once, and that reminded her of all she personally risked, and all she should be and wasn't. And that had her torn between crying and heaving. "Just give me a second, okay?" Her hands shook on the wheel, but she pulled out into traffic. "I'm, um, working through this. I've trusted

Renee all my life." Chloe choked up, paused, and then finished "I believe in her, Jack." A tear trickled down Chloe's cheek.

"Okay, honey." He sounded tender, gentle, as if only now did he feel how close to the bone this cut Chloe. How close to the bone his lying to her had cut. "We'll go with that for now. You take all the time you need. I'll just hang on here until you're ready to…until you're ready."

A moment of grace. He wasn't abandoning her or intruding. Just standing by, giving her time and space to work through this and choose what she wanted and needed. She loved this about him. His unassuming support, and his no feeling he had to jump in and fix everything. He trusted that she could sort through it and work it out on her own. There was goodness and strength in that. It was more moving and powerful than if Jack had bulldozed in and tried to fix the unfixable. Trust betrayed no longer exists.

If Renee had betrayed her, all the good done before the betrayal wasn't just wiped away. There had to be logical reasons. Unfortunately, none offered would be acceptable to the Governess—or to Chloe. She would have covered for Renee in any way humanly possible—done anything doable for her—but if Renee hadn't trusted Chloe with the truth… That might hurt most.

"You still there?"

"Yeah." She choked on a swallowed sob. "I'm afraid I need another minute."

"No problem. Take what you need."

She needed him. Darkness fell around Chloe and the temperature quickly dropped to freezing, seemingly pressing heavy weight against her skin. A storm was building in the western sky. Tatiana could be held prisoner or sold, Emma lay comatose and critical, Erik had done exactly that which Chloe had begged him not to do yet again, Renee had deceived Chloe and Emma, Harrison had lied to Chloe and the Governess, and Chloe and Jack had broken their special bond. This had been one bitch of a day.

Skirting Central Park, she drove into the private garage at Eleanor Towers, then got out of the car and passed the keys to her garage supervisor. "Thanks, Craig."

"You're welcome, Princess Chloe." He took the key and walked her to the elevator.

"How's the baby?"

"He's fine." Craig beamed. "Sitting up and scooting all the way across the room on the floor."

Chloe laughed. "Keeping Debra busy, I'll bet."

"Oh, yes, ma'am." He laughed, a content man.

Discontent, she stepped into the elevator. "Night."

"Good night, Princess." Whistling, he parked her car.

She keyed the elevator and pushed the button for the fifth floor, wishing for one moment in her life—just one moment—she could know Craig's kind of contentment.

Phone service was dead on the elevator. Oh, damn, Jack! When she got off, her phone was ringing. "Jack?"

"Elevator, eh?" He chuckled.

"Yes. I'm sorry. I forgot again." The bell chimed and she stepped out, her apartment key in her hand. Breezing past a security camera—the building had several on each floor—she nodded at Aubrey, the night monitor until 11:00 p.m., and then stopped at her apartment door.

It stood slightly ajar.

"Oh, God." With her free hand, she reached into her purse and retrieved her Glock.

"What's wrong, Chloe?"

Her throat went dry. "My apartment door is open."

"Is your staff in?"

"No, they're off and Frank's at the hospital with Emma."

"Don't go in," Jack said. "I'm two blocks away. Just go to the security desk and wait for me there."

The coward in her wanted to do just that. But if she did, she'd always be afraid. She couldn't live her life afraid. Yet every horrible thing the Duke had ever done—every single bruise on Emma, Tatiana being kidnapped—haunted Chloe, and she stiffened, summoned courage and faced it. "This is my home, Jack. I will not be afraid here. I can't."

She wasn't a rookie. She'd been trained by the best in the business. Pumped up, she kicked the door wide open.

It banged against the wall.

"For God's sake, talk to me so I know you're okay."

"I'm going inside." She clipped the phone to her pocket. "You'll be able to hear me." Taking in a steadying breath, she held the gun in a two-handed grip, hoping to hell she didn't have to shoot anyone here. She'd done plenty of shooting on the range, and she'd fired her weapon on assignments, but she'd never had to kill anyone. And if she did have to kill someone, she damn well didn't want it to be in her home.

"Entry is clear." She moved on to the living room, skirting wide of the sofa. Jimmy Valentine had warned them repeatedly in training that pros loved to recline on the sofa and shoot straight through it. She stepped up to the alarm system control panel. "Alarm is inactive but shows no signs of entry. Someone beat the damn system, Jack. They've been all over my apartment. I can't explain it—there are no signs of damage—but I know it. I feel it."

"Don't go any further," Jack said. "Remember Emma, okay? Wait for backup. I'm in the garage, heading up the stairs."

"Take the elevator." It was faster.

"No phone service." His voice was breaking. He was running up the stairs, full out.

"You can slow down." Okay, so she'd be elated when he got to the penthouse, but she wanted him to *get* to the penthouse. The man had just been released from the hospital.

"Second floor."

She walked on through, flooding the apartment with light as she went. "Living room is clear. I'm moving to the kitchen."

She checked under the table, brushed past the fridge. The motor clicked on and the icemaker dropped ice. The sudden plop nearly scared her out of her skin.

"Fourth floor landing." Jack reported in.

God, he was fast. Keeping the gun elevated, ready to fire, she set the phone in its base to charge and tapped the speaker button. Her hands were shaking. The flowing drapes and draping tablecloth in the dining room had her checking the floor for feet. "Dining room is clear."

"I'm at the door. Let me in."

An icy chill swept up her spine. "I left it open." She headed back the way she'd come, her senses wide open to catch so much as a hint of a glimpse of movement, a whisper of sound, but there was only dead silence.

"The damn door is locked," Jack shouted. "Get out here."

Someone was inside with her. She moved quickly through the kitchen, checked the sofa, the living room, her heart pounding hard in her ears. At the door, she shoved the locks and jerked open the door.

Jack grabbed her, jerked her out into the hallway and then pulled her into a bear hug, twisting so that his back was at the wall beside the door. "Damn it, woman." He tugged her closer, his heart hammering against her breasts. "The next time I tell you to wait for backup, you wait for backup or I swear to God I'll shoot you myself."

He was terrified, pasty white, not flushed from the run, and holding her so tightly she couldn't breathe. "Ease…up."

Jack loosened his grip a fraction and searched her face. "You're okay, right? You didn't see anyone?"

She nodded, her chin bumping his chest. He was shaking all over. Fear for her. Even now… Her heart tender, she rested her cheek against his shoulder, her fingertips curled at his waist, holding him close. Absently stroking her hair, he clicked the flash button on his phone and then dialed 911.

A woman's voice carried to Chloe. "Emergency services. Medical, police or fire?"

"Police," he said, paused, then added, "Home invasion. Eleanor Towers. Penthouse. The intruder is still inside." His panic was subsiding; Jack was getting his color back. "Princess Chloe St. John," he said, then relayed her street address.

The woman said something, and then Jack responded, "No need to hold on. I'm a federal agent, requesting backup." He hit the flash button again, then asked Chloe, "What's security's number downstairs?"

Chloe gave it to him and he reported the break-in. Building security procedures went into effect. The outer doors would be locked. There'd be no ingress or egress until the security team had checked the entire building.

Four men flooded the hallway, all in uniform. Aubrey, the portly nighttime security chief, drew his gun and took aim on Jack. "Back away from her," he ordered. "Do it now."

"No, Aubrey," Chloe said. "Jack's with me."

They fanned out and checked the apartment, their voices carrying to her. Shouts back and forth that everything was clear. She looked into Jack's eyes. "I don't believe it. Someone was in my apartment with me, Jack." She'd sensed him, almost smelled him there.

"Stay on guard and be ready to shoot." He went inside.

Chloe followed, systematically checked her apartment, but found no one. "All clear," she shouted.

"All clear." Jack joined her in her bedroom. "You okay?"

She absolutely refused to say she wasn't okay another time, though she seriously doubted that she'd ever really be okay again. "I'm not scared, Jack. Not anymore. Someone was here. I feel utterly violated, and I'm pissed off."

"That's a normal reaction." He checked beneath her bed.

"Maybe, but it's different when it's *your* reaction." She stopped in front of her dresser, dragged her fingertips over the gleaming wood. Something was wrong. What was it?

"I expect it is different."

She pegged it. "Oh, no." She checked the gold tray beside her jewelry box. In all the upset, she'd forgotten. "My Rose pin is gone." The tracking device Alan had made her was gone.

Jack frowned. "The one you were to wear at all times?"

"I forgot it, okay?" She tapped the tray. "I left it right here." She looked at him. "I leave everything I wear all the time on the tray…so I don't forget it." *Lame. So lame.*

Aubrey talked back and forth to Ed, who was manning the monitors in the security office, then tapped on her bedroom door, but didn't enter. "Princess Chloe?"

"Yes, Aubrey." She turned toward his voice.

"The rest of the apartment is clear. Ed reviewed the tape. The only person who entered the building since the last security sweep was a plumber. Ed monitored him on surveillance. He went directly to 503, came out half an hour later, and exited straight out the north entrance."

"That's the penthouse next door," she said. "It's unoccupied."

"The crawl space." Aubrey ordered Ed to check it.

"There's a crawl space above the penthouse?" Jack asked.

"In Eleanor Towers there is. Yes, sir," Aubrey said.

"Where's the access door?" Jack asked Aubrey, but Chloe

answered. "In the hallway outside the master suite. I put a lock on it." She led him to it.

Everything looked fine from the floor, but Jack stood on a chair to get a better look at the lock. "It's broken."

Chloe's stomach crunched. Had that happened today? Or earlier and gone unnoticed? She wasn't sure, and that felt like the biggest violation of all.

"I want the surveillance tape," Jack told Aubrey.

"Sir, I appreciate your concern, but this is a matter best left to professionals."

"I am a professional," Jack said. "FBI."

Frowning, Aubrey glanced from Jack to Chloe. "We're dating," she said, explaining their connection.

"She could be a target," Jack added. "One of my cases has heated up. They might try to use her to get to me."

"All that Marcus Sterling business?" he asked Chloe. She nodded and protectiveness replaced his wariness. "Ed will dub you a copy of the tape. I'll put all the guards on high alert."

Jack hoisted himself through the opening, then disappeared. Standing below, craning her neck to look up, Chloe got nervous. "You okay up there?"

"I'm fine, honey."

Minutes later, Jack appeared at the opening. "Scoot back." She did, and he grabbed the doorjamb and swung down. His feet hit the floor and he stepped to the sink to wash his hands. "Apartment 503 has a busted lock, too. I'm guessing the plumber wasn't a plumber." Jack snagged a paper towel.

For Chloe, that was the worst possible news. Their covers had been blown. Emma had been attacked. Chloe's home had been invaded. The mob wasn't involved because of Marcus. There was only one realistic explanation left.

The Duke wanted her neutralized. Whether by attack

like Emma, or by abduction like Tatiana, he wanted Chloe neutralized.

Protecting herself took on a new urgency. Was Ryan Greene or Harrison Howell the Duke?

Chapter 11

By 9:00 p.m., the adrenaline surge abated and Chloe crashed.

Functioning on sheer grit, she called the hospital to check on Emma—*no change*—and then left Jack in the kitchen. He'd insisted on preparing dinner for them while she showered.

Someone violating her home made her feel as if everything in the apartment had been soiled, including her. This stranger had touched her things, and by extension had touched her. She hated it. No amount of soap could remove the slime, but Samantha was always talking about the healing power of *prana*—energy from flowing water—and Chloe was definitely going to give it a shot.

The hot water melted some of the tension from her muscles and the lack of sleep for the last two nights caught up with her. She was just too exhausted to think.

"Ten-minute warning," Jack called out from the door.

Chloe actually smiled. Jack cooking for her was extremely intimate and should worry her, considering they'd blown their chance for a magical relationship. But it didn't. It just felt comfortable and good. Maybe magical wasn't realistic, and comfortable and good was enough. Maybe. But magical had been stellar. She sighed longingly, missing it, mourning it.

She slipped on her favorite robe, a clean-lined Chantelle, then strode into her bedroom, skirted the king-size bed and walked on to the large walk-in closet. As soon as she opened the door, she noticed something horribly wrong that had escaped her earlier. "Son of a bitch!" she shouted in pure frustration, then stormed out to the kitchen.

"You roared?" Jack stood at the stove, stirring.

"I might just kill her this time." Outraged, Chloe snagged the phone, punched three on speed dial.

"Kill her whom?" he asked. "Over what?"

The phone at her ear, she parked her free hand on her hip. "Every fricking Vera Wang I own has been stolen from my closet."

"The intruder stole your clothes?" Jack added that information to the break-in mix, and it clearly wasn't computing.

How could he understand? Her mother hadn't raised him. "My home has been invaded twice today, Jack." She let out an exasperated huff. "Mother?" she said into the phone.

"Chloe, one in your position should begin a telephone conversation with a greeting."

Chloe ignored her. "Did you take my damn Vera Wangs?"

A slight hesitation and then she confessed, ignoring the outrage in Chloe's voice. "Yes, I did. Why? Oh, dear. Did you think you'd had an intruder?"

Chloe could choke her. "I *did* have an intruder." She'd had two because her mother certainly hadn't broken the access-door lock here or on 503. "Why did you take my clothes?"

"I'm saving you from yourself, Chloe. Vera's designs are

beautiful, of course, but they're all wrong for you. They're too sexy, darling. Your look must always be regal."

"My look is mine, Mother. I want my damn clothes back."

Another hesitation, one that stretched twice as long as the first one. "All right," she finally said.

Too easy. Way too easy. "Did you take my Rose pin, too?"

"Your Rose pin?" Her mother sounded clueless. "Oh, do you mean the gold rose you wore at the date auction?"

"That's the one, Mother."

"No, I don't know anything about your pin."

So her mother had taken the clothes and the intruder had bypassed diamonds, emeralds and rubies for a gold rose? That sounded screwy, but what didn't sound screwy right now? "Fine." Chloe calmed her voice. "Send Gerard with my clothes first thing in the morning, Mother."

"If you promise to dress regally for formal functions."

"Fine." Chloe glared at the wall and put down the phone.

Jack looked and sounded stunned. "Your mother broke into your home and stole your clothes?"

Chloe sighed. "My mother knows no boundaries."

"Honey, I don't mean to be critical, but why should she? You haven't set any boundaries."

She heard the unspoken question as clearly as if he'd asked. Why hadn't she set boundaries and given her mother no choice but to live within them? "Old habits are hard to break, Jack. I've been swallowing anger at that woman my whole life."

He stirred the pot. "You've been trying to win her approval your whole life. I watched you in the Hamptons."

Year after year. And she'd always failed. "Pitiful."

"No." He turned down the fire and cupped her chin in his hands. "Normal," he said. "Kids always want their parents to be proud of them. Even royal kids."

She grunted. "I might be a coward, but I'm not living in

fantasyland and that's the *only* place my mother would ever approve of me."

"Why is that?" Jack stroked her hair. "She should. You're an amazing woman, Chloe."

She snitched a sip of his iced tea, then leaned against him. "It doesn't have anything to do with me," she said. "I just get to feel the effects of it." She rubbed circles on his chest. "She's been failing to win approval her whole married life. So she's tried to make me perfect, and I am not."

"Whose approval does she want?" Holding her, Jack reached over and adjusted the burner, turning it down to Warm.

"The royals," Chloe said.

Jack wasn't getting it. He had that blank look men get when women talk about fashion or feelings or other topics only women seem to gravitate to and want to grasp.

"My father's family rejected my mother. Insufficient blue blood," Chloe said. "Since costing him his family and his crown, she's spent thirty years trying to please them, but they've never accepted her, much less approved of her."

"What about you and Erik?"

"We've never met them." Chloe shrugged. "Our inheritances were contingent on us never entering the country." Compassion softened Chloe's voice. "All of this eats at my mother—for my father, and for Erik and me. For herself, too, I expect, though she'd never admit it. Add my arrest—I'm already a huge disappointment to her because I'm not a perfect princess—and, well, I think that's more than enough disappointment for one person to have to live with in one lifetime, don't you?"

Jack didn't answer, just held her and kissed her temple.

Chloe lifted a shoulder. "Anyway, that's why she wants me to be perfect. The perfect princess," she explained. "To show the royals that they were wrong about her."

"I see." The look in his eyes turned tender.

He did see. Far too much. "Thanks for the hug."

"That's what partners are for." He winked. "Grab those plates, will you?"

"Sure." She looked down. "I should go throw on some clothes first."

"You're fine. Just sit down and let's eat."

Happiness lifted Chloe. This dinner was going to be like those in Lucas's kitchen: warm and cozy and comfortable. And after last night and today, and all that had happened between her and Jack, that was nothing short of amazing.

They were midway through a chicken casserole that her housekeeper had left in the freezer when Jack stared down at the floor. "What's that?" He stood up and walked over to a sleek bronze silk chair.

Something shiny was behind the rear left chair leg. Chloe shrugged. "I don't know."

He picked it up and brought it to her. From his expression, he knew exactly what he held in his hand.

Chloe looked down at it and gasped. "The royal crest."

"I'm guessing that the odds of it being your mother's are minuscule. It's clearly a man's ring."

Betrayal burrowed in and cut her deeply. "It's Erik's."

"What are the odds that it was here before today?"

Chloe sucked in air, trying hard to breathe past the heartbreak and disappointment choking her. "None." She forced herself to meet Jack's gaze. "He had it on last night. And he had it on today when I saw him and Brit Carouthers at lunch."

Jack pinched it between his forefinger and thumb. "Does Erik have more than one of them?"

"No, Jack," she explained, her fuse short. "It's an heirloom that passes from generation to generation, father to eldest son on his twenty-first birthday. There is only one."

"I'd better report this." Jack reached for his phone. "Chloe," he said while waiting for someone to answer. "There's something that's going to be hard for you to handle, especially with Emma and Renee on your mind."

She could feel it coming, pounding through her, hard and unrelenting. "I know, Jack."

He went on as if he hadn't heard her. "Your brother is in bad company. In the end, he might not be squeaky clean."

Chloe's heart hurt. She hurt all over, feeling fear in her every cell. "Do you think that *Erik* is the Duke?" She shook, and answered herself. "I don't believe it."

"Why not?" Jack asked, the phone still ringing in his ear.

"He's too young, for one thing."

Jack raised his eyebrows. "Is he, Chloe?"

She paused. They'd never been this close to the Duke. The evidence of his former activities suggested only he was male—and the Governess's consultants disagreed on that. "I don't know."

"Erik was at Hollow Hill."

Staring at the food on her plate, she felt her stomach get queasy and set down her fork. She couldn't possibly swallow another bite. This wasn't going to be a dinner like at Lucas's, after all. "Yes, he was at Hollow Hill."

The phone still rang, and Jack's expression tightened. Clearly worried, he closed the phone and pushed back his chair. "I have to go. I hate leaving you alone, but I have no choice."

"What's wrong?" She couldn't believe it. Since Marcus's death, there had been more crises than in Chloe's whole life.

"I can't reach the Governess." Worry lighted in his eyes. "I've been waiting for a callback and trying to get her all day. So has Renee."

"All day?"

"I've worked for her a long time and I've never been unable to reach her. Not once."

Chloe nodded. "What if the Duke discovered her identity, too?"

"Don't even think it," Jack said. "The consequences would be catastrophic."

That rattled her to the core. "Should I come with you?"

"You can't." He came around the table to her. "You know the rules." He planted a kiss to her temple. "But thank you."

"Does this mean you forgive me?" she asked.

"Do you forgive me—enough to trust me?"

"I think so," she said, being as honest as she could.

"When you know it, you tell me." He winked and moved away. "Lock the doors and turn on the alarm." He paused, then added. "Call one of the Roses to come stay with you."

"I will not." Chloe was insulted.

"I just meant the company would be good."

"I'm going to the hospital to see Emma." She shooed him out the door. "Find out what's happened to the Governess."

"Don't mention finding that ring to Erik," Jack said. "Or to anyone else."

"I won't." She walked out with him, determined to keep that promise for two reasons. She had to keep it, for the assignment, and she didn't want anyone to know that her brother had betrayed her again, much less twice in one day.

She mentally reviewed what she knew of the Duke, and though it rattled her to the bone, not one snippet of evidence on any case proved that he could not be Erik.

The daughter and sister in her battled against the Rose agent. Bias with objectivity. Her head with her heart. No part of her wanted to believe it was possible.

Jack waited for her to dress, walked down with her, then seated her in her car. "Lock your doors."

"I will." She looked up at him, knowing the pain of the last twenty-four hours was revealed in her eyes.

He cupped her face. "I'm sorry. Sometimes the job sucks. But even at its worst, it's better to know the truth."

"I know you're right. It's just going to take a little time for my heart to catch up to my head." She kissed him. Tender and sweet. "Thank you, Jack."

He stroked her face. "My privilege."

She keyed the engine, waved to Craig and then left the parking garage, doing her damnedest to blink back tears.

Frank met Chloe at the elevator and walked with her back to the ICU waiting room. "Miss Emma's still unconscious," Frank said. "Doc Scoffield put her parents in a room to get some rest."

"Can I see her?" Chloe asked.

"He said you could, and he's blocked out everyone else, like you said. Mrs. Dalton-Sinclair didn't much like it, but she don't know he put you on the list." Frank frowned, his weathered face wrinkling. "Why did you do that, Princess?"

"Because I don't know who hurt her," Chloe said without apology. "And until I do, no one is getting close to her except her mother, father, you and me. And no one includes Dayton."

"Her bodyguard?"

"Yes."

A little surprise ran through Frank's eyes, but he didn't utter a word or question Chloe further. "She's pretty banged up. Be prepared for that."

"I saw her at her worst, remember?"

"No, you didn't." His Adam's apple bobbed. "She's got a lot of tubes stuck in her now. She's real swollen and the bruises are big and dark." He blinked hard and fast.

Chloe patted him. "Don't worry, Frank. She'll be fine."

"I shouldn't have fussed at her about my damn coffee."

Frank had obviously been beating himself up over that.

"She loved it. That's why she got Daniel to help her pull one over on you. And she loves you as much as you love her, too."

He sniffed, his eyes shining overly bright. "Damn right."

Chloe identified herself to Emma's guard, Mac Dayton, who was the size of a tank, then went into ICU. It was a large room, with the heads of the beds lining the walls. Glass walls separated some, and some were open bays. Three other patients were in the unit and hooked up to monitors. Chloe recognized some of the machines, and didn't have a clue about the others.

"She's over here, Princess Chloe," a round-faced nurse with springy black hair said, then led Chloe into a private area. "She's not in pain, okay?"

Chloe nodded. Still, the sight of Emma against blinding white sheets, looking so small and frail and battered, was almost more than Chloe could stand.

The nurse positioned a chair beside her bed. "You're welcome to sit with her a few minutes. Talk to her, if you like. The experts say it helps." The nurse left the room.

Chloe sat down, scooted closer to Emma's bedside and touched her hand. "Hey, you," she said, her voice thick and husky. "I know it's easier for you to do this unconscious thing than to wake up and feel the pain, so I'm cutting you slack on that. But don't keep it up too long, okay?"

She stroked the back of Emma's hand, made sure no one else was within hearing distance. "I know it's been hard on you, Emma, not playing the piano, and I'm guessing you already know that playing professionally is in the past because of these new injuries. But I'll listen any time you want to play, and I want you to remember that there's a lot more to you than your music. You fake it 'til you make it, getting used to this."

Chloe checked again to make sure they were alone, then whispered, "I'm scared, Emma, and I need your help. My whole life, you've always been there to help me." Chloe felt a tear drop to her cheek. "What the hell were you doing with Brit Carouthers, anyway? Why didn't you buy him off at Perrini's? Why did you leave with him? Is he the Duke?"

That was doubtful, but possible. "I'm trying to find out, Emma," Chloe said. "The trouble is, the more things I check out, the more strange things I uncover. I verified Brit's alibi, so I don't think he beat you up. Do you know who did? What was Tatiana doing with you? Where did they take her? Did you guys find out where they're holding the Russian women?"

Chloe waited, knowing there would be no response. "Since you got hurt, everything's gone to hell. Renee's lying to me, Erik is betraying me, and I think he and my mother broke into my apartment. She stole every damn Vera Wang in my closet. And Harrison lied to me twice, and the Governess is missing. That's so not good. Ryan lied, too. He said Tatiana was at his office, but she's been missing since your injury. What if the Duke went after her and the Governess? God, Emma. I don't know what to do next."

Control. Get calm. Emma's voice sounded in Chloe's head. Chloe tried hard. "Jack is helping me. I have to be very careful with him. He lied to me about London, but he's still in my heart, Emma. Like no one else has ever been in it. That terrifies me—and don't tell me to fake it 'til I make it. That won't work on this. I can't fake anything with Jack. He sees straight through me, and I don't want to fake with him, anyway. He broke my heart and he probably will again. The hell of it is, I think he might be worth it." She jerked her emotions back into line. "But, why bother? I'll just disappoint him. Hell, I've disappointed everyone my whole life." Chloe sat back.

"Okay," she said. "Okay, one thing at a time. I'll talk, you listen. I'd better start with Renee. I heard Franklin Greene call her a bitch behind her back to Julio. She says they haven't had a run-in, but there has to be a reason he hates her. And anything that Franklin hates, Ryan hates, too."

She had to tell Emma about Erik. "Wonder Boy is in this business cartel with Brit and Ryan. I asked Erik to stay away from Brit, but he refused. Jack and I found his crest ring in my apartment. He might be dirty, Emma. He might even be the Duke. I don't want to believe it, but I can't find a decent reason to deny it. God, but that would kill Mother."

More disappointment. Chloe couldn't bear the thought of it. Wonder Boy never had disappointed their mother; Chloe had paid dearly to see to it. If he fell off that pedestal now…

Chloe sniffed, grabbed a tissue from Emma's table and dabbed at her eyes. "Please wake up soon, Emma. The suspect list on the Duke is narrowing, and everyone still on it either works with the Roses or is among our friends and my family. Erik, Brit, Harrison, and Ryan."

Chloe licked at her lips. "There's one more thing." She steeled herself to say it. "Renee set us up to fail with the red wigs and interview mix-up. Since neither was an accident, I should determine why she sabotaged us—yet I can't make myself do it. I believe in her. But what if I'm wrong? Did you or Tatiana find proof Renee had switched sides? Is she working for the Duke? Oh, God, Emma. Did Renee have someone attack you and abduct Tatiana?"

Emma tapped Chloe's hand.

Chapter 12

After Emma's tap on the hand, Chloe had nearly flown out of her chair. She'd wanted to tell the nurse, to ask Dr. Scofield if that tap meant Emma was out of the coma, but so long as Emma was comatose and guarded by Mac Dayton—a man both Frank and Lucas had checked out—she was safe. Safe was best for Emma.

So Chloe had kept quiet and left. As soon as she had gotten into her car, she had called Jack and told him, and he'd deflated her hope, saying, "Patients in a coma jerk. I'm 99.9% sure the timing was coincidental. I'm sorry, honey. Try to get some rest. You're exhausted."

And so she'd driven home, showered and snuggled down in bed, totally depleted physically and mentally. Her mind churned, and she begged it to make sense of everything while she slept. She didn't remember her head hitting her pillow, which is why the phone ringing beside her bed startled her. The bedside clock read 3:40 a.m. "Yes, what?"

"Princess Chloe," a woman said. "Pardon the intrusion."

Chloe recognized her voice. "What is it, Olivia?" *Oh, God.* "Is Emma—"

"She's fine. I mean, there's been no change. This is unrelated," Renee's assistant and oldest friend said. "Jillian Baker from the Women's Center called the club, very upset."

Jillian supervised the shelter's night shift. "Why?"

"One of the women who's been staying at the shelter is missing."

"Do you have Jillian's number?" Chloe didn't want to go down there unless she absolutely had to do it. Four hours' sleep in two days just wasn't enough.

Olivia read off the number.

Chloe thanked her, hung up, and then dialed the Women's Center. "Jillian, it's Chloe."

"Oh, thank goodness. I don't know what's going on, but I know it's bad." Jillian had revved up to borderline hysterical.

"Calm down and tell me what's happened."

"One of our women, Nadia, had a five o'clock modeling audition yesterday. She never came back."

Chloe remembered Nadia. She was a center success story, an aspiring model who'd come to them to conquer bulimia. She was staying at the shelter while completing the eating disorder program. "Where was the audition?"

"The Black Swan, over in the Meatpacking district."

Two doors down from Hollow Hill. Chloe sat straight up.

"I went down there," Jillian said. "But the man claimed Nadia hadn't been there—her or Karen Grant. I know he was lying to me, but what could I do?"

"Who's Karen Grant?"

"A friend of Nadia's. She's the one who called and told me

that's where they were. They were auditioning for a photo shoot in Hong Kong."

The Far East. The biggest buyers of brunette Western women. "Is Karen a brunette, Jillian?" Nadia was, and if Karen was, too...

"Yes, she is. Why?"

"No reason," Chloe said. "Did Karen say anything else?"

"They scheduled to leave tomorrow for a shoot in California. Then, they hoped to go to Hong Kong for two weeks. But when I went down to the Black Swan, the man doing the auditions said he'd never seen Nadia or Karen. I'm really worried, Chloe."

Chloe was worried, too. "What was the man's name?"

"Karen called him 'Brother' on the phone. I didn't hear anyone call him by name."

"What did he look like?"

"He was handsome. Blond, tall, well dressed. He had that rich look. You know what I mean. You just know."

Chloe did know. It wasn't clothes or jewelry or anything the naked eye could see. It came from inside, an inbred confidence. Chloe called it the X-factor, and she didn't know why so many wealthy people had it, but they did. Sadly, she lacked the trait. "If I e-mail over photos, would you recognize him?"

"Oh, yes." Jillian hesitated and then added, "I didn't like him, Chloe. He sounded sincere, but working here, you learn to read people fast. The truth never touched his eyes."

Jillian had an amazing bullshit detector from hearing every possible story human beings could contrive. Stories from the women and from the men hunting down the women hiding from them. "I'm going to send those photos. You take a look and call me back." Chloe reeled off her number.

"Okay." Jillian paused. "Chloe, we have to find them."

"Focus on facts not fear. That's our best chance."

Chloe hung up the phone and booted up her computer. She

nearly shot the keyboard when she discovered the Internet connection was down again. Some things simply couldn't be controlled by money.

She dialed Harrison. He sounded wide-awake. "I need some special help, partner." She didn't relay that they had two new missing women. "Can you e-mail or fax photos of Brit, Erik and Ryan for me?" She gave him Jillian's contact info.

"Sure. What's up?"

"I'm not sure yet. I'll let you know as soon as I have anything solid." She turned the topic to avoid questions. "Any word on the Governess?"

"Not yet. But she kept an appointment on her schedule this afternoon, so apparently, it was short-term non-availability."

"Oh, good." Chloe didn't believe it.

"It'll be an hour or two before I can get these out."

"Thanks." Chloe broke the connection and called Jack, who sounded as if he'd been sound asleep. After relaying the information about Nadia and Karen, she told him what Harrison had said about the Governess.

"Chloe, the Black Swan is right by Hollow Hill."

"I know. Should I brief Renee?" That was standard operating procedure, but this assignment had left S.O.P.s in the dust long ago.

"About this development, yes," he said. "Maybe she'll reveal why she sabotaged you and Emma."

Chloe was sorry she'd asked and hoped nothing Renee said or did now would worsen her situation. "Okay. I'll do that."

"Just call her for now," he said again. "I'll meet you at the G.R.C. at three-thirty this afternoon."

"Why so late?" She shoved her hair back from her face and shifted her pillow under her neck.

"I want to get some qualified people in on this."

Some FBI people, Chloe felt sure. "Okay," she said, hoping

these qualified people were good and that they found Nadia and Karen before they were taken out of reach.

"We'll check transportation, but they'll probably opt for private planes."

"Jillian said this 'Brother' seemed rich."

"Definitely need to watch the planes, then. If they get these women out of the country, we're screwed."

"No, Jack," Chloe corrected him. "The women are screwed. They'll be sold and held prisoner until they die."

"Exactly," he said.

"I'm going down there—to the Black Swan." Chloe made the decision on a dime. "Maybe I'll recognize this Brother guy, or learn something that will help us."

"No, Chloe," Jack insisted. "Absolutely not."

Her hackles tap-danced up her neck. "Excuse me?"

"You'll be walking into an active mission and you could hurt far more women than Nadia and Karen." He paused to let that sink in, then added, "Do not go down there."

"A related classified mission that the FBI is already on?"

"Yes. A sting operation."

"Tell me they'll make finding these women a high priority."

"Absolutely," he said. "You have my word."

After all the people who'd betrayed her—him included—she wasn't crazy about trusting anyone on anything. But it was a small leap of faith. She'd be watching. "All right, Jack."

"Call Renee, and then get some sleep. You've had a rough couple days, and I need you conscious and alert."

She was equally dependent on him being conscious and alert, but she didn't feel the need to constantly remind him of it. Of course, *his* abilities weren't in question. She grunted. "I'm acutely alert, okay? Will you quit worrying about your back?"

"Baby, the day we do that will be the day we die."

A cold rush ran through her. He wasn't being sarcastic, just sharing wisdom he'd picked up on the job. "Got it." She committed the advice to memory. "Will you sleep, too?"

"I will. Good night."

She hung up, and then dialed Renee. Her husband, Preston, answered, sounding sleep-fogged, and Chloe winced. "Pres, it's Chloe. Sorry to disturb you, but I need to speak to Renee."

"Just a moment, Chloe."

A pause and then Renee came on the line. "Chloe, is it Emma, darling?"

"No. No, there's been no change," Chloe assured her, then filled her in on Nadia and Karen Grant.

"Where are the women now?"

"They've disappeared and the man running the auditions, Brother, denies seeing them." A slight variation was necessary here due to the classified nature of the sting. "Jack's put some people on it."

"Oh, good." Her relief was evident. "So no immediate action is required."

Surely if Renee were involved, she wouldn't be relieved. "That's correct. Just an FYI to keep you up on developments." Prickly, Chloe asked, "How is the peace accord coming along?"

"It's not." Renee sounded sad about that, and Chloe well imagined she was. Preston's return should be a happy time. Instead, Renee stood right between a rock and the hard place. Who could be happy with their spouse and child at war? "Is there anything I can do to help?"

"Pray. Otherwise, no, darling." Renee's gratitude was genuine. "These things work out in their own time, bit by bit."

"Okay. I'm here if you need me. You know that, right?"

"Of course, darling," she said. "Good night."

"Night."

Chloe cradled the receiver, thoughtful and solemn. If she wanted to know why there was tension between Renee and

Franklin, she needed an alternate source. Olivia wouldn't utter a word… But Senator Ellie Richardson might.

Ellie had served with Renee and Olivia in the Peace Corps in Colombia. She could have useful insights. Resolving to phone Ellie's office as soon as it opened, Chloe settled down to sleep.

At 8:00 a.m. Harrison still hadn't sent Jillian the photos and Chloe's Internet was still down.

Chloe had breakfast and then dressed in sporty cocoa-brown slacks and a cream top Adele had designed. While phoning the hospital to check on Emma, she had an extra cup of coffee, hoping for a caffeine jolt.

No change.

God, she was sick of hearing those words. Chloe spoke briefly with Emma's mother, who was even sicker of them, then left a message on her mother's voice mail not to forget to send Gerard over this morning with Chloe's Vera Wang couture. Then she dialed the security desk and told Scott, the daytime security chief, to expect Gerard and a delivery from Adelphio: Chloe's gown for the Halloween Ball.

It was next to impossible to gear up for the Halloween Ball while Emma lay in a coma and Erik's innocence was in doubt, not to mention Renee, Nadia and Karen, the three Russian women and Chloe's suspicions that Ryan, Brit, Harrison or Erik could be the Duke. And the Governess still being out of pocket didn't do a thing to restore Chloe's flagging confidence.

Jittery, she reconsidered. Maybe she should switch to tea.

She steeped it and added lemon, steeling herself, and then dialed Ellie. If Renee was on the wrong side in this, shock wouldn't begin to cover all Chloe would feel. She just couldn't believe it of Renee, but what she believed was insignificant. All that mattered was what she could prove.

"Senator Richardson's office. This is Liz. How may I help you?"

"Liz, good morning. This is Chloe St. John."

"Princess Chloe," she said. "Wonderful to hear from you."

"Thank you." She sipped from her cup. "I need to speak to the senator, if she's available."

"She'll be disappointed to miss your call, but the senator is in Tuscany until next Monday. Shall I relay a message?"

"No, thank you. It was purely social," Chloe lied. "I'll phone again after she returns. Goodbye, Liz."

"Goodbye."

Chloe couldn't phone Olivia. That would be a hotline right to Renee. So she called Alan Burke. "Morning, Mr. Gadget."

"Chloe, hi. What's up?"

"I need to do a little breaking and entering—on the QT."

"Jimmy's never going to get off his knees with you, is he?"

"Right now, I need all the novenas and candle-burning Jimmy can give me." Divine intervention on this assignment would be totally welcome. "It's important, Alan." Everyone knew Olivia had the most extensive database on the elite in the city. Names, addresses, phone numbers, cell phone numbers, children's names and ages, family trees, food and drink and restaurant preferences, and even what type flowers and chocolates people preferred. "I need Ellie Richardson's number in Tuscany."

"And when should I tell Jimmy you'll be in for training?"

Chloe frowned, wishing he could see it. "I'm coming in this afternoon—and I need another Rose pin."

His tone turned serious. "What happened to the original?"

"Someone stole it when they broke into my apartment."

"Damn, Chloe. You okay?"

"I'm fine." She didn't dare admit how *not* fine she really was. "But as you can see, I've been a little busy."

"I didn't hear about the apartment."

"No one knows it. Keep it that way," she added. "I want the Roses alert, not terrified."

"Okay," he said, sounding wary. "Does Renee know this?"

Oh, hell. Now she was stuck. "Not at this time, Alan."

On the other end of the phone, his silence roared.

Chloe waited him out.

"All right. I'm supposing you know what you're doing."

Scary assumption and he didn't sound convinced. She faked certainty and shoved it into her voice. "I know exactly what I'm doing," she said with conviction. "Has Tatiana been found?"

"She was with Emma on the hotel security tape, Chloe."

"Did it show her leaving?"

"No."

Disappointing, but not surprising. "I guess I just need that number, then."

He read it off to her and she jotted it down in her book. "Thanks, Alan. Not a word on anything we discussed."

"Not to anyone?"

"No."

"Damn it." He sounded disillusioned.

So was she. "Yeah." She hung up, knowing he'd be in a tizzy all day, figuring out why Chloe wasn't briefing Renee.

Can't be helped. Chloe put through the call to Tuscany and got Ellie's housekeeper on the phone.

"No, Princess Chloe," Ellie's housekeeper said. "That's what I'm telling you. The senator never came. She got on the plane in New York but she no get off the plane in Tuscany."

"Did it stop anywhere in between?"

"No, ma'am. It was a direct flight. The driver, he wait and wait, but no senator."

"If you hear from her, will you call me?"

"Of course."

"Thank you." Chloe gave her the number then ended the call—and read an incoming text message from Jillian, asking her to come to the Women's Center ASAP. Then Chloe reported the missing Ellie discovery to her secretary, Liz.

"I appreciate your telling me, Princess Chloe."

"You already knew," Chloe realized. "Damn it, Liz. You already knew."

"The investigators are keeping it out of the press as long as possible to avoid getting a million false leads. Senator Richardson has been missing since yesterday afternoon."

A slow sinking feeling shrouded Chloe. The Russian women. Nadia and Karen Grant. The Governess. And now Ellie, too?

Coincidence? Chloe mentally ripped through four years' worth of speculation on the Governess's identity, and while both women obviously held jobs high in government, Chloe couldn't see Ellie issuing some of the orders that the Governess had issued. She couldn't see Ellie risking her senatorial career by deliberately involving herself in assignments going up against the very rich scum that had to be, at least in part, her political base. Career politicians didn't risk re-elections.

And yet Renee had cut a deal with the Governess. She'd run G.R.C.'s spy agency and the Governess secured Preston's early release from prison. So it *wasn't* impossible that the two women were one and the same…

Could Ellie be the Governess?

Oh, but it was time for a face-to-face with Renee.

* * *

"You want the Jaguar, Princess Chloe?"

The smell of car exhaust was strong in the garage. "No, I don't think so, Craig." Matching her car to her mood, she needed the tank. Maybe in it, she could plow through all the twists and turns this assignment had taken. "The Hummer."

"Yes, ma'am." The tip of his stocking cap bobbed.

She smiled. "How is Anthony doing?" She bet the baby was growing like crazy.

Craig beamed with fatherly pride. "He's great. Seven months old today."

"Already?" She laughed. "I can't believe it."

He nodded. "Right now, the little guy has a double ear infection. The doc says he might need tubes put in his ears."

"Really?" That sounded serious.

"A lot of kids need them, he says. We shouldn't worry."

"Well, that's good news. Does your insurance cover that?" She didn't recall anything about it specifically in the policy.

"Oh, yes, ma'am." He smiled. "We've got great medical. It's the life insurance that sucks."

"It does?" She'd have to check into that.

Craig nodded. "I worry every day that something will happen to me before Anthony grows up." That worry shone in his eyes. "Debra would never make it alone."

Chloe frowned. Debra was a stay-at-home mom, which was great for Anthony but it left her and the baby more vulnerable. "I'll see if we can't make it better," she told Craig.

"You will?" His eyes lit up with relief and then regret. "I didn't mean to sound ungrateful, Princess Chloe. And I don't want to stir up any trouble." He forced himself to meet her gaze. "I like my job here."

"Craig, telling me there's a problem isn't stirring up trouble. If I don't know something is wrong, I can't fix it. It's important that you're happy here. I want you to work at Eleanor Towers a long time." She smiled. "And it's not good for Anthony to have his dad worried. I'm sure Debra would rather you weren't, too."

"Yes, ma'am." He let out a laugh and looked at her with appreciation. "Thanks." He hooked his thumb toward the cars. "I'll go get your Hummer." He ran off with a lighter step.

Chloe dialed the resident manager. "The life insurance for our employees is substandard. Fix it."

"It's too expensive, Princess Chloe."

"Fix it, Charles." She put a bite in her tone. "When our employees have to worry that their children will go without if something happens to them, they're not happy. If they're not happy, then I'm not happy. You don't like me when I'm not happy, Charles, and if this isn't fixed by five o'clock today, I'm going to be very unhappy."

"I—I'm taking care of it right now. Just this minute."

"Thank you, Charles," she said stiffly. The guy was a miser. She appreciated his concern about their money, but not at the expense of their employees. "Call me when it's done."

"Ten minutes. Maybe five."

To seriously get his attention, she starched her tone and pushed. "Is that the best you can do?"

"I'm increasing the coverage as we speak. There is no faster way to handle this, Princess Chloe."

"Charles, you do remember that I own this building, right?"

"Oh, yes, ma'am."

"And that I monitor your management closely?"

"Yes, ma'am."

"Yet this is the second time I've had to call you down for shorting the employees, and I distinctly remember telling you after the first incident to not do that again."

Dread filled his tone. "Yes, ma'am, you did."

"I won't ask you for an explanation; there is none. But understand this, Charles. If my employees are shorted a third time, at the end of that call, you'll be unemployed."

"Yes, ma'am."

"Phone me when this is done." She hung up the phone, still furious. People like Craig were solid, loyal employees, damn it. They deserved better than this. At least Craig had talked to her about it. How many things like the life insurance did she never hear about? As soon as this assignment was over, she had to address that. A survey? Personal visits? Something…

Lucas Perrini swore it was better business to keep your people happy than to spend your time hiring and training new people. Chloe had taken that advice to heart—because it sounded smart, but even more so because it sounded right.

While Craig retrieved the car, she waited, her mind shifting to the latest missing women, Nadia and Karen, and recalled Jillian's text message. Chloe dialed her.

The exhaust smell was so strong it was making her stomach queasy. A gust of cold, crisp wind whipped through the garage-door opening to the street. Sweeping her hair back from her face, she stepped outside.

"Women's Center."

"Jillian, it's Chloe," she said into her cell phone. "I got your text message. What's up?"

"Oh, Chloe, you won't believe it. They found them!"

The FBI found Nadia and Karen. "Are they okay?"

"Yes. Yes, they're fine. That Brother guy took them to LAX, and Nadia said he told them he was going to the restroom, but something must have happened. The FBI found out—I don't know how—that there was a private flight chartered for Hong Kong, and they had these agents waiting for Nadia and Karen. Somehow, Brother must have known it, because he never came back. He just disappeared."

Jack. Chloe's throat went tight. "Brother got away, then?" Disappointment ripped through her relief. Two men rode bicycles down the street. Neither wore a helmet. She hoped they didn't crack their heads.

"I think he did get away. The important thing is Nadia and Karen are safe. They'll be here shortly." Jillian blew out a relieved breath that crackled through the phone. "God, that was too close a call, Chloe."

"Yes, it was." Closer than Jillian, Nadia and Karen would ever know. "I'm really happy they're okay." She'd be damned elated if she knew what happened to the three Russian women.

"We're having a celebration lunch for them. That's why I told you to come to the Center. So you could be here for it."

Chloe checked her watch. She had to meet Jack at 3:30, and a lot to do before then. "I wish I could, but I can't. Toast them for me—and no more answering those kind of ads."

"I don't think we'll have this problem again. Nadia swears she's sticking to just reading novels until hell freezes over." Jillian giggled, joyful from the heart out. "Oh, I still haven't gotten those photos from you."

"A friend is sending them. Check e-mail and fax, and call after you look at them."

"I will."

Chloe peered through the parked cars. It was taking Craig a long time to retrieve the Hummer. "Everything okay, Craig?" She walked back from the street toward the door to see deeper inside the garage. Why hadn't he answered her?

Instinctively, she eased her hand into her brown Gucci. If something was wrong and she had to shoot through her purse, she was going to be thoroughly pissed. But she didn't dare to pull her gun on the street. Some idiot would shoot her. "Craig?"

The starter grinded.

Oh, he was inside the car. He hadn't heard her. She stepped

back outside into the sharp, biting wind. It was bloody cold today. Shivering, she hunched her shoulders and snuggled deep into her coat.

The starter grinded again.

She hadn't driven the vehicle much lately, but— *Oh, God.* A memory from training returned to her with a vengeance. A memory of grinding ignitions being a signal of— "Craig, no! *No!* Get out of the car! Get out—"

The Hummer exploded.

Chapter 13

A man, about thirtysomething, dressed in baggy pants and a blue stocking cap, dropped a remote on the sidewalk.

Chloe heard it hit the concrete, glanced down and then up to the guy's face. It was hard-angled and scrubby; he hadn't shaved—and recognition lighted in his eyes. Horror followed.

He knew her. She glanced back down to the concrete. *The detonator.*

He ran.

She pulled her gun and chased him, skirting a cab and bumping her hip on its front fender. The driver blew his horn, and the runner looked back. He locked onto her with his gaze and kept running, bumping into two men and a woman pushing a shopping cart down the sidewalk. He rolled off her, scrambled up onto his feet, then ran on. "Stupid bitch," he shouted back at Chloe, widening the gap between them.

Chloe's side ached. Damn it, if Jimmy saw how out of shape she was, he'd give up novenas and take to saying rosaries.

"I'll be back after you. You're a dead woman," the runner shouted back over his shoulder—and ran right into a stack of boxes outside the front door of Carmine's Deli.

He fell, and Chloe caught up, drew down on him, her heart jackhammering against her ribs. Winded from the run and the adrenaline surge, she warned him, "Do *not* move."

He darted a gaze up at her. "You won't shoot, rich bitch."

Saving her breath, she fired, putting a bullet in his toe.

He yelped.

"Next one goes between your eyes." Dialing her cell, she called Jack. The runner shifted off a box of zucchini. Half of it spilled on the sidewalk. "I said don't move. You just tried to kill me," she spat out. "And you did kill my garage attendant. Are you sure you want to try me?"

"I'm not moving." He held up his hands and stayed put, sprawled on his back. The left knee of his pants had ripped and his skin was scraped and bloody. "I'm totally still, okay?"

"Quaid." Jack sounded rushed.

"I need you now."

"Thrilled to hear it, Princess, but I'm a little busy at the moment. Is this personal or professional? Just want to run the right set of fantasies through my mind."

"Jack, please." *Hold it together. You can do it, Chloe. You can do it.* "I'm standing outside Carmine's Deli, holding a man at gunpoint on the street—well, on the sidewalk, actually. He just blew up Craig in my fricking Hummer."

"Are you all right?"

He had to be kidding. "Do you want me to just go ahead and shoot him, or do you want to get your ass over here and tell me what to do? I've got a nervous breakdown scheduled for 1:00 and, I swear by all that's holy, I will *not* be late for it."

"Two minutes, Chloe," Jack said, serious and sharp. "Just give me two minutes, and then call the police."

She looked up at the people clearing the corner. "I think someone's probably already called them."

"I'll handle it, then," he said. "Just try not to shoot him before I can get there. I'd like to find out who hired him. But if you have to shoot him, kill him."

"Okay. If he makes me shoot him, I'll kill him." That turned the runner sufficiently ashen. "I've got it. Hold on a second, and I'll ask your question." She didn't bother asking his name; he'd just lie to her and piss her off even more. She tilted the phone away and spoke to the man sprawled on the vegetables. "If you don't answer me, I have to kill you. You understand?"

He nodded.

"Who hired you to blow up my car?"

"Chloe," Jack said. "These jerks never answer questions. Think retribution. He's not going to turn and burn his ass."

But she hadn't already shot those jerks in the toe and she had this one. He knew *her* retribution would be immediate. His boss's would be delayed. "Let's give him a chance," she said into the phone. "I really don't want to kill him. I'm sure it was just a job and nothing personal. Now if I'd gotten blood on my slacks, then he'd already be dead." She paused a second.

"Chloe? Honey, you sound a little…strange."

"Not at all. They're a new design." She paused again. "Adelphio." The runner looked waylaid, baffled and terrified. *Excellent.* "But I didn't get blood on them, so it's okay for him to live—if he answers the damn question."

"Greene." The guy yelled up at her. "Greene hired me."

"Damn," Jack said, hearing the man. "I don't believe it."

Pleased with herself, she looked down at the runner. "Which Greene? Franklin, Ryan, Julio?"

"I—I don't know."

She tilted her head, stared at him down the length of her nose. "That's not the answer I want to hear. Do better."

Fear flashed over his face. "I swear, I don't know. I didn't see him."

A man. "Well, what did he sound like?" Chloe persisted, ignoring the people veering far and wide away from them.

Carmine came to the door. "Princess Chloe?"

"Just a second," she told the runner, and then turned to the round man wearing a white butcher's apron, standing in the doorway. Carmine was about sixty-five and had a jovial face that at the moment was twisted with worry. "Good morning, Carmine. You doing okay?"

"I'm fine, thank you." He nodded. "Um, are you going to kill that man?"

"If he moves, yes, I am," she said frankly. "Or if he doesn't answer my questions. Otherwise, no."

"Why?" Carmine asked in a totally reasonable voice.

"He blew up my Hummer." She forced her voice calm. Her heart felt stuck in her ribs. "Craig was in it."

"I'm sorry to hear that. He liked my pastrami."

"He was a nice man." Chloe glared at the runner. "He had a wife and a seven-month-old son, you son of a bitch."

"I'm sorry to hear that, too." Carmine frowned. "Well, okay, then." He hugged the inside of the door. "Um, do you mind if a couple customers come out?"

"I'm sorry to inconvenience them, but unfortunately I do. This murderer could grab them, or try to escape. Someone else could get hurt." Surreal conversation. Absolutely surreal, but it fit in with the training tactics she was employing. Jimmy swore they worked, and he'd be proud of her handling of this—unless he somehow tapped into her insides. They were like jam. "Best keep them inside for now, where they'll be safe."

"Okay, then." Carmine nodded. "I'll just close the door, and you let me know when it's all right for them to leave."

"That'll be fine, Carmine."

He closed the door halfway, and then opened it again. "Oh Princess Chloe?"

"Yes?"

"If you have to shoot him, try not to hit that third box— the one with the big pineapple on the side. They're hell to ge right now, and Mr. O'Grady needs them for his digestion."

"No problem," she said. "When I shoot, I don't miss."

"Good. Thank you, then." He moved back and shut the door

Chloe looked back to the runner, still sprawled on the zucchini. "You were saying…"

Gape-jawed, he looked at her as if she'd lost her mind "You are one weird-ass, wacky lady."

"Of course. Didn't Greene tell you that?"

"No, he sure as hell didn't." The runner sounded angry about that omission, too.

"So now you know." She dismissed the topic, and returned to the one of interest to her. "You were going to tell me abou Greene's voice."

"He had a guy voice." The runner shrugged. "You know?"

She didn't know. "Old or young?"

"I don't know." The runner shrugged and a zucchini rolled off the curb and plopped into the street. "How can you tell?"

Good question. Unfortunately, she couldn't answer it "Why did you choose the Hummer?" Even she hadn't known she'd be driving it today.

"I didn't. Greene told me you had seven cars. Rig 'em all. So I did."

A spark of panic rose in her. Which problem did she focu on? The runner, or the garage? No one in his right min walked into a garage billowing smoke, right? It was safe t wait for the police, wasn't it? *Damn it.* Unsure, she dialed 911, requested a bomb squad and homicide.

A male officer came on the line. "Are you the lady holding a man at gunpoint outside Carmine's Deli? Princess Chloe?"

"Yes, I am." *And I'm going to throw up or fall on him any time now because my stomach is stuck somewhere in the middle of my backbone and my knees feel like spaghetti. So tell Jack to move his cute ass and get here soon, or I'm going to be a totally neurotic, raging bitch.*

"Did the man you're aiming at set the bombs?"

"Yes, he did. And he killed my garage attendant, Craig." *He was always so nice, and I don't even know his last name. God, that's awful. Debra and Anthony, and he probably had a mother, too. Oh, God. They loved him, and someone's going to have to tell them he got blown up getting me my car. That's no reason to die. That's nothing to have to one day tell his son.*

"You already shot the bomber once?"

The bomber. The runner. She made the mental shift. "Yes, I did." *Jack, would you please get your ass here?* This had to be the longest two minutes in history.

"In the toe?"

Carmine must have called. He'd watched her shoot the bomber from the window. "That's correct." *Breathe deeply, you almost coward. Do it for Craig. Do it for Anthony and Debra.* A knot of tears welled in her throat. The gun shook. Oh, no. She was going to lose it, and cry in front of this murderer.

Don't you dare, Chloe. Don't you damn dare.

"Um, was that deliberate, or did you miss?" the police officer on the phone asked.

Emma's voice sounded in Chloe's head. *Fake it 'til you make it.*

Chloe could do that. Hell, she lived her life faking it. She held the gun steady and frosted her tone. "I don't think he wants to find out."

"You're okay, right? The FBI called and said you were okay with the gun. You aren't shaken up and ineffective, are you?"

Ineffective? He meant *dangerous.* "I'm fine. Pissed down to my Jimmy Choos, mourning a man who died for getting into my car, but otherwise, I'm just fricking fine."

"We're on our way."

"Excellent." She bared her teeth.

The man on the ground cringed.

"Chloe?" Jack walked slowly toward her. "You okay?"

Seeing him did something to her, and all the hurt in her heart rushed up her throat. "He killed Craig. He put bombs on all my damn cars, too," she said, shaking. "I shot him in the fricking toe and I ought to shoot him in the fricking head. Anthony doesn't have a father now, and this idiot won't tell me which fricking Greene hired him to kill me."

"I don't know which fricking Greene hired me."

"Shut up until I tell you to talk," she shouted at him. "Don't you see this gun?"

"Okay, honey," Jack said. "He's probably telling the truth." Jack walked closer. "The police are here now, and they're going to arrest him, so you need to put your gun away. You're making them a little nervous."

She held her aim steady. "He'll run."

"I won't run," the bomber swore, then looked at Jack. "How can I run? She shot me in the damn toe."

"See, he can't run," Jack assured her. "And if he tries to, then I'll shoot him."

Chloe swerved her gaze to Jack. Why did he seem uneasy, almost afraid of her and what she would do? Odd…

Oh, dear God. She'd gotten emotional and dropped her

training role. She was acting like an amateur. And yet she had to accept that this situation was different from any of her assignments. They'd been setups and then FBI or police handled the nasty parts. No one ever knew Chloe had been evidence gathering or building the case. This started with Marcus and it was the first time in her career she'd been targeted for murder. It upset her, yes. That someone else had died in her place tore her apart. But that one of the Greenes would put out a contract on her had a different emotional impact. It thoroughly pissed her off. And whichever one it was would live to regret that.

She pulled herself together and put her gun in her handbag. "Greene," she told Jack. "Male. He doesn't know how old."

The police moved in and removed the suspect. An officer approached Chloe. "Ma'am, we'll need a statement."

"We'll provide it as soon as possible," Jack said.

Chloe launched into a full-fledge description of events, including the license numbers of two vehicles that had been parked on the street at the time of the explosion, then asked, "Is the bomb squad taking care of my cars?"

The officer nodded, his nose red from cold. "They've secured the area. Now they're diffusing the devices."

Chloe saw Carmine's face at the glass door. "Oh, hell. I forgot." She walked over and tapped on the glass. "Carmine, it's okay. Your customers can go now. Thanks for waiting."

Carmine opened the door. "Did you stop being a princess and go to work for the police?"

"No," she said. "You can't stop being a princess, Carmine. You're stuck with it for life."

"Okay, then." He stepped back and shut the door, keeping his customers safely inside.

"Why is he doing that now?" She looked at Jack. "The bomber is gone."

"Maybe the situation is just a little too weird for him."

"You're joking, right?" she said. "This is New York."

"Right." Jack shrugged and wrapped an arm around her shoulder. "I'm glad you didn't get yourself killed."

"Me, too." She blinked hard. "But it should've been me. Poor Craig. His wife and baby… Oh, Jack. It's so awful."

"I know." He tucked her under his arm and led her toward his car. "Are you okay? You weren't hurt in the blast, right?"

"No. I'm as okay as I'm going to get until one o'clock."

"You're going to have to postpone that nervous breakdown, if that's what you're talking about," Jack said. "I have news."

"What kind of news?" She walked the sidewalk with him, tucked under his arm, and felt relief. Her knees were going to make it after all.

"We found Nadia and Karen."

"I know. Jillian told me before the explosion."

"Did she tell you we identified Brother?" He stepped up to a jet-black Lamborghini Murcielago and opened the door for Chloe.

"No, she didn't." Chloe slid inside and, after Jack got in and closed his door, she picked up the conversation. "I'm guessing she didn't know it."

"Well, I should say that we've almost identified him, but there is some disparity—"

"Disparity?" And he was worried that she wasn't quite together? "Jack, you either know who he is or you don't."

"There are two men," he explained. "We pulled photos from the surveillance tapes at the airport. Nadia and Karen were brought in separately. They were separated in New York and not reunited until they arrived at the airport in LA. Nadia identified one man as Brother, and Karen identified the other."

Chloe frowned. Why hadn't Jack started the car and gotten the heater going? She was suddenly freezing to death. "Are you telling me there are two men named Brother?"

"Or more." Jack took her hand. "It appears that whatever man escorts the women to export them is known to the women as Brother. It's a position, not a name."

"Clever," she grudgingly admitted. "It makes them much harder to identify."

"It does." Jack hesitated and then frowned. "Chloe, I'm afraid we know the men they identified."

She tried to feel surprised. She wanted to be stunned that anyone she knew could do such a horrible thing as to sell women. But she wasn't. She just…wasn't. "Who are they?"

"Brit Carouthers is one of them." Jack stopped, waited.

"Harrison?" She guessed the second man.

Jack nodded no.

"Then where is he?" she asked. "He's been M.I.A. ever since the Governess went missing."

"That's where he is," Jack said. "Looking for her."

"So he's not the Duke?"

"No."

She was glad to hear it. She liked Harrison, and being as close to the Governess as he was, if he were the Duke, well, it could be complicated. "I knew that sorry bastard Brit was trouble, and I tried to tell Erik, but no, he refused to listen to a word—" The truth slammed through her in crashing waves and she stopped suddenly. *Breathe, Chloe. Breathe.* "The second man is Erik, isn't it?"

Regret filled Jack's eyes. "I'm sorry, honey."

The heart her brother had broken so many times she'd been convinced he couldn't break it again shattered.

* * *

In the secret offices at G.R.C., Chloe and Jack mutually agreed not to mention that Ellie Richardson was missing along with the Governess. With everyone unable to reach her, the Governess being missing couldn't be hidden, but hopefully Ellie's absence could be kept quiet.

Jack did the briefing with Renee and spent fifteen minutes relating details on the Governess, Chloe's Hummer blowing up, and Brit and Erik's photos in the L.A. airport being identified by Nadia and Karen. Afterward, he touched base with Chloe.

"Well?" Chloe asked. "Is she going to recover?"

"She's working on it. But she said something odd, Chloe."

"What?" Swirling her chair away from the computer, she faced him.

He closed the door and hitched a hip on the corner of the desk. "I told her about Erik, and she said, 'Son of a bitch. I wonder how her mother will blame this on her.' I assume that meant your mother will blame you for Erik's actions."

"Unfortunately, Renee's comment isn't odd, and you assumed right. It doesn't matter how Erik screws up, it will ultimately be my fault. It always has been."

Jack unbuttoned his suit coat, letting it fall open, and leaned against the edge of her desk. "Why?"

Chloe opened her mouth to answer and realized she had no idea what to say. "I don't know," she confessed. "I've never known."

"And you accept that?" He folded his arms, his expression intense.

"Yes, I pretty much have." Chloe stood and shrugged. "She should be proud of one of us, and it was crystal clear early on, it wasn't going to be me."

"Could that be because you've kept the truth about Erik's

indiscretions from her?" Jack's voice sounded soft but struck a hard note in her heart.

She wanted to deny it with a resounding no. But thinking back, she couldn't. That's exactly what she'd done, though she couldn't say why, and she had no idea how her mother would have reacted had she known what all Erik had done.

"Never mind," Jack said, reeling her closer to him. "You don't owe me any answers, but you do owe them to yourself." He ran his hands down her arms, shoulders to elbows. "How's Emma?"

"The same." Chloe's insides twisted and she inched between his spread thighs, looped her arms around his neck and rested her head against his shoulder. "I swear, I've never hated the words 'no change' until now, but I'm making up for lost time."

He rubbed little circles on her back. "Intense, eh?"

"So intense it feels like stone slabs on my chest and I can barely breathe."

"What are you doing on the computer?" He buried his nose at her neck and breathed deeply.

A shiver coursed through her. "Running copies of a few reports. I know the Duke is in there. I'm going to find him."

"Believe me, after four years of searching for the bastard, I hope you do. I hope anyone does." He brushed her throat with the tip of his nose. "You smell good."

"Thanks." Smiling, she turned her head and captured his mouth.

This kiss was tempered, cautious and timid, as if they both feared asking for too much would result in being wholly denied. When she snuggled closer, he grew bolder, sweeping her mouth with his tongue, and Chloe met him, stroke for stroke, need for need, and passion ignited hunger, and hunger an unquenched thirst. All that they seemed to tangle with words became so evident and clear through lips and mouths and hands eager to touch everywhere at once. Their bodies and hearts communed unencumbered, and Chloe knew that this man would always, forever be in her heart.

Jack separated their mouths. "I need some serious time in bed with you."

"Soon." Chloe gave him a siren's smile. "First, reports."

He groaned. "You have no mercy." He let go of her. "I'm going to work in the office next door, or we're going to melt the bolts off the door."

She laughed. "What are you doing?"

"Checking in with agents to get the latest updates from the field."

"Work fast, and let's go home." Chloe smiled. "If they find Brit or Erik, let me know, okay?"

"I will." He walked out, turned around and came back in, then kissed her hard. There was no tenderness and gentleness in this kiss; it was steeped in raw passion, and Chloe returned it fully, and gave him more.

He lifted his mouth. "I'm glad you're alive, Princess."

She nuzzled his neck. "Me, too."

Jack walked out and closed the door behind him.

Still zinging from his kiss, Chloe turned back to the computer, selected all of the previous six months' mission reports entered on Rose assignments, burned them onto a CD, and then printed out a hard copy for review.

Somewhere in them was the key that would tell her the Duke's identity and whether or not Renee or Erik or one of the other Roses had crossed over and betrayed the rest of them. Chloe just had to have the courage to look with her eyes wide open to see the truth, and then she had to have the strength of will to report her findings.

While waiting for Jack, she spent the next forty-five

minutes reading reports, and the subsequent thirty minutes reading the Roses' mission notes. Oddly, Brit Carouthers had been mentioned several times on several missions, and so had Ryan Greene, though pretty much in passing and never with anything that would point to either of them as the Duke. That didn't bode well for Erik.

Someone tapped on the door.

"Come in, Jack." Chloe lowered the report and looked back. "Oh, sorry, Olivia."

"No problem," she said. "Rubi Cho is on the phone. She wants to talk with you."

Chloe blinked. "I wonder what she wants? An update on Emma?"

"As of ten minutes ago, there was no change."

Those hated words, yet again. "Thanks." Chloe turned to the desk, swallowed her dislike of the woman and lifted the phone. "Rubi. This is a surprise. What can I do for you?"

"Two things to talk about," she said in her clipped tone. "One, congratulations on snagging a dinner date with Harrison Howell."

She'd seen them at Perrini's, no doubt. "You know him?"

"Oh, yes," she said. "It's very QT, and I'd never violate his trust, but the man is…" She paused.

Would Rubi expose him as a representative for the Governess? She mentally slapped herself. How could she? Rubi didn't know the Governess existed.

"Very low key," Rubi continued.

Chloe decided to play dumb. "Are you warning me that he's a fortune hunter?"

She laughed. "Hell, no. He doesn't need your money, Chloe. He has more than enough of his own."

"From what?" Couldn't hurt to get the scoop from an outsider and see if it matched what he'd told her himself.

"One of those dot-com companies. I forget which one, but he's got more money than God."

Loud noises sounded in the background. "Where are you?"

"L.A. Ryan Greene chartered three planes full of friends and a film crew out here for a party. I got a tip about it and managed to get a seat on one of the flights."

"What's the party for?"

"Celebrating some major real estate deal he closed," Rubi said. "Ashley's covering it for *Chic*. He even hired some models so she'd have professionals along to do a shoot."

The hair on the back of Chloe's neck stood on end. "Were they on the plane with you?" This couldn't be dismissed.

"Two were. The others came on the earlier flights. Erik and Brit acted as hosts on those."

Were the modeling jobs Nadia and Karen had been offered legitimate? Or were Rubi and Ashley in danger of becoming victims? They had family and connections—their absence would be noticed. The Duke wouldn't dare be stupid enough to snatch them—would he?

"Is Tatiana with you?"

"No, she's gone."

"Gone where?"

"That's the other thing I wanted to ask you about. Erik says she's vanished."

Chloe's heart skipped a beat. *Speak up and risk being a fool. Or stay silent and live with regret.* Rubi was fishing, hoping her statement would trick Chloe into revealing something. But now Chloe needed Rubi's help. Damn it, she didn't know what to do. "Rubi, I need a favor."

"Does this mean we're friends?" That was Rubi's term for people who gave her scoops.

"No," Chloe said. Why lie? They both knew the truth, and being honest would set the stage for their future interactions.

"But it does mean I'll contact you with the next interesting tidbit that comes my way."

"That could work. What's the favor?"

Chloe pushed. "Are you in or out?"

"Oh, what the hell? Call it junket fever. I'm in the mood to take a few risks."

"Find Erik at that bash and latch on to him." *Think, Chloe. Think.* "He's been drinking too much, and my mother's going nuts."

"No."

"Damn it, Rubi. You said you were in. Where's your integrity?"

"I'm in for the truth. Don't peddle me a sack of lies."

"You know Brit's history. I don't need to explain. Erik's too tight with him. I'm scared he's getting in over his head."

"Now, that I believe, and since I happen to agree with you, I'll run interference for you with Boy Wonder. I'll recruit Ashley, too, so we can be less obvious."

That was a bonus Chloe hadn't expected but certainly welcomed. "Did Erik bring Chelsea with him?" Chloe asked. That would tell her a lot—or it could.

"No, and she was plenty pissed about it, too. He refused to let her come."

Not good. "Did he say why?"

"I talked to Chelsea, not Erik," Rubi said, clarifying. "He told her this wasn't her kind of party. She's the one who called me about it."

Erik was protecting Chelsea. Keeping her safe and away from this. *Definitely not good news.* "One more favor." Chloe sat on the edge of her seat.

"You're pushing the bounds of our non-friendship, Chloe."

"I know I am." She licked her lips. "But I have to ask."

"Yeah, I'll bet you do. I'll bet it took a lot for you to ask me for anything, which tells me a whole lot is happening." Chloe didn't respond, and Rubi's sigh crackled through the phone. "Okay. What?"

"Don't get on one of those private planes to come back to New York. Swear you won't do that."

"If you expect me to take a commercial flight when I can travel with Ryan Greene, the sexiest man on the planet, you're going to have to tell me why."

"I can't." Chloe let out a pent-up breath. "Rubi, you know I wouldn't ask if it wasn't important. But it is important. It's really important."

"To whom?"

Crossroads time. She could lie and be refused, or tell the truth and maybe gain Rubi's cooperation. "You."

"Me?" Surprise rippled through her tone. "How is this important to me?"

"It is, but I'm not free to say how." Chloe's hand tightened on the receiver. The bones in her fingers ached.

"Can't or won't?"

"Can't." That was it, as far as she was going to save Rubi's ass. She wasn't overly fond of the woman to begin with, and even less so after she'd done the article on Hollow Hill, exposing Chloe's cover. But that was no reason to stand by and watch her be sold as a slave.

Silence stretched between them. Chloe's palm grew damp against the receiver, and though the temptation burned strong to blow it and explain to Rubi, she held her tongue.

"Okay, Chloe," Rubi finally said. "But later, you damn well better have a great explanation for this." She sighed. "I won't take a private flight, and I'll take care of Erik." She told someone she didn't want another drink.

"Thanks, Rubi."

"Thanks, hell. I want to know what's going on, and I expect you to tell me, and me alone, just as soon as you can."

"When I know, you'll know." That was as committal as she could get and implied the information would be coming from another source. That was critical.

She went over to the office Jack was using. Sitting at a computer desk, he rocked back in his seat with the keyboard in his lap and the phone crooked at his ear. Hearing her enter, he looked back. A few words, and he put down the phone. "What's up?" he asked Chloe.

"I think Nadia and Karen had a modeling job with Ryan." She filled him in on Ryan Greene's party and three flights.

Jack frowned. "It's got to be a cover."

"I think so, too. Erik is nuts about Chelsea, she wanted to go with him and he said no." Chloe then went on to relay the rest of the information and everyone she knew to be involved.

Jack paused. "The women they plan to sell were on those planes."

Chloe leaned against the door and folded her arms, keeping the pain of Erik's involvement inside. He would be held accountable, and when he was, her mother would be heartbroken and casting blame. Her poor father would be devastated. "They divided them between the three planes. My guess is the two models on Ryan's were legitimate and will return to New York."

"Why?"

"They knew his name." She sighed. "The women on the other two planes didn't know who they were with. Brother, right?"

"Yes." He seemed surprised, and pleased at her deduction.

"So is Ellie Richardson the Governess?" Chloe asked.

Jack frowned at her, lowered his feet to the floor. "You know I can't answer that."

"You don't have to," Chloe said. "It's a logical deduction,

too. They're missing without word one from their abductors. What are the odds of that happening to them simultaneously?"

"Not as unrealistically high as you'd think, considering they're both neck-deep in Intel matters and half the nuts and extremists in the world are after them."

Anger ripped through Chloe. "Don't treat me like I'm stupid, Jack. My IQ is just south of the stratosphere, okay?"

"Stupid has nothing to do with it. Don't ask questions you know you shouldn't ask," he said. "Questions you know damn well I'm not at liberty to answer. I don't want to lie to you."

Much better. Much, much better. "Don't you dare deny they're one and the same woman."

"I don't acknowledge being asked the question."

"Fine."

"Fine." He frowned deeper. "How do you know the senator is missing?"

"She didn't show up in Tuscany. Her housekeeper told me, and I informed her assistant. But she already knew it."

"Well, she's not missing anymore." He passed Chloe a copy of a statement sent to him from the senator's office.

Chloe read it quickly. "She wanted a few days' respite to deal with a personal issue?"

"Apparently so. But the Governess *has* been abducted."

"So why did Ellie's Tuscany staff think she was missing?"

"I don't know. You'd have to ask them, honey. Though, it's a matter between her and her staff, don't you think?"

She did think so, and that aggravated her because she knew as well as she knew she hated Jack's tie that he'd held back information from her on this. Chloe understood—it was the nature of the job—and so it shouldn't hurt. But it did. Damn it, they were partners and he was handling her.

He paused a moment, then asked, "Can we get someone on the inside in L.A.?"

"Ashley's there, remember?" Chloe shoved her hair back from her face. "She's not answering her cell. I was waiting to talk to you before trying her again and filling her in." Chloe should leave the topic of the Governess alone, but she couldn't. "So is someone looking for the Governess?"

"Half the world is looking for her, honey. She knows way too much for it to be any other way."

"Including Harrison?"

Jack nodded.

"Why did you two each think the other was the Duke?"

"Proximity and information. We kept running into each other in the Duke's haunts and we knew too much to be outsiders. We didn't know we had the same boss."

The Governess didn't need the Roses looking for her. She had a team of professionals who specialized in dignitary abductions on it already.

"Well," Chloe said. "We'd better review these mission reports. The Duke may be buried in them, remember?"

"Right." Jack logged off the computer—its screen had been blank since she'd opened the door—and then stood up.

"I thought we could go over them at my apartment. It's more private than here, and since we're looking at the Roses…"

Jack gave her a slow, sexy smile. "Excellent idea."

With secret smiles and eager steps, they walked up to street level and passed by Olivia's desk.

Renee was standing beside it. "What are you two up to?"

"Work." Chloe lifted the bag. "Research."

"Ah." She looked nervous. Unhappy and nervous.

"Any word on Emma?" Chloe asked to take the focus off events here.

"No change," Renee said. "I'm so sick of hearing that, I could scream."

"I know what you mean." Chloe stepped back. "We'd better get to this," she told Jack, and then they departed.

Renee watched them go. Chloe sensed her gaze on her back, but rather than feeling protected by it, as she always had, she felt uneasy. For whatever reason, Renee had elected to keep her problems to herself and not share them with Chloe as she normally would. Yet it didn't take a rocket scientist to know those problems were serious—just someone who knew Renee well. And even if Chloe hadn't known Renee well, and hadn't felt the fear in her, then watching Olivia and the protective way she was handling Renee would have said it all, anyway.

Not only did Renee have serious problems. She was in trouble. Gauging by her and Olivia's expressions, wicked trouble.

Chapter 14

Chloe and Jack made love, dozed for a full hour, then christened the dining room table.

It stood covered with papers and white cartons from Chinese take-out, and she and Jack sat at it—him in his shorts, her in her robe—and they ate, talked, read, teased and kissed and touched, then ate, talked and read some more.

When they'd reviewed all the mission files handled by Madison Taylor-Pruitt, Becca Whitmore, Porsche Rothschild, Alexa Cheltingham and Vanessa Dawson, they took a break to stretch and walked out onto the terrace.

Manhattan's lights mesmerized Chloe. They'd always seemed magical, and with the air clear and crisp, tonight was no exception. She inhaled.

"Beautiful view." Jack stood beside her at the terrace rail, looking not on the city but at her.

She stepped over and circled his waist with her arm,

nuzzled into his arms. "I love Manhattan at night. It has a high-voltage current that just sizzles through your body and energizes you." She glanced up at Jack and smiled. "There's no place else in the world like it."

"I see it a little differently." He shrugged. "Night cloaks all the rough edges and ugliness," he said. "Everything looks a little softer, a little less lethal than in the bald light of day."

Not exactly cynical, but damn close. "You like the rooftop terrace on your Long Island house better."

"I love the sounds of the water, yes." He planted a kiss to her temple. "But for you, anything."

Thrilled by that comment, she smiled again. "Jack, why aren't you looking for the Governess?"

"I am," he said, seeming surprised. "I believe the answer to who has her is in those records." He nodded toward the table, where reams of reports totally obscured its top.

"Well, we'd best get back to them then." Chloe went to move to the door.

Jack clasped her upper arm, held it until she looked back at him. "I need something to hold me over," he whispered. Closing his arms around her, he claimed her mouth.

Chloe sank into the kiss, into the sweetness and gentle hunger in it, and she sensed that with him she could care too much. Feel too much. Love too much. That was a journey she didn't want to take alone.

Her hands on his chest, she pulled back and looked up at him. "Are you going to hurt me, Jack?" she asked bluntly. "It feels as if we're together again, but are things like they were? Can we go back to that simple magic again?"

He tilted his head. "Honey, I think simple magic is like innocence. Once it's gone, you don't get it back." He stroked her hair. "But that doesn't mean what we have can't be good. Maybe even better."

She wanted a simple "yes." She wanted that badly.

"I didn't mean to upset you." He frowned. "I was trying to be totally honest."

"So it is different for you. Between us, I mean."

He hesitated. "Yes, it is. And if you're honest about it, you'll admit it's different for you, too."

She didn't want different, damn it. She wanted something, someone in her life to be the same. She wrapped her arms over her chest against the chill and moved to the door, then stopped. But she couldn't make herself look back at him. "I've cared so much for you for so long," she said softly. "My judgment about men has been lousy in the past, but you were always different. You've always been in my heart, Jack. I can't…" A knot swelled in her throat and she couldn't talk anymore with her voice cracking, so she fell silent.

"What?" he prodded. "Tell me, honey. You can't what?"

"Take you lightly." Without looking back, she opened the door and walked back inside, then returned to the files.

They sat across from each other at the table, pretending to be calm and relaxed and normal, studying the files and not thinking about what had been discussed on the terrace.

"Let's review before going further," Jack suggested.

Determined to separate the professional from the private, Chloe nodded. "Shoot."

"Alexa Cheltingham and Vanessa Dawson." Jack shifted his gaze from the papers to Chloe. "What do you think of them?"

"I think I hate my job when it involves looking for dirt on my friends." Chloe stiffened her shoulders. "But this isn't about what I think. It's about what I know. And I know I have several people in mind who could be the Duke. Erik—my parents are going to be devastated if it's him, right after they disown me—Ryan Greene, though it pains me to say it and his involvement is highly unlikely."

"Why?" Jack snitched another bite of crab. "Marcus went straight to him for help, right?"

"Yes, but he's so successful. What does he gain?"

"Excitement? The thrill of the edge?" Jack suggested.

"Money motivating them isn't plausible. They're all wealthy men."

"My guess is it's power. The Duke does what he does to prove he can." Jack rubbed the bridge of his nose. "Who else?"

"Brit Carouthers."

"Easy target. Indisputably involved, but not sophisticated enough to be the Duke."

"In here," she tapped her heart, "I agree." Chloe frowned. "Reviewing the files, I have to add Madison's uncle, Bing, to the list of those involved with the Duke. He was tied to the Russian mafia, too, though in fairness, he didn't know it until right before he died."

"Did anything unexpected come up in settling his affairs?"

"A lot," Chloe said. "The attorneys are still sorting it all out, but there's a multi-million dollar project in south Florida—a joint venture with the Greenes."

"Which ones?" Jack asked. "Franklin, Ryan or Julio?"

"Madison isn't sure yet. There's a string of dummy corporations. She's still following the paper trail. Actually, Alan Burke is helping her with it."

Chloe pulled out her cell phone. "Let me get an update on that." She dialed Alan, asked the question, and then waited for his reply. When it came, it surprised her. She scribbled down the message as quickly as she could write. "Thanks."

"Well?" Jack said, surprised that she had been able to get farther on this than the FBI.

"The good news is that so far they've discovered no felonies in her uncle's past business transactions. The bad news is, they've found ties to a lot of other people—all of whom are in our circle of friends."

"Like whom?"

"Franklin, Ryan and Julio Greene." She hesitated. "And four more."

"Let me guess," Jack said, then ticked them off on his fingers. "Brit Carouthers. Your favorite ex-fiancé, the late Marcus Abbot Sterling, III, and—I'm really sorry about this—Wonder Boy."

She nodded. "And the fourth?"

"Not yet proven, but strongly suspected," Jack speculated. "Tatiana."

Surprise rippled through Chloe. "How did you know that?"

"Experience." He didn't sound particularly pleased by it, but he sure as hell wasn't surprised. "She does the books, she knows where the skeletons are buried." He leaned across the table. "I know investigating your own sucks, honey. But this requires personal insight you have that I don't. I'm counting on you, and so is Emma. I believe Tatiana faked her injury the night Emma was beaten, and I'm convinced we've got to nail Tatiana or she's going to get someone killed."

Emma was far from out of the woods. "I agree with you." A lump settled in Chloe's throat. Sparring with Tatiana was one thing. Nailing her was another.

Jack stood up. "I've got to go."

Chloe grabbed her purse. "Me, too."

"Are you going to talk with Erik?"

"Not yet. He's in L.A., but that's just as well. One never asks Erik a question one can't already answer." Sadness crept into her heart.

"Bad track record?"

Chloe paused, then revealed the truth that only Renee and Emma knew. "He's the reason I got kicked out of Harvard."

"I remember the incident from your dossier. The dime bag in your dorm room was his?"

She nodded. "I told them it wasn't mine, but I wouldn't tell them whose it was, so I got the boot."

Jack's jaw went tight. "Why didn't Erik tell them?"

"Because Erik is…Erik."

"You shouldn't have covered for him, Chloe."

"I know that now." She frowned. "I'm asking myself if he'd taken the hit for what he'd done at Harvard, or any of the other thousand times I bailed his ass out and covered for him, then maybe he wouldn't be in this nightmare now?"

"I should have known." Jack stuffed a hand in his pocket. "Why didn't you tag him—and don't you dare protect him again now. Tell me the truth."

"My parents adore him, Jack. They would have been crushed. I was already a disappointment." She let out a heart-felt sigh. "At the time, it seemed like the compassionate thing to do."

"Selfless." Jack stared at her a long moment. "I've heard about it, but I've never really seen it before." He grunted. "God, but you awe me, Chloe. I see you struggle with the way your parents treat you, and yet you still go to extreme lengths to protect them."

Chloe looked up at him. "It's easy to love when it costs you nothing. But when it costs you everything…well, you're content because you know you did what you believed was right."

"Is Erik smart enough to be the Duke?"

"He's brilliant," she said frankly. "But so are Ryan and Julio and Brit. I'm counting Franklin out because he's just not vicious enough."

"And Tatiana?"

"Hands down, she's by far the most brilliant of them all."

"Then you'd better find her and have a chat with her."

"Rubi says she's not with them. But one doesn't ask Rubi questions one can't already answer, either."

Jack led her to the door. "You're coming with me, right?"

"I can. Where are we going?"

"We go see a Rose who knows all about Marcus Sterling."

"Whatever for?" Chloe couldn't make the connection.

"Because he's dead and he can't come kill you or me." Jack frowned. "Quit smiling. I'm not kidding."

"I know. But I know you, too. You're not going for just those reasons."

"I'm not?"

"No. There's more. With you, there's always more."

"Well," he circled her waist with his arm and led her out the door and to the elevator. "As it turns out, you're right. Because he's dead, he also can't make any swift moves to cover his tracks. That makes him our best shot for finding out what this operation is all about."

"You do believe the Duke is running this show—and he has the Governess, don't you?" She hoped so, because she believed it down to her strappy gold Jimmy Choos.

"I know the Duke is running this show and, yes, I do believe he abducted the Governess."

In the garage, Chloe saw the burned-out shell of her Hummer. Authorities hadn't yet towed it away. "I can't believe Craig's dead." Her eyes filled. "God, Jack, I think of his wife and new baby and I just want to hide in a cave or kill that bomber myself. I'm so ashamed."

"Of what?"

"I'm an agent, for God's sake, and I couldn't even protect my garage attendant. He died for me."

"You didn't plant the bomb."

"He was worried about dying before raising the baby. He was worried Debra couldn't make it without him." Chloe would see to it that Debra and Anthony were fine financially, of course, but that wouldn't give her the comfort of her husband or her son the comfort of his father. Tears spilled down Chloe's cheeks. "He's too little to even remember his father."

When they got into Jack's car, he turned to Chloe. "Honey, shh. Don't cry." He hugged her. "Listen to me, Chloe. Listen to me," he whispered close to her ear. "He's not dead."

She went still, her cheek against his shoulder. "But—"

"He used the remote starter, Chloe. Craig wasn't in the car yet when it blew. He got knocked on his ass, and he's currently in an undisclosed hospital under guard. He saw the killer, so he's being protected."

Relief washed through her, then anger. "Damn it, Jack. Why wasn't I told? I've been feeling guilty as sin and—what about Debra and Anthony? Does she know? Oh, God, tell me you've told Debra."

"It was done for his protection and yours. Until we had him secure, no one was told, not even his family."

"But Debra knows now, right?"

"Yes. She's with him now."

Okay, so Chloe could see the logic in this move, but it still had her fuming. "I'm glad Craig's alive." That was definitely an understatement, yet it would have to do. "But you definitely make it hell for a woman to trust you, Jack. We're partners, damn it. Stop handling me."

"Fair enough." He went to crank the engine.

"Wait." She got out and ran a check on Jack's car. Finding no devices, she went to get back inside, but Frank pulled up alongside them in the limo. "Get in."

"Why?"

"Your man Mac Dayton suggested it would be safer," Frank said.

Jack moved his car into the garage and then joined Chloe in the limo and shut the door. "What's up, Frank?"

"Mac said for me to tell you that you've entered the red zone. Then he told me to get my ass over here and drive you two."

"Okay." Jack looked worried.

"What's the red zone?" Chloe asked.

"It's a term we use mainly with serial killers."

"Damn right."

Chloe glanced through the lowered glass to the back of Frank's head. "Oh, God, we've got a serial killer now, too?"

"No, honey. No," Jack said. "We've got someone blinded by rage. That's the red zone. They'll do anything to anyone, and are so angry they might not even remember what they've done."

"Who?" The Duke, the Governess's abductor? Chloe wasn't sure and couldn't confidently tag anyone.

"I don't know and he doesn't either, or he'd have said so."

"The Duke has to be one of the guys I mentioned in our circle. Otherwise, nothing makes sense."

"Damn right," Frank mumbled from the front seat.

Jack glared at Chloe. "You know everything about this assignment is classified. Why are you—"

"Jack, don't suddenly get stupid," Frank said. "She didn't say a thing to me."

"Then how do you know about any of this?"

"Because I ain't stupid." Frank shook his head. "How the hell can anyone be around all this and not see it?"

He had a point. "You know that makes you a danger."

"I know you ain't stupid, either." Frank looked in the rearview mirror at Chloe. "I've watched over this woman from the time she started breathing. You think I'd do anything to harm her?"

"No, I don't. But you having knowledge creates…complications."

"So give me a badge, or keep your mouth shut about it. Either way works for me, and the shut mouth's been working fine for four years."

Jack's frown creased his forehead. "Let me think on it."

"Fine," Frank said.

Chloe smiled, and whispered close to Jack's ear. "He works for Renee, too."

Jack nodded and pecked a kiss to her lips. "Thanks."

"So where we going?" Frank asked.

"Hang a right, Frank." The limo pulled out into traffic. "Chloe, it's time to issue a Rose alert. Get these women in one place so we can find out what's not on paper. Try Perrini's, in an hour," Jack said.

Chloe put out the calls, and noticed something else. Peppermint. Why did she smell it now? "Frank, do you have Peppermint Schnapps in your flask?"

"No."

"Where's the peppermint, then?"

"It's on the carpet, Chloe," Jack said.

"Oh, Miss Emma's peppermint foot treatment," Frank said. "She always takes her shoes off and the oils get in the carpet."

The limo suddenly lurched and made a hissing noise. Frank pulled over as far as he could, given there were no parking spaces, then popped the hood and opened the door, totally disgusted. "She's running hot." He pushed the emergency roadside service button on the dash, then flagged down a taxi that had been just behind them.

Frank tilted his head. "I'll phone as soon as the car is repaired, Princess, and then meet you."

"Are you warm enough without a coat?" she asked.

He opened the back door of the cab. "Got one on the front seat," he assured her. "Be safe."

Chloe smiled and got inside the taxi.

Jack went to get in, then stopped. "Chloe, wait. We need to take care of something first. Come with me."

Surprised, Chloe said, "Okay." She reached into her purse to grab a tip for the driver, planning to ask him to wait.

Jack stepped back so she could get out, and extended her his hand. "Hurry, honey."

The driver stomped on the gas. Chloe slid on the seat.

Frank and Jack lunged for the door, but caught only air.

The cabbie burned rubber and momentum slammed the back door shut. The locks clicked.

Jack yelled. "Get out, Chloe. Get out!"

Pinned back to the seat by the speed-demon maniac driving, Chloe slid from side to side with every turn as they whipped in and out of traffic, weaving lane-to-lane down Amsterdam. Figured the lights were with them this once. She had to get out of this damn cab before he got to wherever he intended to take her. She grabbed for the door handle.

There was none.

She was locked inside.

Chapter 15

The backseat of the cab was empty.

Empty. How the hell was she going to get out? There was nothing—and her handbag wasn't heavy enough to break the glass. Frantic, Chloe screamed at the maniacal driver. "Stop the damn car!"

He ignored her, drove faster, jerking the wheel to slide past a sedan and cut off a truck. She dug through her purse for her gun. Her hands shook so hard she could barely hold on to it.

If you're locked in a vehicle, don't try to kick out the side windows. Go for the rear windshield. It's bigger and that makes it weaker. Kick it out. It won't shatter, it's safety glass.

Jimmy's voice. His training. Chloe forced herself to calm down and think. She wasn't a helpless victim; she'd had tons of training, and she could use it, if she stopped reacting on emotion and got her damn act together.

Fake it 'til you make it, baby.

Got it, Emma. Chloe twisted on the seat, bumping her shoulder on the clear, bulletproof plastic covering the back of the front seat. It was a barrier installed in all cabs to protect the drivers from attempted robberies. Finally in position, she kicked at the rear windshield. *Come on, Jimmy Choo. Don't let me down!*

She kicked again and again, and finally kicked her heel through the glass. Then she kept kicking at the edges of the hole, making it larger and larger.

The driver screamed, "Knock it off or I'll shoot you here."

"Go ahead, asshole," she shouted back, swiveled and kicked the back of his seat.

It cracked.

It wasn't bulletproof! She kicked it a second time and shouted again. "I said go ahead." With luck, he would believe it was just temper; he wouldn't realize he was vulnerable.

He lifted a gun off the seat, looked back at her. "One more time, Princess."

She held her Glock inside her purse, pressed its nose flat against the break in the plastic and fired.

He yelled and swerved, his gun hitting the floorboard with a thud. "Bitch!"

Chloe didn't have time to throw up as she braced for impact. There was traffic ahead, and it wasn't moving. She had to get out of here, or she was going to end up dead, anyway.

Shrugging out of her jacket, she rolled her sleeves over her hands to protect them from the rough edges of the glass, then pulled herself through the back windshield. Belly down, she pressed flat against the trunk and held on to the glass frame, her hands wrapped in her coat. Sliding, she looked through the cab to the congested traffic ahead, estimated their speed at about thirty miles per hour. Less than a minute until the cab crashed into the stopped cars.

A blue car pulled up alongside her. "Here!" a thin man with hair the color of carrots shouted. "Come here."

A convertible. She walked her hands along the windshield opening, until she was at its side. "Pull up!" She shouted at the man driving. "Pull up!"

He inched ahead. The cars were stopped not twenty yards in front of them. "Hurry!" he yelled.

Chloe jumped. Her feet hit the floorboard in the convertible. She crumpled, fell headlong against the backseat, scraping the driver's head and landing with a *swoosh* and a heartfelt groan. Pain shot through her side.

He slammed on the brakes.

His tires churned smoke, squealed on the pavement. "Ohhhhhhh dammmmmmmmmmmn."

Chloe covered her head with her arms, slid off the seat onto the floor and prayed she didn't become a missile. There was no way she could get a seat belt on in time.

The car screeched to a stop, its front end inches away from the back end of an 18-wheeler. Chloe pulled herself onto the seat, looked up at the truck, which seemed to stretch skyward forever, and nearly fainted.

The cab veered sideways and crashed into a parked black van, drove it into the red Jeep in front of it. Chloe watched, unable to look away, involuntarily jerking at each crunch of metal colliding with metal. Her mouth gaped open as the driver crawled out and took off, limping. She couldn't even move to chase him.

The guy driving the convertible looked back at her. "You alive back there?"

She nodded. "I'm alive." And if she said it a few more times, she might just believe it.

"What happened?"

"The cabdriver abducted me." She couldn't believe it.

"Why?"

She shook her head to clear it, and began feeling the cold. Where was her coat? Had she lost her coat? "I don't know."

"Oh, man." His eyes glittered excitement. "I know you. I know you from the newspaper!" Excited, his voice hitched. "You're Princess Chloe."

She nodded. "You saved my life," she said. "Thank you."

"No way." His cheeks flushed. "You were already out of the cab. How'd you break the window?"

"I—I don't remember," she said, deciding stupidity was her best option. But she did remember, of course, and inside she spoke the truth. *Jimmy Valentine, I'll love you forever for all you've taught me, and I swear I'll never miss another training session as long as I live.*

What he'd taught her had saved her life.

A silver car screeched to a stop beside her.

Were more of them after her? Chloe scrambled for her gun, but her purse was still in the cab. She stiffened, preparing to bolt over the door and hit the street running.

Both front doors flew open as Jack and Frank bounded out of the car. "Chloe!" Jack reached her first, grabbed her in a hug and lifted her out of the car. "What—how did you end up in this car?"

The driver just stared at them. "I didn't force her."

Frank came up, touched her arm. "You okay, Princess?"

"I'm fine, Frank. A little bruised, but fine."

The driver explained what had happened, and Jack and Frank looked to her for confirmation. She nodded.

Two police cars pulled up and Jack went to intercept the officers. They all went over to the mangled cab. Chloe saw Jack make a call. He gestured to her, and the officers nodded.

"What happened to the cabdriver?" Frank asked.

"He ran off." She pointed, but the man disappeared. Damn. Some spy she was.

She reached out a hand to her rescuer. "Thank you again for helping me. You're quite the hero."

"You're welcome, Princess Chloe."

Jack strode back to them and handed Chloe her purse, which now sported a clean bullet hole. "Can you wait and make a statement?" he asked Chloe's hero. The man nodded, wide-eyed. "Thanks. We have to go. Chloe, they've agreed to talk to you later."

Chloe sighed, grateful Jack's mysterious connections were at work.

"Jack, take her to the car," Frank said, then asked the driver for his name and address. "Princess Chloe will want to express her gratitude."

"No, that's not necessary. She was hanging out the back window. Anyone would have pulled alongside, though I'll tell you, I never expected she'd jump."

"She often does the unexpected," Frank said. "It's put plenty of gray hair on this old head."

Chloe smiled. He'd been telling her that her whole life. She walked over and climbed in the passenger's seat beside Jack, who was behind the wheel. He took her hand in a death grip.

"Frank's a little shaken up," he said. "Don't mention anything about me driving."

She nodded, shaken up herself and touched that Jack was being so thoughtful toward Frank. "It scared him," she said. "He loves me."

"Yes, he does," Jack said, then slid her a killer look. "The next time I tell you to hurry and come to me, for God's sake, hurry and come to me."

Jack was scared, too. She hugged him and dropped kisses

to his cheek, his nose and eyelids, letting him know she was fine. "I will, Jack."

Frank crawled in the backseat. "Next time Jack tells you to come on, you move your ass, Princess. You hear me?" He grumbled and groused. "Scared ten damn years off me."

Chloe smiled at Jack, then turned serious and glanced at Frank. "I'm sorry. I just didn't think fast enough."

"Damn right."

"I'll be more careful in the future."

"Damn right."

"Damn right." Jack agreed with gusto. "And no more chances until we get all this nailed down."

Chloe found a napkin in the glove box and wiped at her hands. They were filthy. "Who fears me enough to pull that?"

"That worthless brother of yours ain't looking too good, Princess."

"No, Frank. He might be angry, but he wouldn't kill me. Erik loves me."

"Erik *uses* you," he countered. "Damn fool boy always has."

"He wouldn't kill me, Frank. I don't believe it." She wouldn't accept it. It just wasn't possible.

"Was the cabdriver a man or a woman?"

Jack answered. "The cabdriver was a man. No identification left in the cab."

"Humph." Frank chewed at his lower lip. "No doubt he was hired by the damn Duke. That cab was following the limo. They must have done something to make it overheat."

Chloe spun around. "You know about the Duke, too?"

"Oh, hell, Princess. If it's got anything to do with you, I've always known it."

Great. So much for not breaching security. "Am I busted?" she asked Jack.

"That's to be determined."

"Terrific." She sighed and swiped the dirt from her palm, dabbed a tongue-tipped napkin against a grimy spot. "This is just turning out to be a banner couple days."

Jack took a call, and turned a one-eighty. "They're ready with the limo. I figure you're going to want to bring it home, right, Frank?"

"Damn right."

They dropped Frank off at the limo, and Jack spoke briefly to one of the men, then returned to the silver car. As soon as Frank left, Jack and Chloe took off.

"Whose car is this?" she asked.

"A friend's. He was in the area."

His friend could be FBI, CIA, Special Detail Unit, or other representatives for the Governess. Just about anyone who walked in the top-secret world. "I should report to Renee."

"I already have, Princess," Jack said. "I'm stuck to your hip for the duration. Could be interesting."

She shoved the napkin into a trash bag that was hanging on the door handle. "If you stick to me, you'd better mean it."

Jack tapped his left blinker. It clicked in the night, sounding louder than in the light of day. "Would it put you in a better mood to know you can break my heart, too?"

Her heart skipped, then thudded hard. "Is it still true?"

"Damn right." Frank's favorite phrase was catching on with Jack now.

Chloe smiled from the soul out. "Then, yes it would help."

"Renee intercepted your call for a Rose alert. She's leaving it to you to handpick the list and make the calls."

Chloe plucked a loose thread off Jack's sleeve. "Sounds like the move of an innocent woman."

"Or one who's stacked events to unfold in her favor."

"She's not doing that, Jack." Chloe held onto faith. Yes, it was shaky. Yes, there were questionable points. Her bones might have doubts, but her heart swore that Renee hadn't switched sides, and Chloe was sticking with it.

"Are you okay to make the Rose calls now, or do you need some recovery time?"

"I was terrified, hanging on the back of that cab. But with them coming at me that openly, I'm afraid there is no recovery time," Chloe said. "The longer they hold the women—especially Tatiana—the greater the odds of them getting caught."

"You were brave, jumping into that convertible."

"I wasn't brave. I didn't want to die. Huge difference."

"Is there?" He glanced over, clasped her hand in his and rested it on his thigh. "Bravery is taking action in the face of danger, not being unafraid of it."

She had been beyond terrified, but she had taken action. Still, if she could have run away to avoid it, she would have. "No illusions here, darling. I'm a coward faking bravery and that's that."

It ticked her off to have to admit it and to have to feel it, so she changed the subject. "I expect Rubi to call anytime and say she's been told to get on a private flight. We both know only one of those three planes will return to New York. The other two will fly to the Far East."

Blinker clicking, Jack turned left. "You're likely right."

"Are we ready for that?"

"FBI is on alert and monitoring." He blended into the heavy traffic, stroking her hand with his thumb.

Glad to hear that they were on point, she checked her watch. Nearly six o'clock in the morning. Another bitch of a night down. She phoned Olivia and gave her a listing of the Roses she wanted to meet at Perrini's at ten o'clock, then phoned Lucas and left a message for him to expect them. She lifted Jack's hand. "I'm starving."

They stopped for breakfast, then checked in with Alan to see if he'd found any evidence definitively naming Tatiana as a member of Ryan's real-estate cartel. He, his father, his brother, Erik and Brit were proven entities. Tatiana wasn't—yet.

Chloe and Jack then checked on Emma at the hospital. Jack had a few words with Mac Dayton while Chloe updated a comatose Emma. Emma likely couldn't hear her, but it made Chloe feel better and she sorted through things, talking to Emma.

Then Chloe and Jack dropped by the G.R.C. to brief Renee on the taxi incident—still no word on the Governess, though Harrison was making progress in his investigation. Chloe gave a smiling Jimmy Valentine two kisses, one on each cheek, for "saves" she'd had as a direct result of his training.

Jimmy beamed.

Chloe showered in the basement's deluxe locker room and dressed in a dove-gray Chanel suit. "In honor of Emma," Kristi said, smoothing the fabric on Chloe's back. Nodding, Chloe thought about Tatiana and the Duke. *The match from hell.* She'd help him make money, he'd get her the power she craved.

"Ah," Kristi said. "You look perfect, Chloe." She checked her watch. "It's time to meet the Roses."

"Thanks, Kristi."

"Don't forget your shoes." She pointed to a pair of gray leather pumps.

"They're not Jimmy Choo." Chloe looked at her. "I have to wear Jimmy Choo. They've saved my ass so many times during all this. I can't risk it, Kristi."

"No problem," she said, disappearing into the room containing all the designer samples sent over. Having a Rose wear your clothes guaranteed success, so the designers were generous to the G.R.C. "Wait here—and pinch your cheeks to put the color back into them."

Chloe pinched and Kristi returned with a pair of gray suede Jimmy Choo heels. Relieved, Chloe slipped them on her feet.

Kristi clasped Chloe's arm. "Get him, Chloe. You get him, and you kill him. No arrest and jail cell for this one."

Chloe patted Kristi's hand. "Honey, I understand the feeling, believe me. I'd love to see this son of a bitch dead. But if I can get him arrested, then that's what I have to do. Otherwise, we're just like him."

Kristi blinked hard, then made the mental shift and nodded.

Chloe found Jack, who'd showered and changed into a steel-gray Armani with a blue tie she loved. *Gorgeous*. Would her heart always flutter on seeing him? Definitely. It always had. "Ready?"

Olivia piped up. "I've gotten all of the Roses except Becca."

"Did you try her apartment in Greenwich?"

"Is she still going there?" Renee asked, looking concerned.

Chloe shrugged. When Olivia started talking, it was apparent to all of them that she'd found Becca. But when she got off the phone, she was smiling.

Renee raised one well-groomed brow. "Well?"

"A certain MI-6 agent answered the phone. Becca's just fine," Olivia reported.

Jack led Chloe out, and when they were in the car, he asked, "What was that about Becca being at the apartment?"

How to explain Becca—and this interesting new development? Chloe didn't even try. "Let's just say we're thrilled that Becca's finally met a man who can more than keep up with her."

The private room Lucas put the Roses in was elegant and quiet.

Madison, Porsche, Alexa, Vanessa, Samantha and Julia were seated around the table. If they were surprised to see Jack with Chloe, none of them showed it. That meant Renee or Olivia had already briefed them that he had security clearance.

"Well, I'm here." Becca swept into the room in a purple

Adelphio suit, which thrilled Chloe. Adele would be beside herself to know the Roses were picking up her designs. She looked preppy and sexy as she slid down onto a chair. "What's up?"

"First, we all have the phone tree going on Emma, right?" When all the women nodded, Chloe went on. "Any news?"

"Not a thing," Porsche said in disgust. "No change."

That earned grunts around the table.

"Her parents haven't left the hospital," Becca said. "That's touching, don't you think?"

Chloe nodded, remembering when she'd been seven and had her tonsils out. Frank had been with her. Not her parents. She had seen them shortly after surgery and not again until she'd come home. But every time she'd drifted off or opened her eyes, Frank was in the chair at her bedside.

Porsche admitted her fear. "I'm scared Emma won't wake up, and if she does wake up, she'll find out she'll never play the piano professionally again, and then she'll want to go back to sleep."

"You're wrong about that, Porsche," Chloe said. "Emma might think about going back to sleep but she'd never do it. She's too strong for that."

"Can anyone really be that strong?" Porsche asked.

"Emma is. Oh, she'll be pissed. She'll hate not playing professionally, and she'll bitch a blue streak about having to go to physical therapy. We'll all have a well-deserved pity party, and then she'll pick herself up and do something else."

"How can you be sure of that?" Porsche didn't look convinced. "She loves the piano."

"I've known her all my life, Bug," Chloe said, using Emma's nickname for Porsche. "It's her way. Emma loves many things. Piano is just one of them."

"I hope to hell you're right," Madison whispered.

Chloe lifted her chin. "You can count on it."

Porsche locked gazes with Chloe. "The Duke did this to Emma."

And the monster Duke could be living in the body of Chloe's only brother. Chloe couldn't respond.

Jack did. "That's what we believe, Porsche."

"Don't you dare faint." Madison shoved a glass of water at her. "Take a drink."

Porsche gulped. Then gulped again. "I'm going to kill that mother—"

"Stop. Now." Vanessa laid a calm hand on Porsche's arm. "Save it. Focus on justice for Emma."

It took a moment for the haze to leave Porsche, but finally she nodded. "Okay. Okay."

They ordered and ate, and talked as they did. "Jack and I reviewed all the mission reports," Chloe said. "Did any of you notice anything recently that's not in your reports?"

"Like what?" Vanessa asked.

"Joint ventures or strategic business alliances with anyone in our circle. Oddities you couldn't explain or didn't consider connected," Chloe suggested. "Anything at all."

"I didn't." Becca took a bite of trout almandine, then swallowed. "Wait. I examined some emeralds for Franklin Greene. Excellent clarity and quality. They were from his mine."

"What mine?" Chloe asked.

"I told you about his mine," Jack said. "In Colombia. The one he owned with Julio's father."

"Ryan tells this story on every first date," Alexa said. "I can't believe you don't remember it."

"I haven't dated Ryan." Chloe took a sip of water.

"Oh, well, do you want to hear it?" Samantha asked.

Jack resisted the urge to roll his eyes by half-a-hair, amusing Chloe. "Sure."

"Wait. I'll give you the short version," Porsche said. "Franklin and Julio's father owned the mine. Franklin was Julio's godfather—a very sacred thing in Colombia—"

"And to Catholics," Vanessa piped in.

"The local mafia—"

"Drug runners," Madison corrected her. "But when you get down to it, aren't they about the same?"

"Whatever," Porsche said. "They wanted the mine, so Franklin told Julio's father to get some protection to cover their assets."

"They hired mercenaries?" Chloe asked.

Samantha nodded, and picked up there. "Julio and his father were heading home and a drunk driver nailed them."

"A T-bone right into the passenger's side," Porsche said.

"The father wasn't hurt, but Julio was hurt badly," Julia told her. "Both of his legs and his left arm."

Jack was rapt. "But Julio's father died in that accident."

"No, not in the accident, but definitely at the scene," Becca said. "This car screams up on them. Someone inside shoots Julio's dad—while he's got Julio in his arms, for God's sake. His dad is dead before he hits the ground, and Julio is beside him on the street, bleeding to death."

Porsche added, "And the drunk driver hauled ass, just leaving them there."

"You've got to be kidding." Revulsion swept through Chloe.

"I am not," Porsche insisted, her hair extensions shaking.

"It gets worse," Samantha said. "The authorities learned the drunk's car was rented by a woman, and next thing they know, she's skipped the country."

"So they couldn't arrest her," Jack said.

"That's right." Becca confirmed it. "Then the drug lords came after Julio—scared he saw them, Ryan thinks, but Julio didn't see them—and Julio's mother and brother, too."

"Good grief." Chloe dabbed at her mouth with her napkin.

Vanessa added more information. "His mother freaked out—who wouldn't—and ran to Franklin for protection. She left Julio with him, supposedly so he could get the medical care he needed, but she was just scared and figured, without Julio, no one would bother her or Paul—her other son. She and Paul took off for Europe and disappeared."

"That's when Franklin adopted Julio?" Jack asked.

Becca nodded. "And hired a small army to protect him and another one to guard the mine. The drug lords apparently figured it was too much trouble to mess with, and left Julio and the mine alone. And that's that."

Vanessa turned to Chloe. "Everyone but Jack knows that on my last assignment I was seeing if I could beat temptation and stay off cocaine."

"You were using?" Jack sounded stunned.

"At one time," Vanessa admitted. "The assignment was to bust up a drug-mule ring in Florida."

"Let me get this straight," Jack said. "Renee sent you, a former drug addict, to break up a drug-mule ring."

"Well, of course, darling," Chloe said. "Who better than Vanessa understands how they operate?"

"That's why Renee chose me for the assignment," Vanessa said. No one needed to remind anyone of Vanessa's super-model status.

"So models were involved then, too," Jack said. "That's a connection."

Chloe nodded, then asked Vanessa. "When you were on the assignment down in Florida, did you see Ryan, Brit or Erik?"

"No, and I would have noticed them." She hesitated a fraction of a second. "I know Erik is your brother, Chloe, but I hate being around those three when they're together. They're absolute animals."

"Thinking back now, do you remember anything that wasn't in the report, Vanessa—anything that might point to the Duke?"

"Not that I'm aware of. Maybe Fluffy Peters noted something in her report." Vanessa named the woman known as the Matriarch of Palm Beach. "She helped me out down there, and she gets the job done."

"Thanks, we will check with her." Chloe looked around. "Anyone else?"

Madison set down her fork. "Ryan competed against me for the Towers."

Jack looked at her. "Privately, or his cartel?"

"He always invests with the cartel."

Jack glanced at Chloe, who asked, "Was Tatiana involved?"

"Of course. She reviews all his financial documents," Madison said. "But I can't say Erik or Brit were directly involved. Ryan did touch base with his father, Julio, Marcus and Brit's brother, Caulfield, though."

Chloe's stomach sank. Brit had replaced Caulfield after Caulfield's arrest. Erik could have replaced Marcus after his death. Regardless, Madison affixed Marcus firmly as a cartel member.

Alexa set down her wineglass. "Ryan Greene was at the Metropolitan Classic Horse Show, where I was investigating suspicious horse deaths. One of the horses had terrible nerve damage—and recovered, thanks to Ross's company's new technology." She blushed when she mentioned Ross. "Maybe Ryan was interested in seeing proof that the technology repairing nerve damage worked. For Julio."

Before Chloe could ask her next question, Jack did. "Didn't a woman die during that mission?"

Alexa nodded. "Dawn," she said. "She could have worked for the Duke, and she would have talked, but she was killed before she could. I believe the Duke ordered her death. I just can't prove it."

"Anything at all unreported?" Chloe asked.

"The photo I gave Renee," Alexa said. "She said to omit it from the report."

"What was in it?"

"A woman and a little boy. She freaked out over seeing it, so I committed it to memory." She shrugged a shoulder. "Instinct, you know?"

Everyone at the table nodded.

"It was of Julio and Marcella Vitiello," Alexa said. "I have to say, I've wondered a million times why Renee was so upset about seeing it. She looked as if she'd seen a ghost. I have no idea why, and of course, she didn't wish to discuss it."

Same words she'd used about Franklin's "bitch" comment.

"Julio Vitiello Sr. owned half Franklin's mine, Chloe," Jack said. "Julio Vitiello is Julio Greene."

She processed that information, and sought verification. "Were Erik and Brit also there?"

Alexa looked as if she wished she didn't have to answer. "They were," she admitted. "Three women were with them. They were dressed like hookers and kept to themselves."

Chloe passed photos to Alexa. "Take a look."

Alexa did. "That's them. Who are they?"

"We believe three Russians who were sold into white slavery."

"Oh, dear God." Alexa cringed. "And Ryan, Erik and Brit are involved?"

Vanessa grunted. "Brit's as twisted as his brother."

Did they think Chloe was as twisted as Erik, too?

Madison touched her arm. "Don't even think it. Wonder Boy is an idiot, but that has nothing to do with you."

The other Rose agents reassured Chloe that they felt the same way, and under the table, Jack squeezed her hand.

"Erik is likely up to his royal neck in this and drowning.

Thanks for not blaming me." Chloe looked at Jack. He, too, knew they were very close to revealing the Duke. He had to be one of the cartel members. And with Renee's reaction to the photo, Chloe suspected she held that key.

"We need to talk to Renee," Jack said.

Chloe hesitated. She was missing something simple but significant and needed a few minutes to get things clear. Talking through it would do that. "First, I need to see Emma."

Chapter 16

On the ride to the G.R.C. to meet with Renee, Jack phoned Harrison for an update on the Governess and looked defeated.

"No word from the abductor?" Chloe whispered.

"No." He glanced over. "Yes, Chloe's with me. Okay." Clearly unhappy, Jack passed the phone. "Harrison."

Chloe bit back a smile. "Hello, Harrison."

"I take it you and Jack have mended fences."

An opportunity to test the waters; Jack was listening avidly. "Sort of. You know how it is. I've been crazy about him since I was a teen. One incident can't negate all that."

"He's giving you fits, eh?" He laughed. "Your cabdriver still hasn't been identified. But the cab was reported stolen just after midnight."

"Oh, thanks for telling me that," she said, acting as if the information were personal. "I enjoyed having dinner with you, too." She avoided looking at Jack. "Mmm, a celebration dinner when this is over?"

Harrison laughed louder. "Give him hell, Princess."

Jack snatched the phone. "*We* would be delighted to join you for dinner when this is over, Harrison," Jack said from between his teeth. "Get off the damn phone and find the Governess."

"Sure. Hey, Jack?"

Chloe could still hear Harrison's words from the phone.

"What?" Now, he was growling.

"If you and Chloe don't get back together—totally, I mean—let me know," he said. "Or if things just don't work out. Or if you decide to see other people. You know what I mean."

"I know exactly what you mean. Don't hold your breath." Jack shut off the phone and tossed it on the seat. "Chloe?"

"Yes, Jack?" she asked, all sweetness and light.

He reached for her hand. "You know you're mine, right?"

"Am I? Really?" Her heart was hungry, but she did have a sliver of pride left.

He pulled over to the curb, pulled her into his arms and kissed her thoroughly, unleashing all the passion he held for her, all the fear and desire and love. She met him with tenderness, with fire, letting him know that she was no longer a child of sixteen but a woman living a leap of faith.

He gasped against her lips. "I love you." Dropping kisses to her jaw, down her neck, he whispered the words she'd craved over and again.

Her hands kneading his back, his sides, slid to his chest. She looked into his eyes. "I love you, too," she whispered, and then kissed him again.

Chloe's cell phone rang. She and Jack groaned, and she answered. "Hello?"

"Did it work?"

Harrison. She smiled. "Like a charm."

"Great. But you need to celebrate later, Chloe. We're about out of time with the Governess. There've been no demands."

If the abductor wasn't making demands, then odds were it was because he already had what he wanted: the Governess. Chances of her safe return were next to nil. "Right." She hung up and looked at Jack.

Her wisest course of action would be to keep her opinions to herself. But Chloe couldn't do it, because if she did and her speaking up could have brought about a positive outcome, the guilt would gnaw at her forever. "I think the Duke has her, Jack," she said quickly, before she could change her mind. "And I think we have him. All roads keep leading back to our favorite suspects, the cartel."

Both she and Jack were pretty damn frustrated, but Chloe pulled out her phone and tried Ashley in Los Angeles. Time to see what she and Rubi Cho were up to. As she dialed, she told Jack, "Harrison says we're about out of time."

"Stands to reason if the cartel is in L.A."

Chloe had failed to reach Ashley at least a dozen times and apparently was going to fail again. No answer. She needed to warn her not to take one of those three private flights back to New York. "Trying her one more time."

When Chloe still got no answer, Jack suggested, "Call Rubi. Ask her to relay a message."

Having to ask Rubi for yet another favor rankled, but Chloe wasn't above it. Not this time. She dialed and waited. When Rubi answered, Chloe said, "It's Chloe, Rubi."

"All's well on the western front."

She sounded half-drunk. Chloe sighed. This, they did not need. "I need to talk to Ashley about the Halloween Ball and her cell is down."

"She forgot to charge it," Rubi said. "Hang on and I'll try to get her. I think—yes, she's still here."

Cold chills ran up Chloe's back. "Is she leaving?"

"Yes. No. Well, sort of. Brit is flying a bunch of us up to Reno to do some gambling."

Shock rippled warnings through Chloe. "Rubi, listen to me. Are you listening to me?" She was singing along with some damn band. "Rubi, listen to me now. Do you understand?"

A pause.

Chloe covered the receiver. "Brit is flying some of them up to Reno to gamble."

"Damn it. He's moving the women." Jack whipped out his cell and dialed a number, quickly sharing the information.

"They haven't left yet, Rubi, right?" Chloe asked.

"Ashley's still here. She was supposed to go with Brit on the first plane, but she's sticking with Erik. She said she had to take care of something first—so she could wait for Erik and the second flight."

Chloe covered the receiver, told Jack, "Brit's in flight. Erik's still on the ground, but taking the second group." Then Chloe asked Rubi, "When did Brit leave?"

"Oh, maybe thirty minutes ago." Rubi stilled, then sobered. "Did you want me to watch him, too?"

"I wanted you to tell me about any private plane trips."

"I thought you just meant with Erik. Is something wrong?"

"I'm not sure. Do you see Ashley? I need to talk to her."

"I'll find her and tell her to call you." Sounding tipsy as hell, Rubi hung up.

Chloe was rattled to the core. "If Brit left that long ago, he could be anywhere now."

Jack put a hand on her arm, gently rubbed it shoulder to elbow. "It's okay. We'll pick them up."

"You'd better tag them to see where they're going or we'll never get those women back."

"We're on it, Chloe." He kept rubbing her arm. "Don't

give up on Erik. He might be on the plane back to New York.
He might not realize…"

"Do you believe that?"

Jack pulled into the hospital parking lot, got out and opened
the door for Chloe before he answered. When he did, regret
burned in his eyes. "We'll have to wait and see. The FBI is monitoring. They got a fix on Rubi's phone when you called her the
first time. They are tagging Brit's flight. I can't predict what Erik
will do any more than you can, but I hope. For you, I hope."

"Just talk straight to me, please," Chloe said. "Do you
believe Erik doesn't realize what he's been doing?"

"No. No, honey, I don't. But with my whole heart, for your
sake, I hope I'm wrong."

His compassion had her blinking back tears. She left the
car, tiptoed and kissed him on the cheek, then hugged him
hard. He wound his arms around her, and she whispered, "My
heart has to fend for itself with you, Jack Quaid." She tucked
her hands under his coat and caressed his back. "I adore you."

"Don't stop." He kissed her, then murmured against her
forehead. "Don't leave me in love without you."

"Never." A rush of joy, warm and bittersweet, swept
through her and she kissed him again.

"Well, it's no wonder you're staying unconscious, Emma."
Chloe squinted against the glaring light shining down on the
bed. "You need my fricking crystal-studded glasses in here,
don't you?"

Chloe saw a string, pulled it, and the bright light dimmed.
"That's better. Now, you have no excuse. You've been lazy long
enough. Wake up. I could use some help on this vile case."

Emma didn't stir. Just lay still and helpless under the white
sheet and blanket.

Chloe pulled the bedside chair closer, looked through the

glass to be sure no one was within earshot. "I've got a real mess on my hands, Emma. Everything keeps leading back to our favorite suspects, and Erik's one of them. Ryan Greene and Brit Carouthers are the others. Marcus was right in there with them, and I think Tatiana was, too. Alan is following the paper trail on that, but I'm ninety-nine percent sure. For a while, Franklin was on the short list, but Jack and I agree that the Duke is too vicious to be him. Still, he's pissed at Renee and that hooks into this…somehow. I haven't quite put that together yet."

Emma didn't move.

"Tatiana's looking really guilty of outing the Roses. She's either been on site or doing the books for the major players on every single assignment. She knew we'd be at Hollow Hill and she did tip off Rubi. Rubi knows too much, and that had to come from Tatiana." Look at all she'd told Jack! "Hell, *she* could even be the Duke. We assumed he was a man, but we don't know it any more than we know the Governess is a woman. Tatiana is certainly smart enough to be the Duke, and we both know it."

The drip into the IV tubing going into Emma's arm was steady and sure. "Emma, your California injury wasn't an accident. This attack wasn't an accident, either. You were targeted. And I think part of the reason is because you and Tatiana were down in Florida with Vanessa. Our favorite suspects were there, and I'm thinking whichever one of them is the Duke thought you were down there looking for him."

Emma didn't move, didn't so much as flutter as she had on previous visits. Chloe again checked to make sure they were alone, and that Mac, who stood his post outside the door, couldn't overhear her. Just in case, she dropped her voice to a whisper and leaned closer to Emma. "Something scared Renee into ordering us to back off. What could have scared her that much? Maybe losing G.R.C., or her place in society? But what could do that? A scandal. But about what?" Chloe sighed, thought about it. Renee loved to party as much as the next person, but she had little time for it, or for more than her obligatory functions. She was a woman passionate about her work, and she was totally dedicated to it.

That, or she's afraid of losing it.

"Emma, things are spiraling out of control. Do you hear me? The Governess ordered me to stay engaged and expanded my assignment, and now she's missing, too."

Chloe shuddered, smoothed the hair back from Emma's face. One dreaded thing was clear. A knot formed in Chloe's chest and throat. She'd refused to believe it, to even seriously consider it. But now she had no choice. "Emma, only one other person was involved on all the missions. Only one."

Someone who should be thrilled because her husband was out of prison and at home, but was nervous and upset. Someone who had always stood strong on principle alone but had caved in a finger-snap on this assignment. Someone who'd sworn every day of her husband's five-year jail sentence that he was innocent and resented the injustice in his incarceration vehemently.

Renee.

And the more Chloe considered the possibility that Renee wanted to get back at the government who had wrongly convicted Preston, the more Chloe believed it possible. But to use women as drug mules, as escorts and white slaves?

That, Chloe could not believe. Still, Renee knew more than she was telling. And that "more" might not be everything, but it was definitely something…

When Chloe entered the waiting room, Jack was talking with Porsche. "These types of injuries can turn on a dime," he said. "They can seem dire one second, then the person wakes up and the whole picture changes."

"Thanks, Jack." Porsche hugged him.

He patted her back, giving her a big brother kind of hug that lacked the caressing Chloe associated with being in his arms. Sweet and compassionate for others, hungry and passionate for her. Worked for her. She smiled.

Jack dropped a kiss to her cheek. "How is she?"

"The same." She looked at Porsche. "Keep the faith," she said, then looped arms with Jack and started walking toward the exit. "It's definitely time to talk with Renee."

"Let's do it."

On the ride to G.R.C., Chloe sifted through all she knew and suspected and many of the puzzle pieces came into focus. Everything, it seemed, tied to everything else.

Two blocks from G.R.C., her cell phone rang. Hoping it was Ashley, she answered. "Hello."

"Chloe, it's Porsche. You need to get back to the hospital right away."

Fear stormed through Chloe and all her muscles locked down. "Is Emma—" Chloe couldn't say it. She couldn't even think it. Emma had to be alive.

"She's conscious, Chloe."

"Oh, thank God." Relief washed through her, and she told Jack. "Turn around. Emma woke up."

Jack whipped a quick left to go around the block. Chloe continued listening to Porsche's report.

"She's fuzzy. Dr. Scoffield's going to evaluate her and let us know her true condition."

"Can she talk?"

"Supposedly," Porsche said. "But she won't speak to anyone until after she talks to you."

"I'm on my way. Does Renee know?"

"Yes—she's here. She walked in about five minutes after you left."

Chloe said goodbye and turned to Jack. "Does this car go any faster?"

"For you, Your Highness, certainly." He stepped harder on the gas.

She laughed, and slapped him on the arm. "Drive, peasant."

He kissed the back of her hand. "Whatever you say. I live to serve, Princess."

Just before turning into the hospital parking lot, Jack turned serious. "What are you thinking?" Chloe asked.

"I'm thinking Ryan Greene is a real Rose lover."

"Well, yeah." Chloe laughed. "Name a deb or heiress he hasn't dated or slept with."

"You." Jack smiled. "You didn't know the first-date story about Julio."

"Okay," she said. "There are a few of us. I'll give you that one. But you know what I mean. He targets Roses."

"He sure does." Jack chewed on his lower lip. "And maybe he does, not because they're debs or heiresses, but so that he stays abreast of Rose activities."

"Tatiana takes care of that for him, I'm sure—especially if she's in his cartel. Hell, with her doing his books, he couldn't hide his activities from her either way. If Ryan's the Duke, Tatiana knows it."

"So say she knows. Why would she keep quiet about it?"

Chloe stiffened. "She's into solidifying her social standing and she's a press darling, Jack. He's the city's most desirable bachelor. It's a PR match made in heaven."

"That wouldn't be enough," Jack countered.

"She has severe princess envy. Ryan elevating her status in society would be more than enough."

"It all fits. She's got to be in on all the Duke is doing. No way around that."

"I agree, but I'm not a fair judge." Chloe fiddled with her

purse strap, needing a distraction to keep her emotions tapped. "I don't like her, and never have. I can't be objective."

Jack searched the rows for a parking slot. "Why don't you like her?"

"Envy doesn't look good on any woman. Not even on a South American knockout dressed in Versace."

Jack nodded. "We've definitely got to talk to Renee before she talks to Emma." Jack pulled into an empty spot and turned off the ignition.

"She's taken care of that for us." *Amazing foresight, Emma. Even coming out of a coma, you've got it together.* "We just have to get in there." Chloe stepped out of the car.

Jack shut his door, glanced up and yelled. "Get down!"

Chloe dropped to the pavement and rolled under the car.

A bullet shattered the headlight.

Glass splattered the ground. Chloe snatched in a sharp breath and pulled her gun from her purse, spilling half its contents. A second bullet hit the asphalt near the bumper. She covered her face with her arm, dodging the spray, scooted backward on her stomach and came out of the car's underbelly at its trunk, then lifted to a crouch.

Jack had moved two cars over, taking cover by a black van.

The gunman bobbed up and aimed.

Chloe fired.

He jerked and tumbled forward, falling over the side of the building and landing on the ground near a concrete bench.

"Stay put," Jack told her. "They usually travel in pairs."

Chloe turned to look and saw the second man one row back, drawing down on Jack.

She fired again. Winged him.

Jack spun around and rapid-fired four bullets.

The man was dead before he hit the ground.

Jack checked the body, then Chloe. "You okay?"

"Freaking fabulous." Standing up, she dusted the dirt and grime from the gray Chanel suit she worn in Emma's honor. She walked over to stare at the man Jack had killed.

Jack phoned in the incident, and then asked Chloe, "Do you know him?"

"He was at the church when Marcus kidnapped me."

They walked over to the building, to where the first man she'd shot lay. "Do you recognize him?" Chloe asked Jack.

"No, do you?"

Shaking, she clicked her tongue. "You will." She reached down and pulled off a really bad brown wig, and then a decent fake mustache. "Recognize him now?"

Jack stared gape-jawed at the corpse of Marcus Abbot Sterling, III. "I don't believe it."

"I know." Chloe had gone to his funeral, still pretending to be his fiancée. She'd mourned him and been determined to find his killer. "But he did go to Ryan for help," she reminded Jack. "Apparently, he got it."

Jack frowned at her. "So…Ryan had his people fake being cops, arrest Marcus, then take him a couple blocks away and cut him loose. Who was handcuffed to the rear door of the police car when it exploded?"

"There was no body left after the explosion, Jack. Only an eyewitness's report that a man had been cuffed to the back door."

Jack looked over to her. "The witness was a plant, too."

"I'd say so," Chloe said. "And I'm sure he was well paid to verify Marcus's faked death."

"Why would Marcus do this?" Jack glanced back at her.

"After he kidnapped me and tried to kill you, life as he'd known it was over. He knew he'd be going to prison for a long time. Only by dying could he live a fabulous life again—and I'll bet Tatiana fixed his finances so that he could do just that.

Which of course, made letting her live even more dangerous
to Marcus *and* Ryan."

"Bring Erik into the cartel, and they up the odds you won't
dig too deep and bring down your baby brother, whom your
parents adore." Jack stared at Marcus's lifeless body. "They
underestimated you, Chloe."

"Most people do." Two police cars turned into the hospital
parking lot and turned off their sirens, but their lights still
flashed. Harrison arrived with them, and Chloe was glad
He'd help slash through the red tape.

He walked over and dropped a kiss to Chloe's cheek just
to annoy Jack. "Glad you're bulletproof, Princess."

"Me, too," she said and meant it. "Thanks for the assist on
this," she whispered, "and with Jack."

Harrison winked. "Anytime."

He worked with the local authorities. By the time Chloe
and Jack filled him in on what they'd deduced, the coroner
arrived and then more officers. Soon the place was buzzing.

Jack got tied up on a phone briefing, and it all kind of hit
Chloe. This assignment, with all its tentacles, was a lot for a
woman faking it to handle—especially a cowardly woman
who was not strong or brave or smart. Certain she'd still be
shaking when she died of old age, she waited for Jack, and
then they went in to see Emma.

"Well, finally she decides to wake up."

Emma smiled through the bruises on her face. "Back off
bitch," she said, her voice stilted. "Hurts."

"I'm sure it does," Chloe said. "You're pretty banged up."

"No mirrors." She lifted a hand. "Tells me...needed
beauty sleep."

"Yeah, but you'll heal." Chloe looked for somewhere to
touch Emma that wasn't bruised.

"Promise?" Vulnerability shone in her eyes.

"I swear it." Chloe gently squeezed her uninjured hand.

"Sorry I'll miss your Halloween Ball."

"You won't. Frank will video it for you," Chloe said. "Who pulled this number on you?"

"Not sure," Emma said through swollen lips. "Mask."

Chloe shoved back her disappointment that Emma couldn't identify her attacker. "Male or female?"

"Male." She paused and sucked in a sharp breath. "Hurts." She swallowed hard. "Grabbed me…from a cab."

That sounded damn familiar. "Tatiana, too?"

"No. She wasn't there."

"Jack saw her. She was lying beside you, beaten."

"No. Not her," Emma said. "Sister of Russian. Tatiana ran. Duke tried to kill her."

"Do you know who the Duke is?"

"No." Emma struggled to stay awake.

"So much has happened." Chloe closed the door, then walked back to the hospital bed.

"I know. Been awake," she said with effort. "Faking it."

"Faking a coma?" Chloe couldn't believe it.

"Safer." She paused to catch her breath. "Dr. Scoffield helped. Two attempts here to kill me, but the guard—who is he?"

"Mac Dayton. FBI. Harrison brought him in." Chloe looked at the man's back. "Frank and Lucas like him."

"Harrison?"

"Mr. Brooks Brothers."

"Mac is…very good." Again she paused.

Chloe frowned. "He hasn't reported any attempts, Emma."

"Parents hired guard, too. Outside unit. Mac warned other guard…coming. Both times. Felt it. Bones." Emma twisted on the sheets. "He reported."

"Harrison and I should have gotten the word."

"Renee said don't sidetrack you. The Duke."

Renee had some damn explaining to do. Chloe forced the tightness out of her jaw. "What happened?"

"Julio Greene in Renee's photo."

The one Alexa mentioned. "I know," Chloe said. "Why is it significant?"

"Colombia," Emma said with a great deal of effort. "Drunk driver witnessed shooting. Parents yanked her out of country."

"Oh, *damn.*" The truth slammed Chloe right between the eyes. "Renee was the driver." Her parents had yanked her and Olivia out of Colombia and they'd both left the Peace Corps. "That's why Franklin cursed Renee when she took off like a shot, driving without her seat belt." Chloe spun out the scenario. "Marcella came to Franklin with Julio. Then she and Julio's brother disappeared in Europe."

"Julio can't find them," Emma said. "Always searching."

"So all of the Roses' assignments have stemmed from that incident. The Duke wants the nerve-damage repair technology for Julio. And he wants Renee and everyone around her to suffer because of Julio's injury and the loss of his family." Damn it, it all seemed so clear now.

"That's right, Chloe," Renee said from behind her.

Chloe spun around. "Renee."

"You're right. I was the driver. I was drunk. I witnessed Julio's father's murder. And I was terrified the drug lords would kill me, too, so I ran."

"Why didn't you report this to the Governess?" Chloe asked.

Renee didn't answer.

"She already knew it," Chloe guessed. "Could that be why the Duke abducted her?"

Tears slid down Renee's cheeks. "I believe so."

"Do you have any idea where she is?"

"No." Renee fisted her hand. "I wish I did, but I don't."

"Who is the Duke, Renee?" Chloe asked. "And don't tell me you don't know. Not telling us all you knew got Emma worked over and almost killed. It cost her the piano. And I've been shot at so much I should be a fricking sieve."

Renee looked at Emma and tears poured down her cheeks. "I am so sorry, darling. I wanted to protect you both by short circuiting the assignment before it started. But things went out of control."

Emma lifted her good arm. Renee stepped closer, and Emma hugged her. She met Chloe's eyes above Renee's bent head. "It'll be okay, Renee. You'll see. Chloe will fix it." And the look in Emma's eyes told Chloe she damn well better.

Chloe held Emma's eyes. She should be outraged—she'd lost being a pianist—but if she was, it wasn't directed at Renee. In Emma's eyes, Chloe saw the great healer Lucas mentioned at Perrini's: forgiveness.

It was humbling.

Renee straightened up, snagged a tissue from the box on the bedside table and dabbed at her eyes.

"Renee, it's long past time for the truth. If you know it, tell me." Chloe searched Renee's face. "Who is the Duke?"

She lifted a shoulder. "I thought Franklin, but he's not."

"Is it Erik?" Chloe asked. Her insides quivered. *Please, no. Please.*

"No. No, I'm sure Erik isn't the Duke." Renee sniffed. "Erik didn't come into the cartel until after Marcus died."

Obviously Jack hadn't told Renee in the waiting room that Marcus had only died minutes ago. Ryan *had* to be the Duke. He helped Marcus fake his death. He brought Erik into the cartel. Tatiana was close to him, not to Julio or to Franklin.

Still, while Franklin had been discounted, Julio had not.

"It's one of the Greenes," Chloe said. "They hired the guy to wire my cars, and they've tried to kill Emma three times."

Renee's eyes widened in shock. "*Three* times?"

"Four," Emma said. "But who's counting?"

"Sweet heaven." Renee frowned. "I believe the Duke is one of the Greenes, but not Franklin."

"Don't parse words with me," Chloe warned her. "If not Franklin, then who? Ryan or Julio?"

"I swear I don't know." Looking puzzled, Renee sniffed. "Why am I smelling peppermint?"

"Jacques sent me a jar of peppermint butter from LaBella." Emma flipped a fingertip toward her toes. "For my feet."

Peppermint. Chloe stilled. The night Emma had been injured, Erik and Ryan had come to the hospital—Erik with roses. But Chloe had smelled peppermint. Emma and Tatiana had had peppermint foot treatments that day…

"Chloe, what is it?"

She looked at Emma, then at Renee. "I know who he is."

"The Duke?" Renee asked.

Chloe nodded.

Chapter 17

Chloe smiled at Porsche, who sat next to Emma's mother, their hands clasped in a death grip. "She's okay."

"You swear?" Porsche's eyes were bright with unshed tears.

Chloe crossed her heart, and then snagged Jack.

Frank stood up, his eyes full of questions. Chloe spoke to him first. "You go in with Emma, Frank," she said. "Do not leave her, and don't let anyone get close to her with a needle or anything else unless it's Dr. Scoffield himself." She passed him her gun.

"Damn right." He tucked the gun inside his suit jacket.

"Tonight, you get Mac to take your place. I promised Emma you'd video the Halloween Ball so she wouldn't miss anything."

That edict worried him. "You sure, Princess?"

She nodded. "He's saved her twice, Frank, and she trusts him. Give him the same instructions I've given you. She's awake now and that makes her more vulnerable." She looked from Jack to Frank, who nodded that he'd do what she said. "Go now, Frank." He turned, and she told Jack, "Come. I'll explain on the way." She headed toward the elevators.

He followed her. "Where are we going?"

"To the Halloween Ball—eventually." When they got outside, she got specific. "Renee verified she was the drunk driver who injured Julio," Chloe said, and then relayed the discussion that had taken place inside ICU with Emma and Renee.

Jack scanned the parking lot. "So where are we going now?"

"Gotham Rose Club," Chloe said, wary that the Duke might have sent in backup assassins, too. The police were still on the premises, but she didn't fool herself into believing he'd let that slow him down. He *had* to kill to save his own neck now. "Tatiana knows the Duke's identity. Emma says she ran."

"Then why are we going to G.R.C.?"

"Because we have to get ready for the ball, and because Alan can satellite-track Tatiana by her Rose pin."

"I doubt she's wearing it now when it's been inactive since she went missing, Chloe."

"You don't understand. She most likely deactivated the pin because she was at risk. If she hasn't been sold with the other women, once she's safe, she'll want the Roses to know it."

"Not if she's part of the cartel."

"She thinks she's too smart to be tied to the cartel. She just does their books. If her pin isn't active, then Alan can contact Tatiana's family. They'll know where she is."

"If she's in hiding, honey, they won't tell you. She won't want you to know."

"Oh, but she will, darling." Chloe nodded, adding weight to the claim. "She is in hiding, and she knows that if she doesn't reveal herself, the Rose agents will search for one of their own until hell freezes."

"I get it." The truth dawned in Jack's eyes. "In trying to rescue her, the Rose agents will lead the Duke right to her."

"Exactly."

Jack parked in G.R.C.'s private garage. Limousines were bumper to bumper, lining the street—Gotham Roses getting ready for the ball. Chloe released her seat belt. "Why hasn't Rubi called back?"

"Good question." Jack checked his watch.

Chloe phoned Rubi, but got no answer. "She's supposed to be back to cover the ball, Jack. Something's wrong."

"What do you want to do?"

Chloe tried Ashley, but her phone was still out of service. It should have recharged by now. As a last-ditch resort, Chloe dialed again, this time a different number, and this time, not sure she wanted an answer.

He picked up. "Hello."

"Erik, it's Chloe." The background noise was deafening. "Where are you?"

"On a plane, heading back to New York."

Her skin crawled. "You'll be at the ball, right?"

"Absolutely, we will."

"We?" God, she didn't want to have to ask.

"A group of us were in L.A. to celebrate Ryan's latest property acquisition. We land in about thirty minutes." He laughed. "I can barely hear you."

She believed that. Shouts and laughter carried through the phone. They were having one hell of a party on board the plane. "I asked who all is with you?"

"Ryan, Ashley and a couple others. Oh," his voice turned devilish, "and your favorite reporter."

Rubi. Chloe closed her eyes and whispered a silent word of gratitude. They hadn't been caught up in the slave-trade sales or he definitely wouldn't be naming them. "Don't be late."

"I won't." He laughed. "Chelsea would kill me."

If what Chloe suspected was true, she might have to wait in line. "Bye." She clicked Off, then told Jack, "They're with him. Thirty minutes out from New York."

"Did he mention Ryan or Brit?"

"Ryan, yes." She got out of the car and walked into Renee's brownstone. "Brit, no."

Olivia took their coats. "Emma's okay?"

"She's fine." Chloe smiled. "How are things here?"

"Busy, as usual. Samantha and Alexa have taken over preparations for you, and Becca is on her way in to help."

Jack touched Chloe's arm. "I'm going to take a quick shower and change while you meet with Alan. Be back in a flash." He headed up the grand staircase that Chloe believed led to Renee's private quarters.

Chloe nodded at Olivia, spoke briefly to a few of the non-agent Roses who were ready for the ball, then made her way to the closet and finally the secret rooms below street level.

Kristi was dressing Madison. "Have you seen Porsche?"

"She's at the hospital with Emma. She'll be here soon."

"Is Emma—?"

Chloe smiled. "She's okay."

Relief flashed across Kristi's face. "God, if I'd had to hear 'no change' one more time, I think I'd throw up. I *hate* those words."

"Don't we all?" Chloe said and meant it. "Where's Alan?"

"Lab," she said around straight pins clenched in her teeth.

Chloe walked down to Alan's lab. He was dressed and ready for the ball in a great-looking tux. "Wow. You look awesome."

"Thanks." He smiled. "Glad to hear Emma's awake."

"Me, too," Chloe said. "I need for you to activate Tatiana's tracker. Emma says she ran. I need to know where."

"I've tried it off and on ever since she went missing, Chloe. It's dead."

"Try again, okay?" She shrugged. "Circumstances have changed."

He keyed something into his computer, and surprised, looked at Chloe. "It's active. She's in South America."

Satisfied, Chloe nodded. "Turn it off and lose the coordinates, Alan."

He looked shocked. "Why?"

Chloe gave him a deadpan look. "Because if the Duke finds her, he's going to kill her. And he is looking for her."

Jack came in just in time to hear that order. "Shouldn't we contact her first?"

"She activated her Rose pin," Chloe said. "She's not running from us, she's running from him. If we contact her, he'll know it. She'll be dead before we can say hello."

Jack nodded. "Where can she go that he can't find her?"

"There is no place," Chloe said. "Tatiana will be running until she draws her last breath—unless we bring him down."

As Alan deleted the coordinates, Chloe watched the screen. Tatiana wasn't a bad person; she just had screwed-up priorities. Somewhere along the way, someone had convinced her that what a woman was inside wasn't enough. She had to hold this special place in society, have all the right moves and looks and attitudes, or she wouldn't be accepted. Maybe there was a grain of truth in that, but it wasn't all of the truth. The inner woman was the one who mattered. The rest was just window dressing for her. In their circle, it was very glamorous, very fashionable window dressing, but still only window dressing.

The screen went blank.

Jack nudged Chloe's arm. "You'd better get dressed, or we'll be late for the ball."

Nodding, Chloe left and returned to the dressing area suites. She showered, styled her hair, did her makeup and slipped into the silver crepe Adelphio gown that Adele had designed just for this event. It clung to Chloe's every curve, draped perfectly. Chloe put on silver strappy Jimmy Choo heels—afraid to jinx her good luck until the cartel was in custody—and flecked a few silver sparkles on her cheek and shoulder.

The look in Jack's eyes was worth the extra effort she'd taken dressing.

"I have to say, Princess, you clean up nice."

"Is that your best pick-up line, peasant?" She lifted her nose.

"Unless you want to skip the ball, yeah, pretty much." He smiled and a sexy teasing light flickered in his eyes. "Beautiful…shoes."

"Aren't they divine?" She twisted her ankle to give him a better view of the spiked heels. "Jimmy Choo."

"Of course."

"Dual purpose. They make my legs and ass look great—"

"I'll vouch for that."

"And they're awesome for kicking out windshields, plastic barriers, front teeth—"

"Front teeth?"

"Samantha knocked out the front eight on the guy Marcus hired to bury you in the concrete foundation at Eleanor Towers."

"Love those Jimmy Choos." He pecked a kiss to her cheek. "Adele outdid herself on that dress."

Enormously pleased, Chloe smiled. "She did, didn't she?"

A flustered Olivia rushed up to Chloe and Jack. "Before Tatiana went to find Emma and disappeared, she gave this envelope to Samantha and told her to give it to you right away, Chloe. Samantha couldn't find you and so she intended to just give it to you at the ball. Then she got here and discovered we've been searching madly for Tatiana and gave it to me to pass on."

"Did she say anything else?" Chloe took the envelope and broke the gold wax seal bearing Tatiana's initial.

"Only that she was sorry, and she had to go."

"Tell Renee to work up a cover story," Chloe said. "Tatiana won't be back."

"Won't be back?" Olivia frowned. "Why not?"

"Personal reasons." Chloe slid the stiff card out of the envelope.

"All right." Olivia silently returned to her office.

Jack adjusted his tie, waited.

Chloe read the card. *"The Towers?"*

"The building where Madison's uncle Bing was killed?"

"Yes." Madison's best friend, Claire, too. "Oh, my God." Chloe grabbed her evening bag and headed for Alan's lab. "Hurry, Jack."

He chased after her. "What is it?"

"It's the building Ryan Greene wanted so badly he could taste it, but Madison—well, Pruitt & Pruitt, but Madison handled it—beat him out of it. The one building Erik said screwed up Ryan's 100% success rate with the cartel. Renovations haven't begun and it's currently empty—the perfect place to hold someone where no one would be around." Chloe entered the lab, saw Alan sitting at the computer. "Alan. Serious weapons. *Now.*"

In minutes and without question, Alan had Chloe and Jack outfitted with enough weapons to take down a small country. "Thanks," Chloe told him. "Not a word to anyone."

"Not even Renee?"

"No one." Chloe nodded. "I'm not positive that Tatiana was our only leak."

Bitterness burned in his eyes, but he nodded his agreement "You should look at Fluffy Peters's report. It came in the day Emma was attacked."

"We will. Vanessa suggested that," Chloe said, then headed upstairs.

Jack followed Chloe up to street level. "Whatever you've got in mind for us to attack, this has got to be overkill."

She frowned. How could he not realize what they were about to be up against? "I just hope we've got enough."

"Chloe, what exactly do you expect to find?"

Upstairs, she held up a wait-a-minute finger, then grabbed a full-length black velvet coat. "Olivia, I need a copy o. Fluffy's report."

Olivia pulled the report and passed it to Chloe.

"Well?" Jack asked.

Chloe finished scanning. "She heard someone was fun neling women through Hong Kong." Chloe grimaced. "Julic has studied international law," she told Jack. "He told me at the auction that he's overseeing Franklin's interests in Hong Kong."

"There's the connection," Jack said. He pulled out his cel and called Harrison.

Chloe turned back to Olivia. "Check travel to Hong Kong on Franklin, Ryan, and Julio Greene. Also on Erik and Bri Carouthers. Actually, make it any travel to the Far East in the last six months."

"You want me to do that now?" Olivia sounded frantic "Before the ball?"

"I'm sorry, but I need to know immediately," Chloe said "Call the info in to my cell."

She nodded. "Okay."

Chloe turned for the front door. "Jack, you've got to d

something about your memory. I know you read the files, and you should know what all this means."

"There were a lot of files, Princess, and you were wearing that slinky French robe." He shrugged on his own coat. "So spare me, and just tell me what you think all this means."

"Darling, I adore you." She smiled. "I didn't realize until this very moment that you *need* me." Chloe smiled, feeling absolutely great. Positively, absolutely great. Maybe better.

"Granted. I need you more than life itself," he said, irked and baffled. "Now what the hell are you talking about?"

Chloe turned and stared at him. "Tatiana *was* the G.R.C. leak to the Duke. She *did* know the Duke's identity. And she's just told us where he's holding the Governess. At the Towers."

"Tatiana to the Governess is a leap. A gargantuan leap."

"I feel it in my bones." That's how she found Emma. How she'd known so much of the specifics on this assignment before it had been verified. So maybe her bones weren't as reliable as Emma's, but they were proving damned indispensable to her. "Where's the silver demon?"

"I had it switched out for my Lamborghini." He pointed half a block down to the black demon.

"Keys." She held out her hand.

He dropped them into her palm, and she grabbed his sleeve, stopped and took off her heels. "Run."

Inside the car, Chloe cranked the engine and buckled up.

"Be careful," Jack said. "This car has a lot of power."

"Great." She stomped the gas and left a quarter-inch of tire tread on the pavement. "We've got to get there before Tatiana gets a conscience and thinks she can better her survival odds by telling the Duke we know where the Governess is."

Jack tightened his seat belt. "Right."

Chloe spared him a glance. "Don't you trust me?"

"Chloe, the car was made to stay on the road, not fly."

He grabbed the dash in a death-grip. "Slow down to warp speed, okay?"

She laughed and went faster. Luckily traffic was moving as they passed through Central Park and eventually got on the West Side Highway. "It's okay. Jimmy's trained me in high-speed and evasive driving."

"I hope to hell you attended those sessions."

"That is so not fair."

Her cell rang just after they crossed the George Washington Bridge and hit the exit ramp leading to the Towers. "Hello."

"Oh, God." Jack rubbed at his forehead. "Now she's going to fly *and* talk on the phone."

Chloe shot him a frown and held it so he wouldn't miss it.

"Chloe, it's Olivia."

She zipped past a Mercedes and cut into the right lane between a green SUV and a white limo. "What did you find out?"

"In the past six months, Ryan and Brit have been to Hong Kong three times—all private flights I found through the filed flight plans. Julio's been once—commercial."

"What about Erik?"

"He wasn't on any of the manifests, Chloe, and there was nothing on his passport records. So far as I can tell, he's never been to the Far East."

Then he really couldn't be the Duke. Not that he'd be lily white in all this, but he might not know what the cartel was doing. Ryan could be keeping Erik legitimate: a front that solidified the cartel's upstanding reputation. Knowing Erik, he hadn't questioned anything Ryan told him. If it raised his cash flow, he was for it. That both relieved her and pissed her off. She'd warned him to stay away from Brit. Now it appeared, she should have warned him—and the Roses—to stay away from Ryan, too. Erik wasn't absolved, but it didn't appear that he was up to his crown in dirty deals with the Duke. "Thanks, Olivia."

"Um, Chloe, wait," Olivia said. "Renee is here, and she wants to know where you are. She thinks you're late."

No way. No handwriting apologetic notes for her. Not on this. "Tell her Jack and I are following a hot lead and Samantha, Alexa and Becca have taken over the ball." Since Chloe was sponsoring the Halloween Ball, it was her duty to prime the Roses and make sure everything was perfect on site. But this was far more important, and Renee would intuit it. Chloe made an instant, instinctive decision. "Tell her about Tatiana's note."

"Will do." Olivia hesitated. "Be careful."

"I will." She hung up and relayed the information to Jack.

"Erik's in, Chloe. Not in the worst of it, but some. I know it's hard to swallow, but—"

"I know." She turned off the headlights, drove down the road to the building, and then pulled up to the fence surrounding the Towers. According to Madison's report, there had been a Doberman on the loose here. The dog guarded against looters.

They got out of the car and Chloe lifted the hem of her gown and tucked it into the waist of her pantyhose; not very glamorous, but damned effective at keeping the dress out of her way. She strapped a Glock to her right thigh, a six-inch sheathed blade to her left, then put a small brick of C-4 into her fanny pack and looped it at her waist. With her favorite stun gun in her right hand, she whispered to Jack, "Ready."

"Move out." He headed for the fence.

"Doberman alert," she whispered, scaling the fence. "Madison's previous report. No sighting."

"Gone." Jack landed on the ground beside her. "Also noted in that previous report."

"Missed that."

He smiled. "Guess you need me, too."

"Guess so." She signaled that she'd enter the building, leaving Jack with the critical job of keeping clear egress. When he nodded, she moved in.

It was pitch black inside. Chloe reached in her fanny pack for a pair of night-vision goggles that looked like Gucci sunglasses and slid them onto her nose. The floors hadn't yet been put in above her head; she could see straight through to the roof. The first floor was stacked with bundles of shingles, pallets of two-by-fours and metal and PVC pipes that would likely become part of the plumbing system. She skirted down a long row of wood pallets stacked with sheets of plywood and Sheetrock.

Something metal clanged ahead to her left.

She stopped and listened. *Silence.* Sweat beaded on her forehead, at her temples, and fear flushed her with heat.

Just do it, Chloe. Fear is okay. It's not cowardice. It's healthy. Bravery isn't the absence of fear…

Her own voice. Not Emma's, not Renee's, not Frank's or Jack's. *Her own voice.* Awed, she stilled. *Focus. Focus!* She slowly worked her way up the rows to the edge of the pallet, then peeked around the corner.

Her heart beat so hard she was certain it was signaling satellites all over the universe. A battery-powered light sat on the floor next to a straight-back wooden chair. A woman sat tied in it.

Senator Ellie Richardson.

But Harrison had reported that Ellie was fine. He'd said she'd taken a few days off to work out some issues. Well, hell, these were issues, all right. Being abducted was one whale of an issue!

Had he been protecting her identity as the Governess? Or knocking out false leads to keep every nutcase in the country from claiming responsibility? Did this mean Ellie was, or wasn't, the Governess?

Could be either. Chloe looked around, certain Ellie would

be guarded, but she saw no one. She moved closer, then closer, up to the last stack of two-by-fours: the one remaining barrier between her and Ellie. She couldn't be alone here. Every ounce of training warned her that was impossible. Yet Chloe hadn't gotten a fix on anyone else near Ellie.

Ellie stiffened, snapped to alert. Sniffed, then sniffed again. "Chloe," she whispered. "Is that you?" She darted her gaze into the darkness but didn't see her. "Answer me. I recognize your perfume."

Her signature fragrance, *Remember Me.* Some habits could be helpful. "It's me." She didn't move into the light. "Are you alone?"

"No," she said aloud. "Two men. One was just here."

Wind rushed behind her long before the man got close. She spun around, dropkicked a metal fitting that collided with the man's forehead, and then hit the concrete with a reverberating clang. Before he clasped his forehead, she fired the stun gun against his back.

He fell to the ground. "Where's the other one, Ellie?"

"Outs—"

Gunshots fired, sounding like firecrackers. *Jack!*

Chloe rushed to Ellie, pulling her knife and slashing at the ropes tying her hands and ankles to the chair. Returning the knife to its sheath, she helped Ellie shed the ropes and gave her a quick once-over. She looked haggard, but not bruised or battered. "You okay?"

"I am now." The spunky senator smiled. "The bastards were going to sell me, Chloe. I discovered the Duke's identity."

More gunfire.

Chloe passed the stun gun to Ellie, then pulled out her Glock. "Stay close. Right behind me. No talking."

Ellie nodded, her eyes overly bright.

Chloe wanted to know specifically which bastards, but

Jack needed backup now. Cautiously, she led Ellie to the door, using the stacks of lumber as cover. But the door stood open, and she knew damn well she'd closed it behind her. The man she'd stunned couldn't have opened it before she'd taken him down. He'd been close to Ellie; he hadn't had time.

Switching to evasive tactics, Chloe took a circuitous route to a window on the opposite side of the building. It was also on the opposite side of the building from the car, but their odds of getting out undetected and without gunfire were much higher.

On the last point before the window, she moved—and nearly collided with a man. Instinctively, she lifted her elbow and jabbed, hitting him full in the chest.

He sputtered. "Damn it, Chloe."

Jack! He was okay. *Thank God.* "Stunned one, one loose." She fired off a report.

"He's dead," Jack said. "Outside."

"That's it, then," Ellie said. "There were only two."

Jack blinked hard. "Ellie? What are you doing here? Where's the Governess?"

Damn. Chloe felt the disappointment down to her toes.

"Charming, Jack. I'm afraid I don't know where she is." Ellie smiled. "But thank you for helping me, anyway."

"I didn't mean it that way. I just expected her." Jack turned and led them out. "This way."

"I know," Ellie said, letting Jack off the hook. "Chloe, I need your cell phone, please."

She passed it to Ellie, who dialed. "Harrison? Oh, good. Get a team to the Towers STAT. Madison Pruitt's new building, on the Jersey side." She paused. "Oh, you did?" She smiled and excitement filled her voice. "He's found the Governess," she told Chloe and Jack. "Is she all right?" Ellie's smile returned. "Fabulous. Did you catch—"

Her smile disappeared. "Well, keep after it, then. No, I won't be here. You've got one D.O.A. and one stunned, so don't linger getting here." A pause, and then she added, "I'm going to the Roses' Halloween Ball." She listened for a long time, and her expression turned serious. "Then I shall be fashionably late to give you time to serve those warrants before I put in an appearance. But I will not give that son of a bitch the pleasure of getting any press on this."

So Ellie clearly trusted Harrison. When she passed Chloe her phone, she asked, "So Harrison works for you?"

"On special assignments for me and the Governess and half my committee."

So Ellie really wasn't the Governess. But the Governess's specialists in dignitary abductions had rescued her, and that was the important thing.

Outside, Jack cut an opening in the fence and they all climbed through and then got into the car.

Jack didn't offer Chloe an option to drive. She supposed he'd had enough excitement for one night.

She settled into the front passenger's seat, then looked back at Ellie. "What son of a bitch are we talking about—*exactly?*"

"We need to move," Jack said, seeing the sweeper's van coming down the street toward them. "Where to?" Jack said, hitting the gas.

"The G.R.C.," Chloe said, seeing Harrison drive pass, going in the opposite direction. "Ellie has to dress for the ball."

"You're seriously up for that, Senator?"

"I am now," she said. "Chloe, please call Renee and tell her I'm all right."

So she trusted Renee, too. And Renee had known she was still missing. Not at all surprised, Chloe made the call and heard Renee's excited squeal. Smiling, she asked the senator again, "What son of a bitch specifically abducted you?"

"Ryan Greene. He's the Duke."

"I knew it." Chloe's stomach clutched. "I just knew it. He

loved the Roses a little too much, you know? You were right, Jack. The bastard didn't want the Roses, he wanted to stay as close as possible to know what the Rose agents were doing."

"Actually, he wanted both," Ellie said. "And tons of press on what a good guy he was so no one would believe even the most indisputable evidence of all the wicked things he did as the Duke. But we've got him now."

Chloe had to ask. She feared the answer so much she could taste it, but she had to know. "How deeply is Erik involved?"

Regret filled her eyes. "I'm afraid Erik was at the Towers, Chloe. I saw him myself."

She was going to be sick. She'd hoped for her parents' sake he'd been the legitimate front, but... Tears clogged her throat. "I'm—I'm so sorry, Ellie."

"Chloe, no." Ellie leaned forward and clasped her arm. "Erik is responsible. You risked your life to save me, and you did."

"She thinks she's a coward," Jack told Ellie.

Shock rippled across Ellie's face. "You've had four years of very successful assignments. And, believe me, the woman who just dropped that armed ape was no coward."

What Ellie had said hit Chloe hard. "How do you know I've had four years of successful assignments?" She *had* to be the Governess. The mirrored events just kept piling on.

"I sit on the Armed Services Committee. I have access to all Intel reports. Of course I know." She smiled.

But there was something in her eye. Chloe saw it and recognized it, and kept her mouth firmly shut.

"You were right to insist Renee is innocent, by the way," Ellie said.

Chloe looked back at Ellie. "I had my doubts," she admitted shamefully, "but she just wouldn't do what the Duke is doing."

Ellie's voice turned tender. "You love her like a mother. That made suspecting her at all difficult, but you did what you had to do, and I'm proud of you, Chloe."

"Don't be proud," she said. "I hated every second of it."

"I'm most proud of that," Ellie said. "It proves you've earned all the medals you won't be getting."

"What?" Jack looked baffled.

Ellie rolled her gaze. "She's undercover. I can't give her the medals she deserves without outing her. But everyone who matters will know she earned them, including you, Jack."

"Yes, ma'am." He pulled up to Gotham Rose Club.

"Ellie, you owe me one," Chloe said. "I want to collect."

"What do you want?" she asked simply.

"Do something—something significant—to stop this black market white-slave trade."

"I will." Ellie looked her right in the eye with a conviction that matched Chloe's. "You have my word on that—and that's not a politician's promise. You can count on it."

"I am counting on it, and I'll be watching."

Ellie smiled. "I'd expect no less."

Chloe debated bringing this up, decided she had to, then plunged in. "I think Renee knew why the Duke was after us."

"She knew the Duke had targeted Roses because she was responsible for Julio's accident. She didn't know which Greene was the Duke," Ellie said. "Actually, she suspected Franklin, and so did I—for a time."

"It's a painful time in her history." Chloe sigh. "She often mentions how relentless guilt is."

"She's lived with it all of her adult life. Sometimes it ravages. Sometimes it nags. But it's always there."

"Then let's not mention it again," Chloe said, obscurely warning her that it wouldn't be in Chloe's report.

"Agreed."

Chloe nodded. Renee had done so much for her, for such a long time. Chloe now fully understood what Renee had meant about never being able to run from consequences. She was right about that. But Lucas was right, too, about the power of forgiveness to heal. You can forgive others and yourself, and accept small moments of grace that come your way. For Renee, this would be a small moment of grace and Chloe hoped that, in it, she found peace.

Frank met them in the G.R.C. parking garage, near the door. "I'll park her for you, Jack. Best get these ladies inside or they're going to be late for the ball."

"How is Emma, Frank?"

"She's fine. Mac and Perry are with her." Frank smiled. "She says I'd best not miss a thing with that video camera or I won't be getting my damn coffee for a month."

He loved it. "Do you need extra tapes?"

"Got 'em," he said. "Picked up a dozen on the way over. That should do it."

Frank was thrilled. Doing something special for his girls. Chloe grinned. "Damn right."

He slid behind the wheel and took off.

Renee came running out and grabbed Ellie in a hug, then ushered her inside, where she and Olivia fluttered around her, giving her everything Chloe expected Ellie most needed.

Standing next to the fireplace, Chloe held out her hands to absorb the heat and sighed.

"What's wrong?" Jack asked. "You seem disappointed."

"Honestly, I am." She watched the firelight play on his face. "I just *knew* Ellie was the Governess, but now…"

"She's not."

"You have to say that." She tapped his chest.

Teasing twinkled in his eyes. "She's a politician, Chloe."

"Yes, darling, she is. But you're not." She hugged him. "Is everything set for the takedown?"

He nodded. Arrest orders for Ryan and Erik have been issued. But Brit Caulfield is out of the country."

The FBI was tagging him to take down the chain rather than just his link. "Let me guess," she said in disgust. "Hong Kong."

Jack nodded. "They'll handle it from here on out."

"When will they make the arrests?"

"At the ball."

She cringed. "Damn it, Jack. I spent months planning that ball, and now it's going to be—"

"The hottest topic of conversation this year."

"But for all the wrong reasons." Still, Chloe supposed she'd have to give Rubi a tip not to be late or leave early. She owed her that for watching out for Erik, not that it had done any good.

"Chloe!" Ellie came running down the stairs. "Chloe, where are the women? Why weren't the women found?"

"We think they're on a plane to Hong Kong with Brit Carouthers," Chloe said. "We don't know exactly where they're going, so we have to wait—"

"No, no, no." She emphatically denied it. "Greene told Erik where they were to be held. He told him!" She squeezed her eyes shut. "I heard it, damn it." Muttering, she tried sounds, and tested words, trying to trigger her memory. "Hell's hill...or something like that."

"Hollow Hill?" Chloe asked.

"That's it!" Ellie clapped her hands together. "I'm certain of it. Do you know this place?"

"It's where we found Emma."

"They wouldn't put them in a room," Jack said. "We'd have caught that, and they know we'll search because we've done it."

An odd thought crossed her mind. She looked at Jack, wide-eyed. "How did Hollow Hill get its name?"

Olivia answered. "There's a city under it. The hill is actually hollow."

"Oh, God." Chloe and Jack hit the door in a dead run.

Chapter 18

Harvey Walker stood behind the front desk. Upon seeing Jack and Chloe approach him, his smile faded.

That suited Chloe just fine. She wasn't smiling, either. She leaned against the desk. "I'm going to ask you once. Only once," she warned him. "Where are the women?"

"I—I—" he sputtered.

She held up a finger. "Only once, Harvey, then you're going down—and I don't mean by arrest." She nodded to her hand, tucked inside her purse.

His eyes widened. "But you're a cop. You can't—"

She pulled her lips back from her teeth. "I'm a princess, and I'll do any damn thing I please." Finally, a use for her title.

Fear filled his eyes. "This way."

They followed him down a hallway, through a door marked Employees Only, then down a flight of stairs. "This is as far as I go," he said. "You know they'll kill me."

"So will I, and I'll do it now." Chloe pulled out her gun. "Dead is dead, Harvey. I suggest you give us directions."

"Down there." He pointed down the hallway, then ran.

Heavy doors lined both sides of the walls. A lock hung outside every door. "Jack, we'd better call for backup—"

"Already there, honey." The phone was in his hand. "Start blowing the locks."

Chloe listened at a door—*silence*—then moved to the next one. Still nothing. "If you can hear me, scream," she shouted.

A din of voices rose—all female.

She and Jack followed the sounds down the corridor to the eighth door. "Back up," Chloe ordered, then repeated it in Russian. "Get away from the door. I'm going to open it." She glanced at Jack. "C-4 or gun?"

"Gun. Less collateral damage."

She nodded, took aim. "Stay back." She gave the women a little longer to move out of harm's way, and then fired.

The lock cracked and fell to the floor. Her heart hammering, Chloe lifted her Jimmy Choo and kicked the door open.

And twenty women, including Rubi Cho and Ashley Thompson, spilled out into the corridor—all wearing Chloe's Vera Wang outfits. Well that explained why Gerard hadn't returned her clothes. Unfortunately, it also proved something significant.

"Oh, Chloe. Thank you." Rubi sniffed. "I'm going to kill that bastard brother of yours."

"He did this?" Disappointment and outrage warred in Chloe.

"The whole damn plane of us. We were coming back to New York for the ball. He and Ryan Greene held us at gunpoint!" Her shock was significant.

It's hell to watch your hero fall, and Ryan had been Rubi's hero. "I'm so sorry, Rubi."

She nodded. "How did you find us?"

"Jack found you. I'm just along for the ride."

Rubi dipped her chin, glanced at the Glock in Chloe's hand, and then looked into her eyes. "Whatever you say."

"Thanks." Chloe pressed a kiss to her cheek. "I'm glad you're all right."

"I'll be all right when I see those two bastards behind bars." She checked her watch. "Damn it. Ashley, come on. We're going to be late."

"Late?" Chloe stood stunned. "For what?" Didn't the woman realize she had to give a statement?

"The Halloween Ball," Rubi said. "I'm not missing it."

"Me, either," Ashley said, her chin high enough in the air to park one of Renee's best teacups on it.

"Seems Ellie's attitude is contagious," Jack said, looking at the two women.

"Yes, it does." Chloe knew exactly what he meant. Ryan and Erik had taken all they were getting. "Okay, but I need for you two to stay out of sight—or else be fashionably late."

Rubi darted a knowing look at Jack. "You're having them arrested at the ball?"

"I'm a reporter, Rubi," he said. "I don't arrest people."

"The authorities are on the way," Chloe said. "Ryan and Erik will be there, of course, but if they see you two, they'll know they've been caught and run before they can be arrested."

"It's Halloween," Ashley said. "We'll wear masks."

"I'll do that, but I am *not* going to miss seeing them handcuffed. Erik punched me, and he's going to pay for that."

"You'll need to file statements," Jack said.

"After the ball," Rubi told him, then she and Ashley left.

The other women began to follow them. Chloe stopped them, explaining in three languages that they needed to wait. Several feared being deported, but Chloe promised her attorney would help them and they wouldn't be sent anywhere. Then Chloe called her attorney and then Ellie to assure it.

Minutes later, the FBI arrived and took charge of the women. Harrison was with them, and he came to Chloe and Jack.

Wordlessly, Jack slipped a possessive arm around Chloe's waist. "Congratulations on the recovery, Harrison," Jack said, referencing the Governess.

"Thanks." Harrison smiled. "Nice work, Chloe. Here and on the senator."

She smiled warmly. "Thank you."

"What about the original three missing Russian women?"

Chloe let him see her disappointment. "They're not here."

"We've done what we can," Jack said. "Do you have this under control?" Jack asked Harrison, tugging Chloe closer still.

"Yep." Jack's jealousy amused Harrison; it shone in his eyes, and if the twitch at the corner of his mouth was an accurate gauge, it was all he could do not to laugh out loud.

"We're out of here, then," Jack said.

Harrison winked at Chloe. She winked back, and walked with Jack outside and back to the car.

Stepping back from the curb, he opened the door for her. "All in all, we got the job done."

"We got the Duke. That's significant."

"Honey, we got *this* Duke." Jack got into the car. "But the thing about these snakes is that they're organized. From the moment Ryan and Erik are arrested, another snake will step into Ryan's shoes, and then the hunt for that Duke will begin."

That was what had happened with Caulfield Carouthers. Brit had stepped right in, not missing a beat. Disappointment shafted through Chloe and fell to reality. "It's like that author said," she told Jack. "So long as there are men, there will be greed. And so long as there is greed, there will be corruption."

Jack cranked the engine. "Yeah, but that author left out the most important part."

She plucked a string of lint from his tux sleeve. "What most important part?"

"So long as there is corruption, there will be Rose agents fighting it, and holding men accountable."

Chloe smiled. "I like that."

"Thought you might." He shot her a slow, sexy smile.

Hand in hand, they drove off into the night, and Chloe felt satisfied at rescuing the women, though the three Russians she'd started out seeking hadn't been among them.

That got her down, but Jack making it clear to Harrison that they were a couple lifted her spirits a bit. Still, she dreaded the ball. With Erik's arrest, her mother would be inconsolable and her father devastated forever.

An imperfect success, but what couldn't be changed had to be accepted.

Perrini's grand ballroom looked magnificent.

"Lucas," Chloe said. "It's gorgeous!"

"Ah, you like it." He beamed with pride at the lavish decorations. "I went with the Celtic rendition of All Hallows' Eve over an American Halloween. It seemed more appropriate."

"It's beautiful." Sparkles and glitter and real women dressed as statues that, when touched with a magic wand, came to life. "Just beautiful."

The band played music that fit with the theme, and Jack dragged Chloe onto the crowded dance floor. Chloe's parents were dancing, too, and seeing them, and Erik and Chelsea laughing and dancing, had Chloe bittersweet.

"This is the hardest part for you." Jack held her closer.

"It really is." She felt choked up. Overall, the mission had been successful, and she'd learned a lot from it. But Erik…

Her parents' hearts would be broken tonight, and Chloe was partly to blame. "I spent too many years covering for him."

"Your mother protected him, too," Jack said. "The women were all wearing your clothes."

Surprised, she asked, "How did you know they were mine?"

He smiled. "They smell like you."

Her *Remember Me.* She sighed and pressed her cheek against Jack's shoulder. "Mother won't see it that way." This time, when she blamed Chloe for Wonder Boy's fall from grace, she'd be right…

Her parents switched partners, and her mother was dancing with Erik. God, but she looked happy. Chloe wished she could warn her, but she couldn't. She hated that.

Erik twirled their mother and moved closer to Chloe. "Hi, Sis. Didn't see you earlier."

"We just arrived." It was incredibly hard to look at Erik much less to speak to him. "You both know Jack, don't you?"

"Of course." Her mother dismissed him. "Chloe, why do you insist on wearing Vera Wang? That dress looks awful on you."

That was the one. The final blow. "It's Adele's design, not Vera's and it's gorgeous." Chloe let go of Jack and faced her mother head-on. "Come with me." She grabbed her wrist and fairly dragged her off the dance floor and into a little alcove.

"I do not appreciate your manhandling me, Chloe St. John. You are a princess, and this is not acceptable—"

"Stop it now and listen to me," Chloe interrupted her. "I've had enough."

"I beg your pardon."

"You certainly should." Chloe frowned. "I'm tired of your cutting remarks, Mother. I had to listen to them when I was at home, but I have my own home now and I do not have to listen to them anymore. I'm telling you that they hurt me. A lot. And I'm not going to listen to them ever again."

"Excuse me?"

"You heard me, Mother." Chloe took in a deep breath. "While this dress is an Adelphio, I love Vera Wang's designs, and I intend to wear them the rest of my life. You don't have to like it, but you do have to tolerate it without comment. And, Mother, the next time you empty my closet to 'save me from myself,' I'm going to ban you from Eleanor Towers." She hadn't taken them, Erik had, but she had lied for him and taken the blame. Jack was right. Boundary lines were in order. Strong ones.

Her face contorted in fury, but she kept her voice low, discreet. "How dare you talk to me like this?"

"You think I like it?" Chloe spat. "You give me no choice. I'm tired of being the thorn in your side, Mother. Damn sick of the poison, actually. So I'm removing myself. As of right now, you can accept me as I am, warts and all, or not. Your choice."

"Chloe Elizabeth St. John." Her father's furious voice sounded at her back. "I will not tolerate you speaking to your mother like this."

"Then I suggest you teach her some manners, Father. Because she deserves far worse than she's getting—and so do you. You stood by for years and watched her treat me like trash under her feet and did nothing. You're not a damn bit more innocent."

His face contorted in anger, but his voice remained low. "You're no longer my daughter."

The words hit her like a brick wall, knocked the breath out of her. She stilled, dragged in air, then turned and fully faced him. "Be careful, Father." He had no idea what was to come, but she did. Without her or Erik, they'd be alone.

"You will not inherit a cent. Not one," he insisted. "And the way you go through money—"

"I go through money?" She laughed. "I have more money than I could spend in ten lifetimes." She looked from him to her mother. "I have always needed your love, but I was never good enough for you to love. Ever."

She started to walk away, stopped and walked back to them. They stood shoulder to shoulder. "I love you far more than you realize. But I'm tired of you looking at me and seeing only a daughter with flaws and faults. You have no idea who I am or what I do. You've judged me based on assumptions, but you've been wrong. I just wanted you to know that." She looked at her mother. "And, Mother, stay the hell out of my closet."

"I didn't take—" She clasped her hands over her mouth.

But it was too late. Pandora's box had been opened, and Chloe had verified the truth. She struggled to stay calm, controlled. "I know you didn't break into my apartment and steal my clothes."

"I did do it," she insisted. "I swear it."

Chloe's father gaped, darted his gaze from daughter to mother. "You stole her clothes?"

"You're lying, Mother," Chloe insisted. "Erik stole all my Vera Wang dresses and my Rose pin."

"No," she insisted, but her voice lacked conviction.

"I found his ring. The royal crest," Chloe whispered. "I know the truth."

Her mother gasped, horrified.

"What is this about?" Her father's face burned red.

"It's about two women who love your son," Chloe said softly, locking gazes with her mother. "Both women have lied repeatedly and taken blame for crimes they didn't commit to protect him." Tears slid down Chloe's cheeks. "And both women, I fear, will regret having done so for a very long time to come." She turned to walk away.

Her mother clasped her arm. "Chloe, please."

She looked back over the slope of her shoulder.

Anguish twisted her mother's face. "I only wished for—"

"Me to be the perfect princess," she whispered. Compassion softened her heart, and Chloe pressed a light kiss to her mother's cheek. "I know, Mother." Pulling up her courage, Chloe said what she should have said a long time ago. "But you need to understand that I know exactly who and what I am. I was born a princess, and I'll die one. But I'm a woman with feelings, too. You're my parents, and I love you. And I know that I can't make you love me." She'd spent half her life trying. "But respecting me is enough." She swallowed hard. "I don't want to lose you, but I won't be treated shabbily anymore. So you decide. If and when you can treat me with respect, call me and I'll come to you." She left them and walked into Jack's open arms.

"Oh, God, honey. I know that was hard." He closed his arms around her and pulled her close. "Parents can tie you up in knots like nothing else."

"Yes, they can." Shaking, she held him tighter, took the comfort he offered, and willed herself to not cry.

"You stood up for yourself, and made them think," he said. "You're brave, Chloe. One of the bravest people I know."

"I wish I were, but I'm not. I'm a bigger coward than Wonder Boy," she said and unfortunately meant it.

"Not hardly." Jack laughed. "You dared to love me. That's exceptionally brave."

"That was inevitable. I didn't have a choice at sixteen, and I don't have one now."

"You've always had a choice, Chloe," he corrected her. "You chose me, and you even trusted me after I screwed up."

Sounded like a solid foundation for a relationship to her. "And you?" She dared to look at him. "Did you choose me, Jack? After all that's happened, do you still choose me?"

"Damn right," Frank said, breezing by with the video camera. "He loves you, you love him. That's the best you can get in a relationship, Princess. Now, wave to Miss Emma."

Leave it to Frank. Chloe and Harrison waved. "Miss you!" Chloe yelled out.

Frank moved on and Jack and Chloe returned to their dance. He tipped her chin to look into her eyes. "Frank's right, you know. I do love you. I will for the rest of my life."

Happy from the soul out, she lifted her chin. "Frank's *always* right." Jack tickled her side, and she snuggled closer to him. "All right, you win." She laughed. "I'll love you forever, too, Jack."

"Damn right." He planted a kiss on her neck, twirled, and continued their dance.

Joy bubbled in Chloe, and she watched Frank working the room with the camera. *No more faking it, Emma. I made it.*

Chloe had made it. She'd dared to dream and had fought for those too weak to fight for themselves. She'd taken on the assignment from hell that terrified her, and with a lot of help she had handled it. Not perfectly, not totally successfully, but she'd done her best, and isn't that all anyone can do? And she'd put her parents on notice. No more treating her like an unwanted puppy. Respect, or nothing; it was that simple, and that complex.

But she did have one regret that would haunt her.

She'd failed to save the three Russian women...

FBI agents quietly entered the ballroom.

Chloe's breath caught. "They're here." She signaled the other Roses. Porsche and Sam covered the southeast exit, with Marlena perched on Porsche's shoulder. Vanessa and Taye took the southwest door. Becca steered Dane across the dance floor to the northeast. Madison and John were already near the northwest. Alexa and Ross had the entrance the orchestra used covered. If Ryan Greene tried to cut and run, he'd have to go through a Rose or a wall.

Ryan was on the dance floor with Glenda Huntsberger.

Four agents walked toward him. The dancers parted, giving them a wide berth, but arrogant as only the Duke could be, Ryan kept dancing.

An agent tapped him on the shoulder. "Excuse me. Ryan Greene, you're under arrest."

Ryan let go of Glenda. Scanned the exits, then headed for the southeast. Porsche stepped near him and suddenly Ryan jumped and fell, sprawled on the ballroom floor.

Porsche leaned down to gather up her seemingly smirking ferret. She smiled down at him. "I'm so sorry, Ryan. Marlena didn't see you coming."

He glared up at her.

Two agents lifted him to his feet, positioned him to put him in handcuffs.

"This is an outrage." He laughed deeply. "I'll be released and back at this ball before you finish the paperwork."

"You might," one agent said. "Let's see, that's thirty years for each charge of human trafficking for the purpose of prostitution and there are forty-two counts, so far." He grunted. "Yes, sir. It could take a while to do all that paperwork."

"Human trafficking?" Ryan feigned shock, but it didn't touch his eyes, and he wasn't laughing anymore. "You're insane."

"And we've got you cold, Greene," the agent said softly. "Save your breath."

"You've got nothing," Ryan spat.

Senator Ellie Richardson stepped forward. Ashley and Rubi flanked her. "I wouldn't count on it."

He turned ashen.

Reading him his rights, the agents hauled Ryan out of the ballroom. Chloe shared a glance with the other Roses. They'd done it. All of them had faced challenges and dangers the Duke had created, and they'd gotten him. This was definitely a time of celebration.

And yet, while the others were definitely bent on doing just that, Chloe couldn't. Not with what lay ahead for her family...

The remaining agents scanned the crowd, no doubt looking for Erik. Chloe's heart beat hard and fast. "Jack, my parents. Where are my—"

"This way." He led her toward the alcove. "Hurry."

Her mother and father stood together, quietly talking. "I wonder what Ryan's done?"

"Or what they think he's done," Chloe's father said. "Ryan has been such a benefactor to the community, it's difficult to believe he's involved in anything scandalous."

Chloe kept her opinions to herself and, with Jack, joined her parents just as the two agents located Erik. He was still dancing with Chelsea in a quiet corner, oblivious to the turmoil going on around him. Vintage Erik.

Chloe wished she could hear what was said as one agent stopped them, his nod respectful and authoritative at once.

Seemingly startled, Erik took one look at his badge and twisted away in fear. The agents moved in, grabbing him.

"Let go of my arm!" Erik's voice rang out, echoing across the ballroom.

The music stopped.

"What are those men doing to Erik?" Chloe's mother turned, started toward her son.

Chloe clasped her arm, held her in place. Standing between her parents, she whispered, "Stay here, Mother."

"But—" Confused, she frowned at Chloe's father, then at Chloe. "I insist on knowing—"

The FBI agent's voice now rang out over the shocked, silent crowd, making what was happening all too clear. "You have the right to remain silent..."

"He's being arrested?" Her mother's face twisted in horror. "Oh, no. This can't be. Why?"

"Be still, my dear," Chloe's father said, moving closer to her mother, sliding his arm around her shoulders, shielding her.

Rubi appeared with a cameraman. He lifted the camera to photograph Chloe's mother. Looking at Chloe, Rubi put her hand over the lens. "No, Rob. Leave it alone. Stick with him."

The photographer shifted focus and snapped photographs of Erik. The flash went off like a strobe.

"Oh, no. Photographs? Now handcuffs?" Her mother darted Chloe a frantic look. "This is what you meant earlier about us protecting him. You knew this was coming."

She had to lie. "I feared it, Mother. I warned him he was keeping bad company and he should stop. He insisted it was business."

"Oh, no. Oh, Chloe. Erik…" Tears coursed down her mother's face. "What have we done?"

Jack passed her a handkerchief. "Don't blame yourself. Erik isn't a child. He's a grown man that you spent a lifetime loving well."

"Thank you, Jack." She took the hanky. "That's very kind," she said, looking regretful. "I haven't always been kind to you."

"Tonight is a good time for fresh starts." Jack smiled, clasped her hand. "I'm sorry for your pain."

"Thank you, Jack."

She gave Chloe an approving nod, then leaned close. "Good man."

"I know." Chloe pressed a kiss to her cheek.

Chelsea stood like a broken statue, torn between shock and shame, too horrified to move, too crushed to weep or utter a sound. She just stared at Erik, clearly not trusting her eyes, as if caught in a nightmare and certain any second she'd awaken and discover none of this was true.

Chloe's eyes stung and bitterness burrowed through the

chambers of her heart. "We didn't let him scrape his knees," she whispered, her voice cracking. "We should have let him scrape his knees. Then he'd never have done these things."

The agents led Erik out of the ballroom, probably to join Ryan. Chloe sniffed and looked up at her father. "You'd better take Mother home."

"They're taking him to jail?" Chloe's mother was beside herself, her whole body shaking. "We've got to get in touch with Peterson Stone immediately to represent him," she told Chloe's father.

"I'd better see to Chelsea," Chloe said. The woman still stood in the middle of the dance floor. The music hadn't started playing again. Chloe signaled Renee and she stepped in to return things to normal. Well, as normal as a scandal of these proportions stood a chance of being.

"Chloe."

She turned and looked at her father. "The incident at Harvard," he said. "That was Erik, not you?"

She nodded.

Tears brimmed in his eyes. "I'm so sorry, my dear."

"So am I." She left them and went to Chelsea.

Jack joined her and they led the woman, clearly in shock, out of Perrini's and put her into her car. "Take her home," Chloe instructed her driver. "And make sure someone stays with her for a while."

Chelsea got into the limousine without uttering a sound.

When Chloe and Jack returned to the ballroom, Renee, with her usual aplomb, had the orchestra playing again and the Rose agents had dragged their men onto the dance floor. The flurry of the arrests wasn't over—and wouldn't be for weeks—but the crisis point was over.

Rubi and Ashley stood near the bar, and even from a distance, Chloe heard Rubi's voice. "Just read my column tomorrow. You'll know more than you dared to imagine about that bastard Ryan Greene."

"I guess he's not her most eligible favorite anymore." Jack smiled.

"I'd say not." Chloe sniffed a final time. "My parents are crushed."

"Your father wasn't that surprised, honey. Your mother was crushed. But he'll help her through it."

He would. Even after all these years, he still adored her mother.

Through the excited chatter, the sound of Rubi's voice had Chloe's mind slipping back to the hallway at Hollow Hill. Remembering the women who'd been rescued with Rubi and Ashley. She'd known the moment she'd seen them wearing her clothes that Erik, not her mother, had stolen her clothes. She gasped. Not one of them had been wearing the red Vera Wang dress.

Her Rose pin!

"Jack. Jack, come on." Chloe ran outside, half-dragging him. On the street, she stopped and faced him. "I remembered. I didn't remove my Rose pin. I thought I'd left it on the dresser, but I didn't. I left it on the dress."

"I'm working at this, Princess, but I'm not tracking—"

"Tracking. Exactly." She gasped. "My Rose pin is still on the red Vera Wang dress that I wore to the date auction. Erik stole all my Vera Wang couture—for the women to wear when they were sold."

"Call Alan," Jack said. "I'll get my resources ready."

Chloe dialed Alan at the G.R.C. "Alan, activate my Rose pin."

"I thought you lost it."

"It's important, Alan. Just do it, okay?"

"Activating it now."

"How long will it take?" Chloe asked, gripping Jack's

sleeve and squeezing. This had to work. It just had to work. It was the only way to find these women and those who'd been taken before them.

"It's done, Chloe," Alan said. "The Rose pin is active."

Her heart slammed against her ribs. She covered them with her hand. "Where is it?"

"Holy cow." His shock rang out. "It's in Hong Kong."

Oh, yes! "Excellent." Chloe smiled at Jack. "Hold on." She covered the phone. "Hook them up, Jack. We've got them."

Jack handled the connections with Alan, then hung up the phone, smiling broadly. "My contacts will handle the retrieval." His eyes twinkled. "Outstanding work, Chloe."

"Yeah, sometimes I surprise even me." She wrinkled her nose at him. "They'll definitely find the women, right? Or at least the people who know where they are?"

"Absolutely. They're all over it. Odds are good they'll retrieve even more women—and that bastard, Brit."

She reveled in the flush of victory. Sweet success. "Then now, my darling Jack Quaid, we're done."

"Oh, no, Princess." He spun her in his arms on the sidewalk. "This assignment is done. We're just beginning."

He had forgiven her, too. She caressed his jaw. "Looks like it's me and you for the duration. Think you can take it?"

"Oh, yeah," Jack said. "But don't forget your Jimmy Choos." He winked. "Why risk breaking our lucky streak?"

"Perfect." Looping his neck with her arms, Chloe laughed from the heart out. *Thank you, Jimmy Choo.*

* * * * *

*There's more Silhouette Bombshell
coming your way!
Every month we bring you two fresh, unique,
satisfying reads that will keep you riveted…
Turn the page for an exclusive excerpt
from one of next month's releases,*
Calculated Risk
*by Stephanie Doyle,
on sale February 2007
at your favourite retail outlet.*

Calculated Risk

by

Stephanie Doyle

I'm dead now. You know what to do, G.G.

Sabrina Masters stared at the e-mail displayed on her computer screen and released a deep breath. Arnold was gone.

A true believer in the art of science and math, he'd been a mentor. Certainly, he'd been one of her few intellectual equals. But more importantly, he'd cared about her. More, she knew, than her own father ever had. At least Arnold always looked out for her.

Her head fell forward because it seemed too heavy to hold up. She could feel the tears well behind her eyes and wanted to stop them. But she decided that Arnold deserved a few tears.

He'd been alone in the world. No wife, no children, no family to speak of. He'd made the computer his wife. The work his child. But the computer wouldn't cry and the work wouldn't mourn for him.

She wondered if he realized now that he was gone that there had never been anyone truly significant in his life. If he did, if that knowledge somehow made him sad, she hoped he at least knew how heartbroken she was.

You know what to do, G.G.

The old nickname brought a smile to her lips. G.G.: Girl Genius.

Sabrina glanced at the number typed at the bottom and instantly memorized it, plugging it into her brain alongside every other piece of information that she'd ever stumbled across. Sometimes she wondered if one day her head might fill up to such a capacity that it would simply explode from the strain. The gruesome image did nothing to improve her mood.

"I don't know if I can do this, Arnold," she stated aloud to the almost empty room, in the practically empty house that was her home in an out-of-the-way, nowhere town in Pennsylvania.

Briefly, she entertained the idea that as a ghost he might be able to answer her. She waited a beat. Nothing. If there was a heaven and Arnold was in it, he was trying to strike up a game of chess with Einstein. Probably convinced that he could beat him, too. The last thing Arnold would care about after his death would be the fate of the nation. Not when he barely had cared about it when he was alive.

You and me, G.G. We're a lot alike.

He used to tell her that all the time. She'd always thought he was talking about their strange intellect. But maybe he wasn't. The idea that they had more in common worried her. In fact, it frightened her.

Sabrina slipped her hand into the back pocket of her jeans to extract her cell phone. She dialed the number Arnold had given her and waited.

"Hello?"

"Is this Assistant Director Krueger?" she asked, somewhat surprised. Arnold must have given her the CIA director's personal cell phone number as a way to cut directly to the chase.

"Yes?"

"Arnold Salinski is dead."

"I know. Sabrina Masters?"

"Yep."

There was a pause on the other end of the phone. Then, "We should talk."

She could practically feel the weight of this moment and the impact it was going to have on her life.

"Yep."

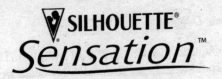

SILHOUETTE®
Sensation™

0107/18a

THE PRINCESS'S SECRET SCANDAL
by Karen Whiddon

Capturing the Crown

Royal PR man Chase Savage was involved in a scandal: he had announced his engagement to Sydney Conner, the illegitimate princess from Naessa, who was pregnant with the late Prince Reginald's heir. But was it true love or just PR spin?

HIGH-STAKES BRIDE
by Fiona Brand

Dani Marlow has had it with men, but is thrown back into the arms of her ex, Assault Specialist Carter Rawlings, when she is linked to a series of fires…first as a suspect, then as a victim. Now Carter faces his biggest challenge: keeping Dani safe while convincing her that their love is worth another chance.

WORTH EVERY RISK
by Dianna Love Snell

Branded with a wrongful conviction, Angel Farentino intended to prove her innocence or die trying. As she ran for her life, she didn't need a sexy saviour distracting her. But undercover DEA agent Zane Jackson had his own secrets—like discovering whether Angel was guilty of a crime, or just guilty of stealing his heart.

On sale from 19th January 2007

Available at WHSmith, Tesco, ASDA,
and all good bookshops
www.silhouette.co.uk

COMEBACK
by Doranna Durgin

Athena Force

Selena Shaw Jones's intervention in a hostage crisis had made her a hero. Now the CIA had approached her again to locate a missing terrorist informant and his case officer. Selena had to put aside her self-doubt because the missing ex-terrorist had vital information…and the case officer in question was her husband, Cole.

DEEP BLUE
by Suzanne McMinn

PAX

Evidence linked to her twin sister's disappearance leads Sienna Parker to the Florida Keys, but she's not the only one fishing for clues. PAX agent Cade Brock is also investigating. And he's in deep water when he realises he is head over heels for Sienna.

CALCULATED RISK
by Stephanie Doyle

Ten years ago girl genius Sabrina Masters was booted out of the CIA for "wilful insubordination." Now, they wanted her back for a mission only she could complete—breaking a twisted code to uncover a terrorist. But she would have to work with Quinlan, her former trainer—and ex-lover. But she was the CIA's only hope…

On sale from 19th January 2007

Available at WHSmith, Tesco, ASDA,
and all good bookshops
www.silhouette.co.uk

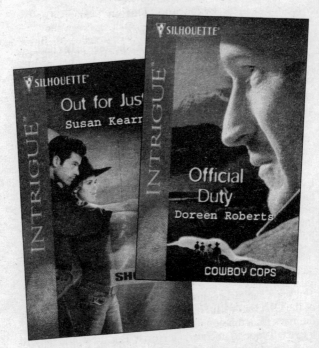

SILHOUETTE®
INTRIGUE™

BULLSEYE by Jessica Andersen
Big Sky Bounty Hunters

When the Secretary of Defence's family was kidnapped on Secret Service agent Isabella Gray's watch, she knew she needed the help of her ex, bounty hunter Jacob Powell. But as their rescue mission intensified, could they resist the long pent-up emotions churning between them?

SECRET SURROGATE by Delores Fossen

When Lucas Creed discovered that his former deputy, Kylie Munroe, was pregnant and moving on, his heart had broken. But after a frantic phone call he took her into his protection, and she dropped a bombshell… As they tried to expose the men who threatened her, would their glacial rift melt beneath an inferno of desire?

MYSTERIOUS CIRCUMSTANCES
by Rita Herron
Nighthawk Island

FBI Agent Craig Horn came to Savannah to investigate a rash of mysterious deaths but he hadn't counted on Olivia Thornbird, a reporter who wanted the truth behind her father's suicide. Then Olivia became a target in someone's diabolical plan and Craig vowed to protect her at all costs.

OPERATION: MIDNIGHT ESCAPE
by Linda Castillo

Special Agent Jake Vanderpol swore he'd buried all tender feelings for Leigh Michaels. Until he learned that the arms dealer she'd testified against six years ago had escaped. For her own safety, she would have to go on the run with the man she had never forgiven. But who would save her heart from Jake?

On sale from 19th January 2007

Available at WHSmith, Tesco, ASDA,
and all good bookshops

www.silhouette.co.uk

'It's scary just how good Tess Gerritsen is.'
—Harlan Coben

Twenty years after her father's plane crashed in the jungles of Southeast Asia, Willy Jane Maitland was finally tracking his last moves. She recognised the dangers, but her search for the truth about that fateful flight was the only thing that mattered.

Closing in on the events of that night, Willy realises that she is investigating secrets that people would kill to protect. And without knowing who to trust, the truth can be far from clear cut...

MIRA